DESPERATE TO DIE

A Dr. Annabel Tilson Novel

BOOK 3

DESPERATE TO DIE

by Barbara Ebel, M.D.

A Dr. Annabel Tilson Novel

Paperback ISBN-13: 978-0-9977225-5-0
eBook ISBN-13: 978-0-9977225-6-7

This book is a work of fiction. Names, characters, places and events are the product of the author's imagination or are used fictitiously. Any resemblance to actual events, persons, or locations is coincidental.

CHAPTER 1

Annabel Tilson read "coughing up blood" on her first patient's ER admission form. She yanked open the drapes to the cubicle with anticipation and formulated the most pertinent questions she could think of. However, how much could she possibly know about the subject? After all, she was only a third year medical student on the first day of her internal medicine rotation.

Her patient, May Oliver, sat slouched over the side of the stretcher with a blue pan in her lap. She gripped the plastic ends up higher as she coughed three times and spit.

"Mrs. Oliver," Annabel said as May used a crumpled tissue to wipe her mouth, "I'm Dr. Tilson. I will be the medical student taking care of you along with the rest of the team."

Simultaneously, they looked into the bucket at the bubbly, rust-colored mucus with streaks of blood. May peeled her gaze away and, with wide eyes, gave Annabel a pleading stare. Her hands trembled and the pan jolted from her lap, but Annabel quickly grabbed it before it slid to the floor.

May sighed. "Thanks. That means I'm going to function as your guinea pig."

"The situation isn't that stark," Annabel said softly. "Actually, every one of us on your team, no matter what our rank, is learning something new from our patients every day. I have less clinical experience than they do, but my path has begun and I treat it with awe, curiosity, and respect."

Annabel let May absorb what she said while she observed her patient carefully. She had learned from previous rotations the essentials of doing a good history and physical and 'general appearance' always came first. The thirty-two-year-old woman would be attractive, she thought, if not for her general physical wasting and apparent malnutrition. Her auburn hair was pulled back with a French clip and she had high cheekbones as well as lackluster eyes. She wore a turtleneck sweater tucked into black cotton pants and a warm jacket and wooly hat were thrown on the nearby chair.

Annabel reached over for another Kleenex and handed it to May. Even though she had scanned the ER notes, her job was to start questioning Mrs.

1

Oliver from the beginning.

"What brought you to the ER this evening?" she asked.

"I finally admitted to myself that something's not right. I've been upchucking blood from my lungs or my throat and today I had a real spell of it … red, nasty, and more voluminous than ever before."

"How long has this been going on?"

"Seems like a couple of months."

Annabel grimaced. "What's a 'couple of months'?"

"Three or four," May said sheepishly.

"Any weight loss during this time?"

May froze, knowing the answer; it was stuck in her throat as she nodded affirmatively and gritted her teeth.

"How much weight loss?" Annabel asked.

"I scaled in here at ninety-five pounds. A half-year ago, I was a hundred and twenty-five."

Annabel tried not to register alarm on her face. "And to be clear, you did not see a doctor before this, so there is no prior work-up record?" It was a must-ask question for her now since she had been burned on rounds once before when a prior illuminating record was available which she didn't know about.

"That's correct. I'm guilty as charged; dedicated enough to have served in Afghanistan but stupid enough not to seek medical care."

"Don't feel bad, Mrs. Oliver. Taking care of yourself last is a common affliction of hard-working and caring people."

Annabel took May's hand and settled her fingers on her wrist. She proceeded to take her pulse and other vital signs so as to not rely on the ones already recorded. Along the way, she asked her patient about other medical problems and surgical procedures. She asked about her family history and medication use and then addressed her social history.

Knowing May's reason for being in the ER, Annabel suspected that her tobacco use would be the most significant piece of the puzzle. The woman probably smoked her way through the armed forces and already did irritating damage to her large and small lung passages. Her patient was younger than the folks who abuse their respiratory tract over decades, but she could still qualify if she was a big chain smoker or used the heavy-duty tobacco brands.

Annabel took her stethoscope off her neck. "Do you smoke?"

May shook her head.

"No?" Annabel asked, doubtful and surprised.

"No. Really. I tried it when I was seventeen. Not only did it leave me in a smoke cloud, but it left an aftertaste and made my breath smell bad."

Annabel grinned; her thoughts exactly. "So what do you do now after serving in the armed forces?"

"First, I finished college. There weren't many jobs available when I graduated, so I started a job as a barista. As it turned out, I stayed there because I worked myself up to store manager. It's a major coffee chain; we're right off the freeway so the place is hopping all the time." She cleared her throat and leaned back on the palm of her hand.

Annabel was glad her patient seemed a bit more comfortable. After completing her history and physical, she left the room thinking of the many possible diagnoses that coincide with a smoking history – if May had smoked. But now she was stumped. She would need the expert insight of her upper level residents or a block of time to search for May's symptoms in the *Principles of Internal Medicine.*

———

Compared to the University hospital where Annabel had rotated in surgery and psychiatry, the government hospital and ER was vastly different. One day at this hospital lent her to believe that the pace was slower and, in general, the patients older and with more chronic conditions. The ER department was busy enough this Monday night but quiet for its size; Annabel realized it was because there were no noisy trauma cases like the bigger teaching facility where paramedics raced in with bloody stretchers, sometimes grappling with CPR and blaring monitors at the same time.

Nevertheless, a steady flow of adrenaline pumped Annabel up for the night, and there was no shortage of patients for her team on call. She positioned herself at a cubicle next to her medical school colleague and friend, Bob Palmer, and swiveled in the chair to face him.

"I still can't believe what you pulled off," she said. "It's understandable we're both now on the internal medicine service, but how you managed to position the two of us on the same team is beyond me."

Bob stopped writing up his patient's admission and turned his head. His tapered haircut was suitable and becoming on his round face and the glint in his eyes always portrayed his sense of humor. He had proven himself to be a dear friend and one she would never need to second guess in a pinch. He had also not held back in the past on respectfully expressing his fondness for her until he began dating an older medical school student during their psychiatry rotation. She wondered if his relationship with her was still intact.

"I went to the doc in charge of these things," he said in a professorial manner. "He was lumping names together for the four teams of four students and he was making up the call schedule for our entire rotation. Everyone is aware of the horrific events that took place on our psychiatry rotation and I told him that you and I share a mutual bond, making it advantageous for us to work together again. We need to overcome the post-traumatic stress of our previous attending getting killed by a patient and there's no better way than to talk about that if and when the need arises. Plus, we seem to have a better than symbiotic relationship as far as learning while on the same team."

He dropped the serious expression, leaned back in the chair, and let a smile creep across his face. She realized the sincerity of his remarks and agreed with his reasoning.

"I can't disagree with anything you've said, so thanks for taking the initiative and doing that. It will be nice to tackle the next few months together. Now hand me some of the extra paper in your stack. My patient's history and physical needs writing up too."

She crossed her trim long legs and yanked a pen from her pocket. They sat in their two cubicles and ignored the 7 p.m. ER shift change taking place behind them. In the next fifteen minutes, they both referred to condensed pocket handbooks as well as iPhone apps on internal medicine.

Annabel stretched and wrapped her hands together in front of her. "Who's your first admission?" she asked.

"Seventy-year-old with a history of colon cancer who comes in with rectal bleeding."

"Understandable history. Mine's only thirty-two. She's coughing up blood."

"Better not say that on rounds."

"Yikes. A week off between rotations and I'm already rusty. What I mean to say is that the patient's chief complaint is 'coughing up blood,' but my term, or the correct medical terminology is 'hemoptysis.'"

"Perfect. Knowing you, that's the last slip up you'll make for four months."

"Bob, you can knock off putting me on a pedestal. You are also proving to be a bright student."

"Yeah. We're both making progress, aren't we?"

"Probably more than we realize, but there are so many more years to train after med school that I often put that fact out of my mind. I think whoever made up the saying 'one day at a time' was a medical student."

"Or in prison. But maybe those situations qualify as one and the same."

"Hah! There is some truth to that. So did you do anything fun over our week off?"

"I took Karla to a concert last weekend and she sprung for a movie and dinner this Saturday. Other than that, I slept in every day like a slug in mud, took my sorry ass to the gym a few times and, I confess, read a little bit for this rotation."

"I guess that answers my curiosity if you're still going out with her. I was conscientious and forged ahead with reading as well."

"What about you? Did you go home to Tennessee?"

"For a couple of days. Except for my sister, my family pampered me more than I deserve. I love going home, even seeing our dog, Dakota."

"Your dad still working full time and running the practice?"

"He's taking less call than his partners but, otherwise, he's working as usual. If he's not in the OR doing cases or in the office, he's attending to something related to neurosurgery."

"Any new thoughts about what you want to do? Like go into his field?"

Annabel furrowed her brow in contemplation. "I really don't know. I still need to experience every specialty. Everything we take, I like, so there's no shortage of ideas. I particularly liked watching the anesthesiologists while we were in the OR during surgery."

"Anesthesia is like multiple specialties rolled into one."

Annabel nodded and smiled. "Something else happened during the break." She clasped her hands together, raised them to her chin, and straddled her index fingers across her lips like a child holding a secret.

Bob tilted his head. "I'm oblivious if you don't tell me."

"Actually, you're not clueless. You told me a month ago on psychiatry that it was obvious I had a thing for our chief resident, Robby Burk, when we were doing surgery."

"Who can forget him? Yes, I was a bit jealous of him for two reasons. First, someday I'd like to be as outstanding a physician as he is and, secondly, he held your undivided attention. I thought you were going to trip over your own feet a few times when he came into sight."

"Bob!"

"Okay, you two," came a voice from around the side of Bob's cubicle. Their chief resident, Donn Schott, stopped directly in front of them. "Up and at 'em. We have a break, so let's go feed our bones and conduct updates on our admissions while we eat." He stood close to Annabel's swinging leg; he tended to clutter into people's personal spaces. She couldn't fault him; he wore thick glasses. Farsightedness was most likely an issue for him.

Donn turned and waved his hand from the side. Annabel and Bob both rose with their sheets and followed him.

"To be continued," Bob said. "The med student's crush on a chief resident."

"Look who's talking. Going out with an older PhD med student."

"But you started the wandering eyes first."

———

In a private lunchroom off of the main cafeteria, Dr. Schott put down his dinner and then lined up two tables together. The clunk of trays going down on the tables sounded from the rest of the team – all four medical students and two residents.

"I intend to get informal rounds done over dinner, everyone," Donn said, "but since you all scrambled around today picking up previous admitted patients from a prior team, we haven't had a chance to effectively introduce ourselves. As you can tell from the premature gray hair on my head, beard, and mustache, I'm not your typical chief resident. I dabbled in selling real estate, acquired my late college degree over a long span of night classes, and finally buckled down when I figured out what I wanted to do with my life. So here I am. You'll notice I'm kind of laid back so never worry about me riding your backs. And, as you can see, I like my food."

All six pairs of eyes settled on his tray of pot roast and gravy lumped on top of mashed potatoes. He was busy buttering three pieces of Italian bread, so his chubbiness was now understandable. "I hand the spotlight over to you two," he said.

"As you know, I'm Melody Burg. You're already wondering about my accent. I'm from Louisiana, so that explains it. Unlike Dr. Schott, I won't eat that drab stuff." She wiggled the bottle of hot sauce she'd taken from the condiment section. "Anyway, feel free to ask me anything. I like to teach, which is why I love being a resident so much more than being a student."

"I'm curious," Annabel said. "You changed your shoes into clogs this evening, but wasn't it uncomfortable walking around all day with short heels on?"

Melody laughed while sprinkling the hot sauce on a piece of chicken. "Sorry, I hope I'm not making too much noise in the hallways."

"No, it's not that. I find heels so uncomfortable on the hard floors."

Melody shrugged and smiled. "Until my feet tell me otherwise, I'm sticking with the feminine touch."

"If heels were for men, they wouldn't be wearing them," the other resident, Chineka Watt, said. "I worked in Chicago and I even wore flats. Anyway, you students will find the subject matter in internal medicine so vast and overwhelming, you'll wonder how to remember half of it. Be sure to soak up and get a working knowledge of caring for patients with the most common medical problems. I picked this specialty because I've watched my mom and dad both deal with hypertension, heart disease, and diabetes."

"Did you grow up in Chicago?" Bob asked.

Chineka opened a salad dressing packet. Her eyes moistened. "I did. My brother died from a drive-by shooting when I was young and then my mom and dad focused on me. They saved every dime they could to send me to a decent college."

"Sorry to hear about your brother," Bob said, "but glad you made it to medical school."

Donn cleared his throat. "Jordan Maldonado, why don't you stop glancing down at your lap and put your iPhone away. I can't stop any of you from the incessant social media but understand this: texting, phoning, Facebooking, tweeting, pinning, and all that mindless clicking is secondary after patient care. You're up next."

"Sorry, Dr. Schott," Jordan said. "The students know me from school;

I'm going to be a cardiothoracic surgeon."

"That's all?" Donn asked.

"I won't be shy to consult the internal medicine service on my surgery patients after I attain my goal."

"In the meantime, you must pass the course and pretend that you care," Donn said, pausing his fork.

"I'm Stuart Schneider," the other student said, not making eye contact. Annabel and Bob knew him to be a quiet colleague, thin as a dime, and in the top of their class as far as exams. "I'm a native of right here in Ohio,, so if you out-of-towners need local information, just holler." He turned to Donn. "I want to do a residency in internal medicine."

Donn nodded. "So what do you two have to say for yourselves?" he asked Bob and Annabel.

"I can't hide my excitement," Annabel said, "to finally learn general medicine, but I hope it's not fraught with monstrous problems like the last two rotations."

"I second that," Bob said. "Dr. Schott, what's our testing schedule and when do we meet our attending doctor?"

"Study routinely because over the next sixteen weeks, you'll only have two exams. Your clinical evaluations are super important and will come from me and your attending. He, however, is not as visible on rounds as some. He's Dr. Sebastian Mejia, a cardiologist. He's side-tracked with acute cases all the time because of his reputation. Much like an obstetrician being called away for deliveries."

Donn raised his cup of coffee and after taking a sip, he put it down and then picked up his tray. "I'm going back over to select a lousy dessert, and when I come back, we're talking about patients, not about ourselves." He stepped out from the table and waddled away.

After the two residents began talking to each other, Bob turned to Annabel. "I'm going to burst a blood vessel if you don't tell me."

"Tell you what?" she grinned.

"About your heartthrob, Robby Burk."

CHAPTER 2

The two female residents, Melody and Chineka, rose from the table and followed Donn to also select a dessert. Annabel swung one leg over the bench and faced Bob.

"I went to the important meeting the Friday before our break," she said, "between psychiatry and this rotation. You know, the conference that was pending with the anesthesia and surgery departments and the Drug Company and FDA ... all about that OR drug that was called into question. Anyway, Dr. Burk attended, and at the end of the meeting, he came over and walked with me to the elevator. He said since he wasn't my chief resident anymore and I was no longer his student, would it be possible to go out to dinner with him sometime before he heads to Africa on his medical trip." She replayed in her mind what happened and how the elevator doors had snapped shut and she rode to the ground floor with a pounding pulse.

Bob's heart skipped a beat, but he forced a smile. "That's a major development in your personal life. Congratulations. Have you gone out with him yet?"

"No. I only got back from Tennessee last night. If tonight is a decent call and I'm able to sneak in some rest tomorrow afternoon, we're going to meet for dinner tomorrow."

"You must be excited. You alluded to other dating this year, but I guess nobody was important enough to mention. Have a great time; I hope he lives up to your expectations."

Annabel nodded. His speculation about her dating all along was correct but finding people on her dating app, Findar, had not been for finding relationship material at all. Something he had no clue about. It had been more for an occasional romp in the sack. Her thinking was that if men could do it, she could do it, too; it had also served multiple functions.

However, Annabel's use of the app, or another one like it, now took a back seat to her starting medicine and making time for Robby Burk.

———

Donn walked back to the table and placed down a piece of pie with a dollop of whipped cream. Dr. Burg and Dr. Watt shared two cookies from a baggie that they bought at the cash register.

"Now we're ready to roll," Donn said. "Each of you students had an admission since this afternoon and, unbeknownst to you, I staged a little trick on you. I use a teaching method on the first day to emphasize a point. Dr. Palmer, it's customary as a student to write up your H&P, or history and physical, after you've seen you patient. Correct?"

"There's no other way," Bob said.

"However, your supervising resident and your chief resident saw the patient before you. How much of your written H&P is then plagiarized from your resident's H&P already placed in the chart?"

"Uhh…" Bob stammered. "If I haven't talked to them yet about the patient and I'm stumped on the possible diagnosis or plan, I do reword what they've written."

"You're an honest young man."

"Mostly," he chuckled. "However, I do sometimes stretch the truth when I'm complimenting people."

"That only goes for women," Annabel said.

Bob rolled his eyes. "She's knows me better than I think."

Donn swallowed and pushed around a few crumbs with his fork. "So each of you must have noted that either Dr. Burg or Dr. Watt's H&P was missing from the charts of your patients today. That's because they are in your resident's pockets, ready to be put in the patient's record." He looked squarely at each student. "Unfortunately, on rounds, students are subconsciously taught to regurgitate the same information that their superior wrote about their patient."

He put a forkful of pie in his mouth, letting them digest what he said. In a few moments, he continued. "My point in doing this today is for each of you to learn the skill of thinking for yourself like a seasoned physician, make educated guesses before you see what your resident has written, and be willing to have a constructive discussion about possible diagnoses and be open to positive feedback."

He focused on Annabel. "Let's start with your admission, Dr. Tilson. Why don't you begin with a short version of your H&P? Remember always that there is no substitute for being at the bedside and no replacement for a careful history and physical examination."

Annabel dug her hand into her jacket and pulled out her cards. Each of her three patients had their own index card where she wrote down their most pertinent information. She held May Oliver's.

"Like I've mentioned," Donn added. "I'm a pretty mellow guy, so right now, this will be informal. Go ahead, Annabel. Tell us what you know."

"May Oliver is a thirty-two-year-old white female who came in with a four-month history of coughing up blood. She reported an unintentional weight loss of thirty pounds and increased fatigability, but she's devoid of a temperature and lacks fever, chills, or night sweats."

"The absence of those latter symptoms makes you believe what?" Donn asked.

"There is no suggestion of an infection."

"Exactly. Already you told us so much. In the back of your minds, you should all be churning out a differential diagnosis for hemoptysis. If you can't do it now, then you'll be snapping it out it in a few weeks. Did you ask her if she had any recent surgeries or chest pain?"

"Not directly," Annabel said.

Donn turned to the resident assigned to Mrs. Oliver. "Melody, why is that piece of information critical?"

"Because you want to evaluate for a pulmonary embolism, which can be life threatening. That would be suggestive with a history of recent immobilization such as a hospitalization for a surgery. She could have developed a deep venous thrombosis in a leg which broke off and got trapped in her lungs, causing her chest pain and shortness of breath."

Donn gave her a thumbs up. "So back to the differential diagnosis. Our attending doctor, Dr. Mejia, has been practicing medicine for a long time, so he could tell you that years ago the most common causes of hemoptysis was tuberculosis or a lung abscess. But these days, it boils down to bronchitis or lung cancer."

Annabel worried about what he'd say next. Surely lung cancer couldn't be a strong consideration. Her patient was too young.

Donn ate another piece of pie and chased it down with a gulp of coffee. "In your short history, however," he said, "you neglected telling us an important point. Your patient's smoking history or lack thereof."

"She never smoked," Annabel said.

"We boiled it down to bronchitis and lung cancer, but the most common cause of bronchitis stems from smoking. See how far we've come?"

He turned his fork over and tapped the tines on the plate. "We're left with a primary working diagnosis of lung cancer. The only type not usually associated with smoking."

———

Their team office was way too small. The hospital was undergoing a facelift and until some areas were spread out into the new wing, the physical space of some departments was tight. When they got back, Donn tucked himself into the end of the sofa and opened up his *USA Today.*

"This is my intermittent diversion all day long," Donn said to no one in particular. "An old-fashioned newspaper which I bring in whether there's rain or shine."

Annabel grinned at Bob. Their chief was hidden behind the colorful front page of the "Life" section with a satirical picture of a movie celebrity.

Donn folded back a corner. "It's nice to see the media ridiculing someone in Hollywood for a change, since all they do is make fun of certain politicians. I'd like to see some of those privileged folks taking on the responsibility of an area of government. They can't act their way through that."

Annabel knew better than to get into that discussion. "Dr. Schott, we don't know where our call rooms are. Perhaps we can unclutter this room and remove our overnight bags."

"Come on with me," Dr. Burg said. "I'll bring you all over. The rooms are finished in the new wing and you won't believe it. Each student and resident has their own call room."

All four students shot a glance at each other with disbelief. Hastily, they gathered their things like the offer may be rescinded and followed Dr. Burg and Dr. Watt out the door.

"Annabel," Dr. Burg said, "my H&P is on Mrs. Oliver's chart now and she's off in radiology getting x-rays.'"

"Should we tell her of our suspicions tonight?"

"No use in telling her our thoughts so late. Sleeping in a hospital is bad enough without wrestling with the idea that you may have cancer." They reached an abrupt transformation into the new wing with shiny new floors and lighter walls. "Here you go, everyone. Pick a room and don't forget the key, which should be right inside on the shelf. Now is my opportunity to change my shoes." She pointed to her duffel bag and disappeared into the first room.

Annabel entered the first door across from her. It was small but appreciated. All four students didn't have to pile into the same room and disturb each other by coming in and out all night for new patients or problems on the ward. She changed into scrubs for the overnight haul, grabbed the key, and headed back out. Bob was waiting for her a few feet away.

"We have a problem," he said as they began the trek back over.

"There's always some kind of dilemma," she said, grinning. "What is it this time?"

"I did not find a separate, upscale coffee shop in the hospital lobby. Not only will we be out of rich brew, but we won't be able to buy our chocolate espresso beans or blueberries."

"You'd think a government hospital would rent out space to make some extra money, being that they're always short of funds. At least I hear from the reports about doctor shortages and overflowing clinics and long patient wait times. I guess the new part of the building is to factor in some of these changes to help expand and hire."

"Maybe so. But none of that is going to solve our immediate dilemma. Especially when it comes to tomorrow morning or rounding without our secret treats."

"I agree. We must come up with a plan. Either buy a stash for the rotation somewhere else or change our addiction to something from the cafeteria."

"Heaven forbid," Bob said. "Do you want to get us poisoned? Did you notice those lousy cookies our residents were eating before?"

"Yeah, I guess you're right."

"So where are you going right now?"

"I have to check if Mrs. Oliver's chest imaging is done yet as well as her other labs."

"And I suspect Dr. Watt ordered a transfusion for our bleeding colon cancer patient."

They parted ways and Annabel went to the ground floor x-ray department. In a stack of new films, she pulled out May's chest radiograph. Even as a novice reader of films, when she put it up on the viewer box, there was no denying the lung mass on the right side.

———

Annabel approached the quiet nurses' station down the hallway from May's room and found Melody Burg dancing her fingers across her iPhone.

"It's not personal," Melody said as Annabel leaned against the counter. "I'm looking something up in the PDR." The PDR, or *Physician's Desk Reference*, was a heavy-weight textbook of pharmaceutical knowledge. Technology couldn't have done a better job than getting the monster on a mobile device for clinicians to carry in their pockets. "I'm checking the dosage of a drug for Mrs. Oliver," she added. "I'm ordering her a cough suppressant and rest to help minimize her hemoptysis."

Annabel nodded at the two simple strategies which would help. "I just pulled her chest x-ray from downstairs, which is waiting to be read by the radiologist; you all were right. She has a lung mass."

Melody slipped her phone back into her pocket. "What do you think is the next step in her work up?"

Annabel thought through the steps: making the diagnosis, staging a disease, treating it by knowing what stage it's in, and then following the course and disease's response. They were still in the infancy step of making the diagnosis and the only way to cinch that was to make a tissue diagnosis.

"I suspect a biopsy procedure is in order," Annabel said.

"Precisely." Melody closed the chart and stood up. "And tomorrow morning, we'll discuss all of this with her." She nodded towards the hallway. "Her boyfriend came and they're inside her room with the door closed. If you look in on her, you can at least tell her that her lab work looks okay."

"I'll tell her and at least meet her friend. She may have him listed as a contact person."

"As for me, I have a break since Chineka, Dr. Watt, is in the ER with Dr. Schott seeing the next patient. I use every minute I can to squeeze in other items that can't be avoided. With that, I'm going to the call room to file my nails."

Annabel smiled. "No wonder you look so meticulously groomed."

"I may be a doctor, but I'm not overlooking my femininity. Women with successful careers anymore think they need to blend in with the guys. I look at it opposite. If they are free to be 'guys,' then I'm free to be myself too." She took a step. "And by the way, downstairs is our team's fifth admission for today, and you're up again next."

Annabel frowned. She needed to speed read through a chapter on lung cancer and now there may be another medical topic to absorb. More importantly, the sleep she desired before her big date tomorrow might not be possible.

———

Outside May's door, Annabel paused before knocking. She was glad she did because it sounded like someone was crying inside. Strange, she thought, since her boyfriend may still be with her. She tapped on the door, poked her head in, and received a neutral glance from both of them. She proceeded inside where a thirty-plus-year-old man rested his head in his hands next to the bed and May fought to hold back her sobbing.

Annabel thought twice about disturbing them but couldn't back out now. "I'm one of the medical students," she said. "Can I help out with something?"

"I'm Jeff," the man said. "May and I are close friends." He looked at his girlfriend, who didn't respond and he shrugged his shoulders at Annabel.

"I came by to check Mrs. Oliver's vital signs from the bedside chart and to tell her most of her lab work fell into the 'normal' category."

May wiped her right eye and stared at the tissue in her hand.

"Dr. Burg ordered you a cough suppressant, which may help you sleep better tonight and if your dinner didn't appeal to you, perhaps we can smuggle in a soft snack from the kitchen."

"I'm not hungry," she said. "I don't think I'll ever be hungry again."

Jeff ran his fingers through straight black hair and then shook his head.

"How could this have happened?" May sobbed.

Perplexed, Annabel asked, "What are you referring to?"

"I do it when the need arises and it's never been a problem. Tell her what happened, Jeff."

"May left her labradoodle at the doggie day care this morning before going to work. She knew she was going to seek medical advice after work about the darn bloody cough she's had, so didn't want Riley left so long. Anyway, I swung by there to pick him up."

Annabel shifted her weight. She didn't want to hear that the poor woman's dog was sick.

"Jeff picked him up all right," May interjected, angry and sad at the same time. "Picked up a dead dog."

A silence lapsed while May wiped her eyes again.

"I'm so sorry. I'm a dog lover, so I can understand your shock and despair."

"Riley was in a large room and most of the other dogs had left. One of the girls who works there came back through with her own dog because she forgot something. Her pet picked a fight with May's dog. The pit bull managed to snap Riley's neck."

Annabel's muscles tensed up and she couldn't finish the breath she'd been taking. She wished she didn't just hear that or picture the tragic event in her mind. Being a dedicated dog lover, she couldn't handle the emotional strain when she heard of pets being hurt.

But by tomorrow, May would be facing her own personal, physical news besides what happened to her four-legged best friend. If anything, Annabel hoped the loss of her dog would circumvent her dwelling on the significance of her own diagnosis, but it was too bad the woman had to deal with both.

CHAPTER 3

At 11 p.m., Annabel longed to stretch out in the call room. Any minute, however, she expected to be flagged down by Chineka Watts or Donn Schott to see her next patient in the ER. Lying down would only taunt her into wanting to stay in that position longer. She might as well go head off the call, show up in the emergency department, and behave like a student thirsty for another admission.

She slipped into the bathroom on the ground floor. If Dr. Burg could spruce herself up during the day, then so could she. Looking in the mirror, she admired her straight, white teeth, the product of wearing braces in high school. That time had also corresponded with her tomboy years but, when college rolled around, as well as her first true boyfriend, the boyish manners and interests had disappeared.

That boyfriend, David, ended up being a patient of her neurosurgeon father after a concussion on the basketball court. She was so grateful they were still good friends and that, in all respects, it had been a mature relationship. Would they still be together if his medical course had not interfered with their dating? Maybe his sudden tragic event and the outcome between them was the reason why she become gun shy about serious male connections since then and why she had jumped into quick flings through social apps. However, the situation should change, she thought, and Robby Burk was just the one to put her back on track. There would be so much in common with him. They could share medical stories and always be on the same wave length as far as "career" pursuits. But she was getting ahead of herself. They had yet to go out on their first date!

Annabel rearranged some of the clutter in her two lower pockets and looked in the mirror again. Her slender build was becoming on her 5'8" frame and her medium blonde hair was peppered here and there with darker highlights like her mother's. It hung to her neck and, depending on the weather, it sometimes formed graceful curls. She stroked her fingers through it while appreciating the shiny luster. Fingers worked better than a comb or brush; her lab coat had no room to carry such things. Pockets were meant for med student items related to patients and learning. Except, of course, for the treats that she and Bob secretly harbored to share. She'd have to look into replenishing their supply since doing psychiatry, especially since he influenced the schedule doctor to put them on the same team. She smiled thinking about him; he always treated her with kindness and concern and was full of positive qualities. No wonder he had a blooming relationship with the med student, Karla.

She stepped back out into the hallway and her phone pinged with a text notification.

You getting some shut-eye yet? Bob wrote.

Ha, no, she replied, surprised at his message. *Going to see another admission!*

They rarely used to text each other on the wards and their chief made it clear not to use social technology to communicate. But, she figured, it was work related.

Waiting on another H and H. Pt may need another transfusion again! Annabel frowned. At least she was not the only student still walking the hallways. She knew the 'H and H' stood for a hemoglobin and hematocrit, allowing Bob to check the patient's blood count to guide him and Dr. Watt about giving more transfusions. And "pt" stood for patient … who was having a rocky course.

Sorry, she countered. *Hope pts and docs get some rest!*

He sent her back a smiley face while she pushed open the silver doors to enter the ER.

"I was getting ready to call you," Chineka said as Annabel approached her. "Another interesting patient for you, but this time, you'll work with me instead of Dr. Burg."

Donn was planted in a chair with a bag of microwave popcorn in his lap. "A seventy year old with Parkinson's disease," he said. "The subject can take up an entire textbook all by itself, but before you go in there, what do you presently know? We can give you a short bio of the essentials."

Chineka leaned over and grabbed a few pieces of popcorn. "He can also use some help with this midnight snack."

Thinking about his question, Annabel nodded.

"The patient comes in for medical reasons," Donn added before she could speak, "but too bad Parkinson's is already her established diagnosis. It would be splendid and memorable if you wove through a patient's symptoms and history to make the original diagnosis of Parkinson's disease."

"She's still going to appreciate it, though," Chineka said.

"What's more, there are always exam questions about it," Donn said, and popped a cluster of popcorn into his mouth.

They kept talking like she wasn't there until Annabel cleared her throat.

"Okay, then," Donn said. "We'll shut up. Enlighten us at this point."

"I'm fortunate because the little I learned in my first year neurosciences, I retained. Although those patients rarely presented to my dad as surgical cases, he used to talk about Parkinson's disease since it's a disorder of the central nervous system.

"It is a neurodegenerative disease markedly characterized by motor symptoms. The term came from the doctor who first described it and was nicknamed 'the shaking palsy.'" Knowing that historical fact, she beamed.

"As you'll find out," Donn said," the non-motor symptoms can be severely disabling as well. But here's the thirty-thousand-dollar question. What's the key, most important reason or etiology why patients exhibit Parkinsonism or Parkinson's disease?"

"From the loss of brain neurons which produce the neurotransmitter dopamine," she said and reached over to snatch some popcorn.

"Here's some butter flavoring." He pushed a small plastic bottle towards her.

"He's not that prepared," Chineka said after seeing Annabel's look of surprise. "He stole it from the ER break room."

"Thanks. Knowing where the essentials are around here is a priority."

Donn raised an unpopped kernel up to the light. "Think of this tidbit as a brain neuron. It's supposed to pop with activity, releasing the sizzling neurotransmitter, dopamine, which plays a role in proper motor movement. When it doesn't, you find patients with rigidity, resting tremors, and bradykinesia. What does that fancy word – bradykinesia - mean, however, Dr. Tilson?"

Annabel shrugged. "Slow movement."

"Ah, ha. But it's so much more than that. Yes, a patient may turn into a slow, mundane walker and eater, but that slowness redefines his or her personality and who they are. The idiosyncrasies of swinging or gesturing with our hands and arms, or even our seemingly insignificant facial expressions, are erased."

"Plus," Chineka, added, "you may also realize that dopamine is more than a neurotransmitter for movement. It enhances our memory, sleep, mood, learning, behavior, and, right now, the pleasure we're experiencing from eating this snack."

"We'll quit lecturing and I'm going to bed for as long as I can," Donn said. "March in there now to see your patient and the family caretaker who's with her. To save you the suspense, the reason the Parkinson's patient is here is for systemic symptoms of a UTI."

He crumpled the bag, tossed it in the garbage, and patted Annabel's shoulder as he passed. She took a big breath with tiredness and excitement. Since it was now the next day, she tried not to think about seeing Robby Burk in the evening. She slipped into a back cubicle to catch up on her new patient's paperwork.

Annabel read all the doctors' entries on her patient and also noted that some lab work was outstanding. Of course, that would be her job to round them up if they were still missing by morning rounds. Time for overnight sleep was slowing ebbing away.

She memorized her new patient's name and age of seventy, wrote them on an index card, and plunged ahead through the blue drapes. Two women were inside; separated only by age and the passage of time, they were clearly mother and daughter. The older woman's hair was drastically short but otherwise they shared similar nasal anatomy, narrow eyes, and golden honey-colored hair. That's who Dr. Schott meant was the caretaker, she surmised - a loving daughter.

"I was waiting for a med student to appear," the younger one said.

"Did my residents prepare you that I'd show up?"

"One of them mentioned it, but I interviewed at this hospital yesterday since I'm trying to change jobs. They explained to me that this place is also a teaching hospital affiliated with the university." The woman stood and shook Annabel's hand and then rubbed her palm on her cotton pants. "I'm Gloria Pratt and this is my mother, Darlene."

"I'm Annabel Tilson. Nice to meet you both." She shifted her position to Darlene, who was bolstered forward on the stretcher with several pillows. "Mrs. Pratt, what brought you in here today?"

Gloria sat back down. "She's not a good historian because of some dementia; some days worse than others. You'll have to get most of that stuff from me. Around eighty percent of patients with Parkinson's disease develop dementia within twenty years of diagnosis and it's been twenty years for my mom."

Annabel scrutinized Gloria, who swung her leg over her knee and bobbed it back and forth. She wore heavy black laced shoes which Annabel thought would be worn by someone much older.

"That must be difficult for both of you," Annabel said. "I understand you take care of her."

"You bet I do. I spend most of my time doing it too. I live in my mom's house where I converted the living room into a nursing home floor. There's a hospital bed there for her where she spends a substantial segment of each day. I work three ten-hour shifts a week when I have a home health nurse cover for me. I need to make the income and it helps me get out of the house."

"Your dedication to her is commendable. You're obviously doing a remarkable job." Annabel figured that Gloria was approaching forty; not a fun way to be spending her middle-aged years.

"Thanks. Although she told me years ago she never wanted to get to this stage."

Annabel nodded absentmindedly while noting Darlene's tremor. It was as if her hand was having a convulsion trying to rest on the mattress.

"Getting back to your original question," Gloria said, "Mom is often incontinent, but the last two days have been worse and I detected a hint of blood in her urine. After I got home today, the nurse who left said Mom had a fever. So here we are."

"Any other symptoms?"

"When I do manage to situate her on the portable toilet, she grimaces. I think she's in pain, it burns, and it smells bad."

"Has this happened before?"

"Sure. We go through the UTI, or urinary tract infection thing, at least once or twice a year, but this time I can tell that maybe the infection spread further."

"I think you're right," Annabel said. "The ER record has her temp at a hundred- nd one."

Annabel continued with a thorough history and had to remind herself to focus on the immediate medical problem. Asking about Mrs. Pratt's

Parkinson's disease was a separate issue that could take her the whole night. That disease and its course could be dealt with on rounds and after she spent some time with her patient after her admission.

She started Darlene's physical exam and found her lungs and heart to sound normal and Mrs. Pratt didn't flinch when Annabel palpated over each kidney. The increased muscle tone in her arms from Parkinson's impressed her and there was marked resistance to passive stretch when Annabel tried to move her limb. Rigidity was a hallmark of the disease.

As she continued her exam, Mrs. Pratt stumbled through a slow progression of words that at least made sense.

"What … is your name?" Darlene asked.

"I'm a medical student. Dr. Tilson."

"Shit," she said.

"Be prepared," Gloria said. "She hasn't forgotten bad words."

"It won't offend me. She must have been feisty in her time."

"No kidding," Grace mumbled.

The woman became quiet again while Annabel studied her rhythmic tremor. She noted it increased while she asked Annabel her name, it only occurred on the right side, and she rubbed her thumb and index finger against each other over and over again.

Annabel stepped back when she finished. "Do you mind if I call you Gloria since you both have the same last name?" she asked the daughter.

"Sure," she said, glancing at the clock. "Like me, I bet you're dying to go to bed."

"I can't count on it," Annabel said. "As far as your mom, do you have any questions? She is being admitted and they've ordered IV antibiotics for her, but we'll know more from the lab in a day or two about the specific organism responsible for the UTI. At that point, we can change antibiotics to something more specific. The other docs may have mentioned it, but her bladder is probably involved with the infection and not her kidneys. She didn't squirm when I examined the area around her kidneys, which was a promising sign."

"I hear you. She probably has just an old fashioned E. coli infection."

Annabel raised her eyebrows.

"I know a little," Gloria said. "I'm a medical assistant and work in an outpatient ambulatory center where I do a combination of administrative and clinical duties. Mundane stuff like updating medical records, doing coding, and other clerical tasks. I like the clinical aspect better like collecting lab specimens, preparing and administering medications, removing sutures, blah, blah, blah. I even get to run the electrocardiograms sometimes."

Annabel laughed. "That explains it. You're qualified to take care of you mother too."

"Surely you are aware that women are the real caretakers. The guys just pretend to be."

Annabel half smiled and also noted the time. She still needed an H&P on the chart, which usually took longer to write than she thought.

"We'll see your mom on rounds in the morning. They'll be moving her soon."

Gloria pulled a plastic bottle of hand sanitizer out of her purse, squirted a glob in her palm, and began massaging it into her hands as Annabel stepped away.

Outside, Annabel found a spot at a desk away from the busy ER staff and began writing.

Chief complaint: Daughter states her mother, the patient, has more incontinence than normal, blood in her urine, and a fever.

She paused, yearning to find out if she was the only medical student still working, and leaned back with her cell phone.

She texted Bob. *Still on the ward?*

I'm leaving now! Patient's red blood count is stable. U?

Starting to write my H&P!

Bummer. You can always delay your date tonight with Burk to another time.

That's a possibility but I'll go if it kills me!

Then please don't go. He finished with a smiley face.

She shook her head. As usual, he made her smile.

CHAPTER 4

Annabel hated the walk to the call room. Away from the wards, the quiet, desolate corridors with their strong white lighting gave her the creeps. Daytime was bad enough, but nighttime seemed much worse. She appreciated their separate rooms, but that compounded the desolation of the new area. Everyone else was tucked in bed and she would be lucky if her eyes closed by 3 a.m.

She threw her white coat on the chair inside, tightened the drawstring on her scrubs, and pulled back the blanket and nestled in. The pillow, mattress, and linen smelled and felt so fresh, she realized she must be the first person to use them.

Her mind jumped ahead to the evening. She needed to plan what to wear; even so far as two outfits, depending on where Robby and her would eat. Most days on the rotation with him, she had worn pants. Tonight called for showing off her legs. She formulated a skirt and blouse in her mind and decided on her emerald green dress if the evening called for a dressier look.

Annabel realized the importance of their meeting. A couple will always remember their first date, she thought; where they went, how it went. That successful first encounter seemed to be an iconic event which launched couples into the years that followed.

But how far physically would they go tonight? It might not be a wise idea to go all the way if she didn't get enough sleep. Passionate sex takes vitality, she thought, and by tonight, she may be lacking sleep and vigor. And should she invite him back to her place or would he suggest his? Both scenarios posed a problem because if they spent the night, she had to get up and out early for clinical duties the next day. But what was she thinking? He had the same early schedule for surgeries.

She tossed on her side. Forget about all these stupid details, she thought. Only imagine Robby Burk … sitting across from him, looking into his eyes, taking in his karma. Sleep swiftly swept over her and when she woke back up, she had to scramble to see patients and be on time for rounds.

Dr. Schott, the two residents, and four students piled into the office where Donn signaled to clear off the couch, desk, and two chairs.

"The floor and any space you can find on shelves is fair game for your gear," Donn said as they moved items around. "If you make the clutter organized, so much the better."

Annabel grinned at Bob. The two coat hooks were not enough for all the bulky winter jackets and Bob threw half of them on boxes in the corner. Annabel stashed three insulated food cooler bags past a book end and moved the desk printer as far back as possible so she could sit in its place.

"Are patients seen?" Donn asked.

Heads bobbed up and down.

"Annabel, did you make it to bed?"

"Eventually," she said.

"Everybody get coffee?" He gestured with his plastic cup.

All heads shook no.

"Eww," he said. "We'll swing by the ICU after we visit all our patients. I'll vouch for us to steal theirs." Blank expressions stared back at him and he rubbed his beard. "We'll plow through rounds. The attending can't make this morning, so you're off the hook with him. I'm briefing him on our admissions later and I'll also check all our patients out to today's call team." Melody and Chineka smiled because they didn't have to do it. They couldn't ask for a bigger break.

Donn took a baby step and flicked his finger on the wall board with their patients' names. "We'll see Dr. Burg and Tilson's patient, May Oliver, first." His finger went to the door. "Onward and outward."

Outside May's room, Donn put up his hand. "We discussed Mrs. Oliver in the cafeteria yesterday," he said. "Dr. Tilson, give us an update."

"Mrs. Oliver is the patient who came in with hemoptysis," she reminded the other students, "which seems to be under better control with cough suppressants and rest. However, her chest x-ray confirms a right lung mass."

"Which doesn't surprise us," Donn said. "That film continues to support the primary working diagnosis we came up with. So think ahead, Dr. Tilson. What is your next move to establish the histology of that mass and whether or not it's malignant?"

Annabel gave Melody a smile. "Fiber-optic bronchoscopy."

"You two discussed your patient. Exactly. We need a tissue sample." He chugged down the last sip of his coffee and squished the cup with his hand. "That suspicious neoplasm doesn't belong there. After rounds, Dr. Burg, write the order for a pulmonary consult. A lung doctor can do the procedure and assist us with their expertise."

He led the group into May's room. Her tray table was beside her as she sat in an oversized armchair. Half-finished breakfast and paper wrappings were scattered on top.

"Good morning, Mrs. Oliver," Donn said. "I see you chugged down your coffee like me." He showed her his cup and dropped it into the wastebasket. "May I?" he asked as he moved the table further to the side.

Mrs. Oliver sniffled and darted her glance at Annabel. Her chest began heaving up and down as she started to weep. "My boyfriend, Jeff, just called me. He called a lawyer a little while ago, got a bit of advice, and I'm going to hire him." She held out her attenuated fingers to clasp Annabel's hand.

Annabel crouched down beside her chair and the bed, took May's hand, and glanced at her group. "Mrs. Oliver's dog died yesterday while it was boarded in day care."

May reached into the pocket of her robe and pulled out her cell. She opened up pictures and passed them her phone. "Here's my Misty. She was the sweetest thing in the world."

"She must have been a great companion," Annabel said, looking at the furry brown dog. "Do you plan on taking legal action against the facility?"

"For sure. I don't want to, but what happened to Misty was negligence. That worker shouldn't have walked through there with her nasty dog." She wiped a tear away and laced Annabel's hand with a firmer grip.

"We're sorry about your dog," Dr. Schott said. He paused, hoping her tears would dry up. "Please don't be surprised if pulmonary doctors come by to talk to you today. We are asking them for their input because an abnormality showed up on your chest films."

"So that may explain this bloody cough I'm experiencing?"

"Most likely. We'll get to the bottom of it."

She let go of Annabel. "Is there anything we can do for you?" Annabel asked.

May only shook her head and looked at Misty's picture. The team started out the door and then the chief resident paused. "We're leaving the hospital since we've been here all night," he said. "Another team will be covering for us, but we'll be by tomorrow morning." His remark fell on deaf ears.

"Annabel and Dr. Burg did a physical exam on Mrs. Oliver," Donn said outside the doorway, "but did the rest of you appreciate her fingers?"

"I was so wrapped up in her sorrow," Bob said, "but nevertheless, I couldn't miss it. Was that finger clubbing?"

"Unmistakable," Jordan mumbled.

"Dr. Maldonado, would you like to expand on that?" Donn asked.

"Clubbing is an enlargement of the terminal digital phalanges," the student said, practically puffing out his chest, "and also the nail bed angle diminishes."

"In non-medical terms," Donn said practically in Jordan's face, "chunky fingertips. Not bad coming from a student. Tell them why I brought it up, Dr. Burg."

Melody demonstrated with her own hands. "Clubbing of the fingers can be seen in some chronic pulmonary conditions, but it's most commonly seen in patients with lung cancer."

"That gives us one more thing pointing to our working diagnosis," their chief said. "And here's another ominous tidbit. We said that the majority of lung cancers are linked to smoking, but of the 15% not related to smoking, the majority are found in women."

Annabel frowned and shook her head for them all. "This poor woman has two too many ominous occurrences going on now in her life: probable lung cancer and the loss of her beloved dog under gruesome circumstances."

The team crowded around the bed of Bob's admission from the night before after he gave them a short rendition of his H&P. A pale old man, Kevin Harty, fumbled with his IV tubing and glared at them. "Take this thing out," he barked.

"Mr. Harty," Donn said, "we'll check your H&H one more time later today. If you have no more bleeding and are stable, we can send you home tomorrow. But are you sure you don't want me to consult the general surgeons?"

"No," he snapped. "They cut out part of my inside tubing down there once already. No more surgery and no more sliding that scope up my butt for a colonoscopy. The last time they did it, the source of the bleeding was not determined.

"Also, my family and the head staff at the institution need to stop sending me here every two or three months when I'm bleeding." His voice trailed off. "Doesn't anyone understand that you can't keep someone alive forever? When it's time, it's time."

"But, Mr. Harty," Donn said, "when you lose blood, there exists the simple remedy of transfusion."

"That's what you say and what you think. But you're not me. I felt my life succumbing to the hereafter when my blood count got real low in the ambulance and they resuscitated me. I am tired. Don't you understand? I am tired and I don't want to do this anymore."

A silence fell on the chief resident's voice. Annabel wanted to reassure the elderly man. She wondered if her grandfather had felt the same way in the end … if he was "tired," and wanted to say good-bye to his life. He had gone downhill with dementia and she wished he had not gone that way. It was difficult for him as well as the rest of the family.

"Mr. Harty," Bob said, "I just told my colleagues in the hallway how you're eighty-seven. The care you received since yesterday will let you go back home, maybe live a few more months or years, and perhaps let you enjoy another grandchild's birthday."

"Where I live is not home. I live in an institution. Do you know what it's like to be lumped in with old people day in and day out who are either physically incompetent or mentally impaired? Or eat meals that are nothing but lumpy starch?"

Bob frowned like he didn't believe him.

"You think I'm giving you a bunch of exaggerated horse manure. The last 'dinner' I sat down for, which they call the lunchtime meal, was a serving of more than two thousand calories. The plate was piled with hash brown potatoes, chicken fingers, and French fries. I kid you not. That stuff all comes from frozen bags which they then dump into yet another deep fryer, and is not fit for human consumption or any other living being. I can assure that the dieticians and cooks in these type of places work on monthly budgets of less than I used to spend on my dog, so they buy boxes of those frozen chicken pucks and starch for pennies. I forgot to mention that on the side was a tiny plate with about three shriveled-up pieces of lettuce topped with a half cup of thick, creamy dressing."

Mr. Harty flicked again at the IV tubing like it was a bug.

"I haven't told you, either, what my routine is when I'm not bleeding … like when I'm sitting around in doctors' waiting rooms because of aches and pains, infections, or new eye problems. And the supposed highlight of each week is bingo, which they make a big deal about; or on Sunday listening to some minister with a guitar who sings and preaches to us about the Bible while his real goal is to have us put his church in our last will and testament.

"Does any part of that sound like it's worth living for?"

Bob held his tongue; he didn't know what to say.

Mr. Harty looked straight past him to Donn. "It should be mandatory for each of these young naive students to rotate through a nursing home and an assisted living facility. Maybe it would make an impact before they go out to practice like Dr. Kildare wanting to save the world by keeping old farts working like machines when they are meant to be respectfully retired."

"Students have elective time to select options like that. They can shadow a geriatric doctor for a few weeks and experience first-hand elderly patients in those facilities."

"Now you're talking sense," he said. "Just warn them not to trip over all the wheelchairs lined up in the hallways with slouched-over bodies, the majority of them mumbling gibberish because of strokes.

"Now that I've got that stuff off my chest, I promise not to bleed today. Yank this IV from my hand and I can go back tomorrow to my miserable existence in assisted living where I came from."

Donn put his hand on Mr. Harty's shoulder and gave it a squeeze. "The food here may not be great, but it sounds better than what you eat routinely. At least enjoy your meals today. We'll see you tomorrow."

Outside, Donn waved them over to the nurses' station. "You students already took psychiatry. Do you think Mr. Harty is depressed? Do you think he needs a psych consult or for them or us to put him on an anti-depressant?"

Since he was Bob's patient, everyone looked at him. "I don't think so and I wouldn't consider it," he said. "Mr. Harty doesn't have the classic signs and symptoms. He gives no report of losing weight and he maintains a desire to eat. He can't help it if he has no control over the… excuse me

... crap he's being served. He doesn't lie around sleeping, his affect is appropriate, and he tries to keep mentally stimulated. If we simply prescribe him an anti-depressant or a sedative, we'd be guilty of trying to push him to the side or shutting him up. We don't want to be guilty of the similar behavior he is presently complaining about from the health care system."

Annabel agreed with everything Bob said and stood staring at him with admiration. Mr. Harty wasn't depressed. He told them valid points for why he was mentally and physically near the end of his life. He said it with maturity and conviction; he deserved respect for his opinion about his own life and not pills that would help silence him.

"What does everyone else think?" Dr. Schott asked, his facial expression giving no hint about his own opinion.

"I agree with Bob," Annabel said. "Based on our limited but well-schooled time on psychiatry, I do not believe Mr. Harty is clinically depressed either."

"I agree," Jordan said, "but I bet they don't like him talking like that where he lives. It may be to his benefit to be on an anti-depressant or some other sedative-like drug."

Quiet Stuart shook his head. "I agree with Bob for now. However, he may develop depression back at the facility, so I'd monitor him closely."

"Nice work. You all gave an opinion with a reason. My question was meant to provoke a discussion. There are physicians who would reach for the prescription pad, but not us, not today, and certainly not for Mr. Harty. Who knows, that man may be working on his PhD in geriatric health care delivery."

As they marched down to see Mrs. Pratt, their Parkinson's patient, Annabel asked, "Who's Dr. Kildare?"

CHAPTER 5

With no major developments from their other patients, the team stopped in the ICU kitchen like Dr. Schott had promised. The unit secretary leaned against the counter eating a donut.

"Don't mind if we clear out this coffeepot," Donn said. "These poor internal medicine students need delayed gratification for being last night's caretakers."

The woman peered over the top of her glasses. "I don't mind. Your baby-faced students work better when they're revved up on caffeine."

"Wanda, us scut monkeys will start another pot when we leave," Chineka said.

"That's my girl," the older black woman said.

Donn split a doughnut hole and popped half of it into his mouth.

"That looks splendid," Annabel said.

"That coffee you're pouring will wash it down. Here you go," he said, offering her the other half.

Annabel waved her hand, declining his offer.

"Annabel has an important post-call day today," Bob said. "She's not going to mess it up with a bigger sinking spell than she needs from empty carbs and a sugar blast."

"You talking about this glazed product? It's a trademark of the donut maker," Dr. Schott said, pointing to the patterned box. "Blueberries are in it, or at least the color blue. It can't be all that bad."

"I'm stirring up some egg whites in ground turkey when I get home," Jordan said, "to maintain my brain cells as well as my physique." He flexed his biceps and stepped to the door. "Mind if I go?"

"No," Donn said. "You're all out of here."

Annabel and Bob trooped down the stairs to retrieve their things. "Jordan's full of himself," Annabel said.

"His preoccupation with himself is going to land him in trouble someday."

"My dad reminds me that medicine and surgery is no longer like the old days. It's all about team work and there's no room for egotistical surgeons or other specialists barking at staff."

"I don't think I could bark at anybody."

"No, Bob, you're better than that."

They arrived at the office where Jordan and Stuart were leaving. Bob grabbed both their jackets.

"Here," he said, handing the lightweight parka to her. "Have a nice time tonight." He forced a smile.

Annabel nodded. "Thanks." She slung her backpack over her shoulder and hurried out.

Annabel piled her books and bag into her red SUV and headed down I-75 for her short journey home. It was noon and since most of the young generation in her neighborhood worked downtown, she found a parking spot almost at the front of the three-story house where she rented the top floor. She walked up to the corner coffee shop and café where she ordered a soothing hot tea and vegetarian sandwich. A chef made the bread on the premises and she savored the taste while thinking about poor Mr. Harty's dilemma with food.

That must be miserable, she thought. Lots of old people lose most of what they love to do and the last thing left for them is the pleasure of eating. Without that, she understood how unappealing daily life must be.

The bulletin board on the wall beside her caught her eye; advertisements for services, real estate, and used items were posted for the Cincinnati area. A letter-sized sheet had a picture of the front façade of a nursing home. The caption said *A Place for Mom*.

Annabel grimaced. I don't think so, she thought. Why does society assume that the oldest generation should be partitioned out like putting restaurant scraps in a doggy bag? Which then may sit forgotten in the back of a refrigerator which has a bad door seal, causing a temperature where the bacteria breed faster. She contemplated her analogy; the food, like the old people, turns moldy.

No way, she thought. She and her sister, Nancy, would never plant their mother or father in one of those wayside places. Besides, her aunt and uncle also lived in the large Tilson house and between the four of them, there was a tremendous amount of support. Sooner or later, she would earn a commendable salary and commit herself to getting them at-home care. She snickered at the advertisement. Luckily, those types of scenarios with her folks were a long way off.

She put down the sandwich and slipped out her cell to confirm plans with Dr. Burk.

Are we still on for tonight? she wrote. *I'm wiped out but can grab a nap and meet you later.*

Her eyes grew heavier by the minute and it was becoming more difficult to stay alert. She checked the message again before sending it. Hitting the "send" button meant it was gone forever, disallowing her to take back typos, scrambled words, or ill-conceived messages. After waiting so long to date him, she would never forgive herself if she did something stupid.

"Want some more hot water for your tea?" The young manager from behind the counter stood with an eager expression. They had conversed in there before; he was always pleasant and willing to please his customers. He wore a dark shirt with the top button open and a bulky ring on one hand.

"Sure," she said.

"You off today?"

"Now I am, but just got off from an all-nighter."

"Bummer," he said and poured water for her. "If you grip that phone any tighter, it's going to explode in your hand."

"Thanks for the tip. I'm waiting to hear back from someone, but my problem is first-date anxiety with him."

"Why? Because you think he's a ten out of a ten and excellent relationship material?"

"Yes, I do."

"Really that important, huh?"

Annabel nodded and placed the phone on the wooden table.

"Want some advice?"

"Why not?"

"Since you're thinking he's Mr. Right, you're probably setting yourself up to be perfect, which is an impossible task. Be yourself and stay with reality. And quit thinking that you're on a mission to snag him into being a life partner. Just enjoy the date and learn more about him. You'll have more fun too."

"Wow," she said. "Do you host a relationship website giving advice as a second job?"

He laughed. "No. I'm in my early thirties and dated a lot in my twenties. I'm the manager here now, so this place takes up most of my time and I also see a lot. Watching young couples in here is remarkable; sometimes I think I can figure out who's compatible and who isn't."

Her phone dinged and she startled. "There he is," the manager said. "You both will probably be sharing the same feelings of anxiety, so there you have it … something in common between the two of you for your first date!"

The message came from Robby. "Thanks," she said. "I'll remember what you've said."

As Pete went back to the sandwich counter, Annabel scanned the text.
Yes. Good. Looking forward. Meet you at the steakhouse on Walnut? 6:30 p.m.?

Yes. I'll nap quickly! she replied.

Having paid already at the counter, she started towards the door but went back instead near the register. Bags and palm-sized boxes of treats sat in wooden cubby holes and she sorted through them. A huge grin spread across her face when she found both chocolate espresso beans and chocolate-covered blueberries.

"Here," she said to the manager. "Two more items."

"Share them with your date."

"They're not for him," she said, "but for a fellow student and myself on rotation."

"Right. I'll be sure to keep them in stock."

Annabel walked up the two flights of stairs to her apartment. Inside, she walked through the kitchen to her one big room with a desk, a bed, and one over-sized comfortable chair. The big tree outside the front window appeared frozen in place with no leaves and a hint of frost. She put her things down, changed into pajamas, and crashed.

Her glorious sleep abruptly ended in an hour when a cascade of emergency vehicles zoomed past on the street out front. Annabel rubbed her eyes and padded to the bathroom, where she stood under a hot shower. She added extra hair conditioner and thought about meeting Robby. She mulled over the advice she received from Pete in the neighborhood coffee shop while she dried. Going back to sleep now was out of the question;

she would be tired later. It would be best to keep the evening short ... like turning their first date into an hour or two of quality time.

Annabel managed to read an equally short amount on lung cancer and Parkinson's disease. She peeled away from her desk; it was time to get ready. She'd never been to that restaurant before; wasn't even a fan of steak. Hopefully, the menu would have decent alternatives. She presumed it wasn't too fancy, so she picked out the skirt and blouse and warm boots.

She rubbed mousse into her hair, glided on lipstick, and bundled up in her black jacket and red warm hat and sprinted out to the car. Annabel was aware of the steakhouse on Walnut, but when she neared it, she realized it was a one-way street and it took her several attempts to come off the parallel street and find it. After-work traffic crawled and then she circled around the block again for a parking spot. Despite trying to put her anxiety under wrap, it was getting the best of her. How embarrassing to be late.

She hurried against the cold wind and entered Kirk's Steakhouse. It smelled wonderful as she looked around trying to spot Robby. "Will someone be joining you?" the maître d asked.

"Yes. I don't see him."

"I'll sit you comfortably while you wait. Table or booth?"

"A booth will be fine."

He guided her over, handed her a menu, and said, "Enjoy."

The first thing she did was place her cell on the placemat. A waitress stepped over and then came back with the white wine she ordered to ease her nerves. Her pulse pounded more definitively in her wrist. Darn, she thought, she was almost twenty minutes late, but he was overdue worse than her. She took a sip. Did this mean she was being stood up? What a horrible thought!

With the volume all the way up, her phone dinged like it was a sedentary tree frog calling a mate.

I'm guessing you are held up, but are you okay? Robby texted.

No problems here, she typed back. *Yes, I thought we were supposed to meet at the restaurant at 6:30.*

I'd see you if you were here. Where are you? Never mind, I'll call.

Perplexed, she held the phone as it rang.

"Hi. Did you think you were stood up, which caused you to leave?"

"No. I wouldn't expect that from you," she said.

"That would be childish behavior. I arrived five minutes early at The

Steakhouse. Did you go somewhere else?"

"What steakhouse? I'm a few blocks off the freeway at Kirk's Steakhouse on Walnut."

After a silence, he said, "That explains it. I'm a few miles west of you. I thought you said you knew this place."

"I did know of this one. I've never been that far over on Walnut to know that there's another steak restaurant in the area. An honest mistake."

"We didn't coordinate this well."

Annabel looked at her watch; 7:30. It might as well be 11 p.m. the way she was feeling.

"Want to come up here?" he asked. "I'm enjoying a craft beer and munching on a plate of appetizers which I thought you'd enjoy."

"Umm," she stammered. "I'm halfway through a glass of wine and am about to eat a warm dinner roll."

"Then I'll head your way. I need to pay the bill. The road going east, however, is down to one lane for repairs so it make take me awhile."

She frowned. However, this date, more than any, was a priority. "Okay, I'm not going anywhere, but I do have to get up at the usual ungodly hour."

"Me, too. I'll hang up and see you shortly."

Robby waited for the waitress and asked for a to-go container and the bill. She disappeared to the kitchen, served another table, and then trotted back with a Styrofoam box, but without the bill. He slid in the stuffed mushrooms and potato skins.

The traffic on Walnut was doubly ensnarled. Someone hit a few road cones and Robby and another man got out of their vehicles to straighten up the mess.

At Kirk's Steakhouse, all Annabel could think of was that the date-turned-late was now nothing more than a bad idea. Already 8 o'clock … by the time Robby arrived, they ordered, and dinner came, she should be in bed. A romantic, enjoyable date was turning into an impracticality after the long hours of her hospital call and tedious wait. Her nerves were spent, and her glow to see him was also gone. With her attention span diminished, her desire for bed had intensified.

The reality of living a life as a medical student and the responsibilities that entailed made her snap to the practical decision. She called his number back.

"Robby, hey, I'm sorry about this. Our plan took a prolonged course tonight and I think we should reschedule. Do you mind?"

Robby sat at a traffic light close to the restaurant. "Yes, perhaps that's best. We'll do it another time. Drive home safely."

"Good night," she said. She left the remains of an appetizer and frowned while paying the bill. Her stomach grumbled and she drove home with a silent radio. How much energy she had invested in their first date that never materialized, she thought. At home, she fell into bed quickly, sorry about the entire night.

CHAPTER 6

Annabel woke up with a headache. Above her right eye throbbed with a dull percussion like a timely instrument. The only scenario that would top how terrible the night before had turned out was if the two of them had eaten dinner and had a dreadful time. She contemplated the whole scenario and then rolled out of bed.

"Damn," she mumbled as she ran the water until it turned warm. When Robby mentioned meeting at the steakhouse, she should have asked him to be specific. Then again, he had told her his plan where he wanted to eat without asking her opinion. How would they get back on track for a date? Would he call her or should she call or text him? And should she wait? If too many days elapsed before they connected again, then the possibility of never going out with him might become a reality.

For the time being, she needed to get him out of her mind. A full day of internal medicine, interesting patients, and scut work was on today's agenda as well as the companionship of her team members. She liked the group and cherished Bob's company most of all. Time to slip out of her apartment and face the day on the wards.

Annabel buzzed in to see each of her patients before Dr. Schott arrived. Her seventy-year-old Parkinson's patient, Darlene Pratt, was a sight she hated to witness; nothing but a vestige of a woman who used to be normal and did nothing to deserve the medical health that befell her.

For a second, Darlene's eyes popped open wider when she realized Annabel had entered and she mumbled unintelligible gibberish her way. Now her short hair was flatter than before like a dried pancake adhering to her skull. Annabel tilted the bedside chart and noted her patient's vital signs since yesterday. Hanging from the pole next to the bed was the aminoglycoside antibiotic they had prescribed her. The blue infusion pump was set to deliver it over an hour and someone had added extra wrapping around her forearm to keep the IV in place.

The clunking of food trays from the kitchen cart outside the door came to a stop and a man wearing silent sneakers walked in and grinned. He placed the tray on the rolling table and left.

"Just in time," Darlene's daughter, Gloria, said as she walked in dragging her feet. The thick shoes she wore added to the noise she created with her clumsy gait.

Annabel nodded hello as Gloria piled her coat and bag on a chair and went around the bed to the tray table like it was an emergency.

"Is my mother's condition under control this morning?"

"She ran a low-grade temperature during the night. Until she has a day or two of antibiotics, that's to be expected."

Gloria raised her mother's bed with the remote controls and straightened her up. "Mom, I'm here. Your daughter, Gloria."

Darlene made a big inspiratory sigh. Her head barely moved as she made eye contact. A slight glimpse of recognition glinted in her eyes.

Gloria uncovered the hot food and checked the temperature of it with her own tongue. Satisfied, she brought grits to her mother's lips.

"She has dysphagia," Gloria said. "You know ... difficulty swallowing. She requires soft food. It's only a question of time when we'll need a tube placed to feed her."

"Maybe that will be a ways off," Annabel said. "I must go meet my colleagues, but we'll be by." She silently applauded Gloria's dedication as she wandered to the office.

The students, not the junior residents, were accounted for. They acknowledged each other with "good morning" and nods of the head. Dr. Schott sat cross-legged in the corner of the couch with his daily *USA Today*. He lowered the paper to see who had come in and raised it back up.

"Nothing should surprise me anymore," he said. "I'm not that much older than the millennial generation, but even I can't wrap my head around the behavior of your age group."

Bob stepped aside for Annabel to find a spot for her things. They wondered what Donn was referring to.

"The title of this article is 'Sex before dating is OK and the rules have changed,'" Donn said. "It says 'While the rule of thumb may have been wait to have sex until a third date, 34% of singles have had sex before a first date, and millennials are 48% more likely to have sex before a first date than all other generations of singles in America.'"

He poked his head out for a second to see their reaction of open mouths.

Except for Annabel, who held her breath.

"This comes from a survey," he continued, "and the woman who helped develop it says 'Millennials especially are unencumbered by fears that may have held people back from sex in the past. They are career-oriented, so sex before the first date could be a 'sex interview,' where they want to know if they want to spend time with this person.'"

Annabel cringed. Hearing what she did for the last six months on an almost regular basis sounded terrible the way it was portrayed. But she knew lots of millennials were doing it like her; this just proved it. She glanced at Bob, who seemed surprised yet not alarmed with disbelief.

Above the paper, the top of Donn's head went back and forth in disapproval as he continued reading. "Forty percent of singles have dated someone they met online. And it says sex now is almost a given and it's not the intimate part. That part is getting to know someone and going on a date!"

Melody and Chineka walked in as Dr. Schott folded over the newspaper. "I can't read another word," he said. "Knowing this gives me the creeps. I'm glad my parents aren't aware of this behavior. I can hear them now. 'What's this world coming to?'"

He sighed and scrutinized each of them. "I hope none of you partake in anything close to this behavior. I'm not preaching, I'm saying it because of the potential for sexually transmitted diseases, the threat of pregnancy with or without condoms, and whether you can trust someone when they say they're on birth control. And besides, a risk exists by being behind closed doors with a person you don't know and who may possess a criminal record. In my opinion, the behavior they speak about and its consequences could put an abrupt stop to a significant career."

A redness swept up from Annabel's neck to her cheeks. She felt flushed and could use fresh air. Between last night and this morning, events related to dating were causing her much angst.

Dr. Schott rose, slid his paper into his briefcase, and waved his arm. "Come on. Let's talk at or near the bedside of our patients."

The residents and Dr. Schott loaded patient charts on the rolling cart behind the nurse's station.

Annabel stared at the floor and hoped that the flushing of her cheeks had diminished. For a major article about millennial dating and current practices via social apps to appear in a prominent newspaper gave credence to the fact that many people her age were doing the same thing. They had even done a study on it. She understood Dr. Schott's points, however; she had gotten herself into trouble a few times with dating or sleeping with someone she didn't know. In the old days, which was probably his point, two people usually stalled before becoming intimate.

"Annabel, you're awfully quiet this morning," Bob said, taking a step closer to her. "I didn't ask you about how it went last night because I thought you'd be brimming over smiling, but you're not."

Her expression soured more than the sour face she already wore. She kept looking at the floor and did not meet his stare. "There was a mix up. We didn't end up having the date."

"I'm sorry," he said, dying to hear why. "I'd be disappointed too." She must be crushed, he thought, waiting for a further explanation. But none came.

Stuart sighed next to her, whipped out his index cards, and thumbed through them. Jordan stopped scrolling through his iPhone, making sure Donn wasn't looking their way.

"I can't believe what Dr. Schott read to us," Jordan said. "I just located the Findar dating app and installed it. Ha, I have to at least check it out. It must be easier for guys to do the behavior the researchers talked about. I can't imagine a female doing it. They must all be sluts. But if they're out there and available, what the heck. I must think about it."

"Jordan," Bob said. "You'll get what you ask for."

Jordan shrugged. "I suppose so. Plus, can you imagine some girl finding out that a guy is on his way to becoming a doctor? Female gold-diggers would come out of the woodwork."

"What do you think, Stuart?" Bob asked.

"Perhaps, after thorough vetting and research," Stuart answered, "you could find decent dating material on a social app but not with the intent of jumping into bed. For six months, my brother's been going out with someone he met online and he likes her."

"We haven't heard from Annabel," Jordan said.

Annabel frowned.

"Annabel is too smart," Bob said, "and comes from a good family. She'd never do something like that. There are plenty of exceptional males around in medicine that would like to go out with her. She doesn't need to stoop that low."

Annabel felt like putting her head into her hands and blocking them all out. If they said one more word, she was going to scream.

Melody's heels click-clacked across the hall as she pushed the cart of charts in front of her. Dr. Schott and Chineka stopped before she did and Donn pulled something out of his pocket. Everyone waited as he ripped open the wrapping to a mint and popped it in his mouth.

"Dr. Tilson," Donn said as he held the peppermint inside his cheek, which made a bulge. "Let's hear your update on May Oliver."

"The pulmonary service visited her yesterday," Annabel said, "and left a note. Like we thought, they recommended a fiber optic bronchoscopy; she's on their schedule for tomorrow."

"I wonder how much they told her," Donn said.

"I don't think the word 'cancer' has been mentioned yet."

"Good. My instincts tell me to give her this time to ponder the possibilities. Although there might be some denial, there is rarely a patient that skips over thinking of the prospect of cancer."

"Her hemoptysis is still present," Annabel continued, "and she complained of waking up with it during the night, but her vital signs are stable, and still no sign of a fever or infection. Her white count is normal."

"With all the reading you did yesterday after call, Dr. Tilson, what did you learn about potential other risk factors for lung cancer for a patient like Mrs. Oliver ... since she doesn't smoke?"

Annabel never came across anything about it in her limited reading. She pursed her lips with frustration.

"No problem," Dr. Schott said. "But you better learn it by test time. Mrs. Oliver went from college to a coffee shop and gives no history of exposure to occupational or environmental toxins which would have ramped up her risk. Specifically, what would that entail, Dr. Palmer?"

"Asbestos," Bob said.

"Good. What else?"

"Radon," Stuart said, "or a significant blast of radiation exposure."

"Nice," Donn said. "What if she had a history of being around asbestos? Dr. Schneider, tell the students the current, new thoughts on lung cancer screening."

Melody left her hand wrapped around the rail of the cart. "There was a trial with select high-risk patients where they received a yearly low-dose CT scan of the chest. Their findings showed a reduction in lung cancer mortality so that routine screening in clinical practice is becoming more common."

The ache in Annabel's head that she woke up with intensified. She drew a blank with common information about her patient's probable diagnosis, but she also realized the abundance of knowledge the residents possessed. They could even rattle off medical studies and findings, which meant pouring over the latest journals. When would she have so much material absorbed in her brain that she could read "extra"?

Dr. Schott opened May's chart, scribbled some order, and then marched in her room.

"I can't believe you came up with 'asbestos,'" Annabel said to Bob. "I had forgotten about that."

"I am more aware because my uncle worked in a World War II shipyard and died from lung cancer." He gave her arm a little squeeze, trying to make her feel better.

"Mrs. Oliver," Donn said. "How are you doing this morning?"

"Please don't call me Mrs. Oliver," she said, turning around from the window. "It makes me think you're talking to someone much older than I am. I'm only thirty-two, in case you forgot. Can you all call me 'May' instead?"

"Thirty-two is my cutoff." He smiled. "May it is."

"Thank you. Since I will live until I'm ninety, there is plenty of time later to stick a 'Mrs.' in front of my name." She slumped into the chair and pulled a magazine from the sill with her. "Just like I planned on Misty being with me until I at least turned forty. The lawyer says I've got a straightforward convincing case against that doggie day care especially because, in this state, pets are considered part of the family and not property. But I don't care about the money from a lawsuit. I would rather have my dog back." She coughed and wiggled her hand for a tissue. Annabel leaned over to the nightstand and passed two of them over to her. "Bloody mess," May said after spitting in one.

"The loss of your dog came at a bad time," Dr. Schott said. "While you were here."

"She would be alive if I had not shown up here."

"Yes, I see your point," Donn said, trying to get away from the conversation and on to pulmonary matters. "Did the lung doctor explain your procedure for tomorrow?"

"He is only going to insert a long gadget down my throat into my airway to look around. If he snags a tiny sample of the material he saw on x-ray, then the lab will take a look at it to make sure it's normal."

"Yes, it will be the pathologist that does that. He or she is skilled at different types of tissue under the microscope. They often deal with cells that are growing too fast and/or where they shouldn't be. Perhaps cells that are abnormal and benign or abnormal and cancerous."

"He said something to that effect," she said. "Did I show you the picture of Misty yesterday?" She clutched the other tissue and rubbed her eyes.

CHAPTER 7

Wide-open curtains allowed the team to appreciate the fluffy cumulous clouds outside. The heat blew up from the floor heating system, but a chill could be felt from that section of the hall. Annabel rubbed her hands together as they waited for Dr. Burg to finish writing an order on May Oliver for the next day's bronchoscopy.

"Dr. Palmer, you're up next," Donn said, "for a report."

"Mr. Harty has been stable since yesterday without any further blood loss. His blood pressure is fine as well and his H&H has not dropped any further. Dr. Watts and I are in agreement for him to go home today. With your permission, sir."

"Most likely," Donn said. "What if you had a patient without the overt blood loss that Mr. Harty presented with? What if you have an outpatient who is suspected of having blood loss from the GI tract? What can you do to begin the workup to find out?"

"Give them one of those fecal occult blood tests," Bob said.

"Yes. A stool guaiac test which they can take at home. However, that should never substitute for a skilled GI doc or one of us internal medicine doctors doing an endoscopic evaluation."

"I guess my patient and Annabel's patient are both examples of folks needing a scope down or up either end of the body for diagnostic purposes."

"So true," Dr. Schott said. "But, as we are aware, Mr. Harty is past that stage and the procedure was not proven useful the last time or two. We also have not talked about his iron deficiency anemia due to his chronic or acute blood loss. Your astute resident is going to send your patient home with a prescription for iron replacement. A better iron level will help with his exercise tolerance."

Bob nodded while Annabel stole a glance outside. Donn turned, heading for the patient's room.

"Besides iron," Bob said to Annabel as they stepped away, "I want to give Mr. Harty a gym pass for a personal trainer who makes his clients bench press 135 pounds in one week."

"I don't think Dr. Schott was referring to that kind of exercise tolerance," she said. "He meant like just getting up to go to the refrigerator or out to the mailbox."

Bob smiled. "I was checking if you were listening on rounds or out there in the clouds."

"Sometimes you're a pain, you know it?"

"I hope so."

Donn glanced back once making sure his group fell in line.

"We're springing you out of here tomorrow," Dr. Schott said, entering Mr. Harty's room. "Are you up for that?"

"I suppose," the elderly man said. "If I had to vote on it, the old people's home is slightly more preferable to the hospital. Say your good-byes because I refuse to come back."

"Maybe you won't have to. Dr. Watts and Dr. Palmer are going to fix you up with some iron and we'll follow you in clinic. Why don't you go back and beat everyone at bingo, card games, and chess?"

"Chess?! I'd be lucky to witness any of them play a decent game of checkers." He glanced at one student after the other. "But you young saplings probably don't have a clue what that is. You all grew up with video games. However, I don't mean to belittle other seniors. We're all in the same boat; we're just paddling with different oars."

"Life is short," Dr. Schott said. "We may make it to your age someday too, and we'll have full empathy and understanding for what you're going through. I often tell my students 'Don't die young and don't get old.'"

"Wouldn't that be nice? Living that way would be a miracle."

The team rounded on Stuart and Jordan's patients. Annabel and Bob exchanged glances; it was getting late in the morning and the students still had notes to write and busy work to do. They were on their way to see Darlene Pratt and Annabel figured her daughter had long since finished feeding her breakfast.

Dr. Schott stopped abruptly. "Here comes our attending doctor in charge," he said.

A man about sixty years old wearing a crisp sports jacket came their way. With his last few steps, his comb over became more obvious and his otherwise serious expression became less intense.

"I'm Dr. Mejia, Sebastian Mejia," he said to the group. He nodded at

Donn. "Dr. Schott, am I in time for a few patients?"

"One interesting patient left," Donn said, "although they're all fascinating."

"Then we'll do a thorough study of one aspect of their disease. And by the way, I'm a cardiologist," he told the students. "I keep hearts ticking."

"I plan on cardiothoracic surgery," Jordan said.

Dr. Mejia directed his attention solely at Jordan. "Are you aware that, more and more, heart problems needing anatomic intervention are being taken care of without the knife? Consider gallbladder removal surgery because of gallstones – a cholecystectomy. Years ago, that small organ used to be taken out with a big open incision. Now they primarily remove it with a couple of instruments through a few holes. These days, cardiothoracic surgeons with less business wish they were poking holes and running catheters and small instruments into the heart like me."

Dr. Mejia turned away from Jordan and made eye contact with Bob, and after all introductions, he asked, "Which student and resident has the last patient to see?"

Annabel and Dr. Watts spoke up.

"Dr. Watts, why is your patient here?"

"She's a seventy-year-old with Parkinson's disease admitted for a UTI."

The attending fiddled with his tie. "Unfortunate but fascinating disease, Parkinson's." He went from shaking his head to nodding. "Dr. Schott, how much have you discussed its equally engrossing treatment?"

"Not too much except that the students understand that patients lack the brain neurotransmitter dopamine and need replacement therapy."

"Dr. Schott even brought popcorn into the analogy," Bob said with a smile.

"Perfectly understandable for Dr. Schott to bring food into the picture. The interesting pharmacology is that we can't just hand out dopamine pills for patients to swallow. Resident Watts, tell them why."

"Exogenous dopamine cannot cross the blood-brain barrier," she said, "so it is an ineffective treatment."

"The blood-brain barrier sounds like some kind of wall built inside the brain," he said. "Talk to these students like they're premed and assume they know nothing. Describe to us what you mean by the infamous blood-brain barrier."

Chineka shifted her weight to the other foot. "It is a semipermeable membrane, highly selective, formed by tightly-connected endothelial cells which separate circulating blood from the brain's fluid outside of cells in the entire central nervous system."

"In other words," Dr. Mejia said, "it is a real membrane barrier with an intense purpose. Your point is that if we give someone a dopamine pill, it can't travel into the brain through the barrier. How do we get around that?"

"Scientists came up with a drug years ago. A 'prodrug.' In other words," she said focusing on the med students, "a different chemical form of dopamine which can pass through the barrier into the brain. The name of it is levodopa and the brain actually converts that drug into dopamine."

"So if human beings are determined enough, they find a way to achieve what they want," Dr. Mejia said. "In medicine and life.

"But the pharmacology story does not end there," he said. "The prodrug, levodopa, undergoes too much metabolism in the gut, so little would be left for availability, so another drug called carbidopa must be added to it. That reduces the body's conversion, outside the brain, of levodopa to dopamine. Therefore, more levodopa is available to pass into the brain. We end up with a domino effect and we can't have one without the other two!"

Annabel appreciated their attending's enthusiasm for pharmacology, especially since he clearly enjoyed using his hands for the procedures in the cath lab. It made her think of the little she knew of anesthesia. They also needed technical skills and an abundance of pharmacology knowledge.

"Part of the responsibility with our Parkinson's disease patient is making sure their dose of carbidopa with levodopa tablets is therapeutic and to watch for potential adverse side effects."

Dr. Mejia looked at Annabel this time. "What are the harmful effects?"

"If too much of a dose or a high level occurs, I suppose central nervous system effects," Annabel said, "since it works in the brain."

"Understandable guess, but you don't know the specifics," he said.

She hoped Bob wouldn't rattle off the answer to this one, too, or she'd surely feel left behind. Dr. Watts spoke up.

"Central nervous system, CNS, effects for sure," Chineka said. "Confusion, hallucinations, sedation; and GI effects may include nausea and vomiting, or other things that happen with Parkinson's itself, making it difficult to separate symptoms from over-treatment or from the disease itself."

"Yes, confusing, isn't it?" Dr. Mejia said. "Actually, Parkinson's is such a large subject that some doctors become experts because they deal with it as a substantial part of their practice or in a center. It's no wonder why, since it is the second most frequent neurodegenerative disorder after Alzheimer's disease and more common in the elderly. Not to say that either sex can't develop Parkinson's in their thirties and forties. However, there is a ratio of men to women of about two-to-one."

Dr. Mejia patted his forward-facing fluffed hair. "What's your patient's name?" he asked Annabel.

"Mrs. Pratt."

"This way," Donn said. They walked around a nurse with a medicine cart as she dropped pills into little plastic cups and then they entered Darlene's room.

"We're being invaded," Gloria said, seeing the whole team. The bedsheet half covered Darlene's bare chest as Gloria held her mother's right arm, trying to wiggle it into a blouse sleeve.

"I'm changing her top because she soiled it," Gloria said. "Come on, Dr. Tilson, take the other sleeve from behind her and pull it on her on that side. Be careful of the hep-lock for her IV antibiotics."

Annabel chipped in to help as the assistant from outside also came in with a pill cup.

"We must get her pills down with something soft," Gloria said.

"Let's try this," the nurse said. She mixed the pills in applesauce and handed the cup over.

Gloria pulled over Annabel's side of the blouse in front, buttoned it up, and then tied on a bib. She spoon fed the contents of the pill container while everyone waited. Mrs. Pratt barely opened her lips, so Gloria clenched her mouth with one hand and slid the applesauce in with the other.

"Mission accomplished," she told the nurse, knowing it was part of the woman's job to make sure the patient took their meds.

The nurse dropped the empty cup into the waste bag hanging on her cart. "Thanks, ma'am," she said and disappeared out the door.

"Like we were saying outside," Dr. Mejia said, "Mrs. Pratt's meds are essential. No different than many other patients. At least in the hospital there is accountability for them being taken in the right dose, the right time, and the correct route."

"I'm Mrs. Pratt's daughter," Gloria said and gave her name.

"I'm Dr. Mejia, the attending doctor on your mother's case. Do you have any questions for me?"

"No," she said. She turned to the sink faucet and poured a few ounces of water into a cup and then added a bit of the protein drink from the tray table. She mixed it with a straw as Dr. Mejia watched and then encouraged her mother to take a sip. "I expect Mom will be out of here soon."

"Yes," Sebastian said. "The team believes so. She is making progress with the IV antibiotic."

Darlene took a sip and then pursed her lips to keep away the straw. Gloria shrugged. "Thanks," she said. "Dr. Tilson, I'm sure, will keep me updated. She's been very helpful."

Listening to Melody's heels on the polished floor, the group trudged out and pulled shut the door behind them. Few patients, Annabel thought, end up with the loving one-on-one care that Gloria showers on her mom.

Donn strolled into the office and waved Bob off the desk chair. "Almost three thirty," he said. "Time for you students to get over to the University for your weekly lecture at 4 p.m. No coming back here either. The days you have your lecture, the residents and I will take care of the patients before we leave." He pulled a baggie forward from the back of the desk, opened it, and slid out a half peanut butter and jelly sandwich.

"That looks good," Jordan said. "Wish I had brought one of those."

"Peanut butter is a great picker-upper. But I go light on the jelly after several times of wearing red strawberry goop on my white coat." He took a bite and closed his eyes for a second, savoring the taste. "Any idea who's lecturing today or what the topic is?"

"One of the staff from downtown," Annabel said. "I guess we'll find out the topic when we go over there."

"Pay attention. A few exam questions always come from lectures."

Annabel bundled up and made sure she gathered her books. All four students went down the staircase, and as they headed for the front door, Jordan peeled off taking a different way.

"He must have parked around back," Annabel said.

Bob shook his head. "Nah, he's playing hooky."

"I don't profess to know as much as Jordan to do that," she said.

"Neither do I," Bob said. "See you there." They braced themselves against the cold and drove separately. By the start of the lecture, they were scouting around at the back of the conference room looking for each other. Bob sat next to her; the first lecture slide was up on the main screen announcing the speaker and the topic of "Human Immunodeficiency Virus (HIV)."

"I'm going to take notes," Bob said and weeded through his bag for a notebook.

Annabel checked her phone, made sure it was silenced, and placed it on the empty seat next to her.

"You're keeping tabs if Robby Burk texts you, aren't you?" Bob asked quietly as the speaker fiddled with the computer setup for the presentation.

She frowned and nodded as they both settled back and listened to information about the clinical approach to a patient with HIV. The MD talked about opportunistic infections because of patients with increased levels of immunodeficiency.

Annabel wanted to close her eyes. A cat nap would be wonderful. She wished she had one of Dr. Schott's pb & j sandwiches to give her a boost, or better yet, a stiff cup of coffee. A caffeine blast. Caffeine, she thought, remembering what she had forgotten about the entire day - the chocolate espresso beans and blueberries. She had bought them for both Bob and her and they were shoved in the outer pocket of her backpack.

Her mouth watered with anticipation and she leaned over to the bag on the floor and discreetly opened the zipper. She grasped both boxes and slinked them into her lap. With a pat on Bob's knee, she got his attention. He also looked like he was about to fall asleep.

Bob's smile grew wider upon seeing both items. He wiggled his fingers, ready to try either one. Annabel gave him the blueberries to open while she pried the box top off the espresso beans.

"Other patients can have a latent period," the speaker said, "when there are no clinical manifestations of immunocompromise. That can last up to ten years."

Annabel shifted the open box towards Bob to take the first ones. He did and then she poured a few chocolate-covered blueberries into her free hand. With much discretion, their hands went back and forth to their mouths. Annabel giggled and leaned closer to Bob. "It's the little things," she whispered.

He nodded, took the clipped pen off his vest pocket, and slipped out an index card. *Thanks,* he wrote. *Delicious!*

CHAPTER 8

To Annabel's disappointment, Robby Burk never contacted her in the evening. Perhaps he was on call, she thought as she prepared for bed. Even if he wasn't, a chief resident's responsibilities were stacked high just like it was her duty to be studying and absorbing everything related to internal medicine.

Annabel woke with a chill and realized she had not turned up the heat the night before. She opened the curtains to the view of the street and the tree and grinned at the falling snowflakes and the flurries bouncing against the window. Some clung to the branches and accumulated on the ground. At least it was better than boring weather; she liked the white landscape rather than the usual dismal gray typical of southern Ohio in the winter.

After dressing in warm black pants and an overhead sweater, Annabel drove to the hospital, traffic slower than normal with one fender bender cluttering up the slow lane. After checking on her patients, she went back to the office and in a short time, everyone arrived except for their chief resident.

"Go grab a cup of coffee or something," Dr. Burg said as Annabel noted the resident's high heels. The weather was no deterrent for Melody's choice in shoes.

"I just saw Dr. Schott," Melody said, "and he's gone off with our attending for a meeting. We'll have rounds in an hour or two after he gets back."

Bob tapped Annabel's arm. "Come on, let's find some decent coffee."

"ICU or the cafeteria?"

"We can sit undisturbed downstairs."

"I'm in," she said and got up.

They hastened down the hallway and then Bob stopped short. "Do you mind if we see my patient, Mr. Harty? He's getting ready to leave and we can say good-bye."

"He makes me think of my grandfather and he helps instigate a floodgate of memories."

"Memories and some old people make you want to hug them like your only dog."

"But some of them can be crabby and cantankerous," she said as they turned into his room.

An aide parked a wheelchair next to the window and helped Mr. Harty put on his jacket. He wore street clothes and sturdy brown shoes.

"Mr. Harty," Bob said. "Dr. Tilson and I are the send-off committee, but we hope to see you in clinic."

Annabel stooped over and pulled up the foot pedals as he stepped in front of the seat and sat down. Bob grabbed the suitcase on the bed.

"I'm all in order," Mr. Harty said. "This young woman is carrying the paperwork that gets passed on to the Mother Superiors in the facility where I live. That's what I call the two women who each have their own office when you first walk in the entrance. Everything goes through them ... like decisions about everything. They're like school principals. For instance, I get reprimanded that storage space is limited so I can't stock up on extra items when there's an internet sale. Such as on my nonskid slippers, which I practically live in. I have two pairs and someone told me I own one pair too many."

The aide began wheeling him out and Annabel and Bob followed on either side.

"Or, for instance," he continued, "I can tolerate an hour or two a day on my small computer. Most elderly folks think they are actively involved with emails and the internet age by just pressing the 'forward' button on the stupid jokes and political rhetoric emails they receive from friends. They can't write decent correspondence themselves, so that's what they do.

"Anyway, the time I spend on my electronic device is the brainiest activity I do all day. Googling things I'm curious about and checking if any unseen family emailed me. Plus, I pulled off a coup and managed to break the facility's space restrictions. I smuggled in a small drop-leaf table to place my Apple computer on. However, the Mothers forbid my chair on wheels to use with the table."

"They prohibited a rolling chair?" Annabel asked. "Why?"

They entered the empty elevator and the aide pushed the ground floor button as Mr. Harty's eyebrows went up. "I suppose they considered it to be a lethal weapon. Heaven forbid, I could break a speed limit rolling around in my confined space and plummet myself out the window or crash into a gawker ambling down the hallway."

Annabel and Bob glanced at each other and couldn't resist laughing.

"I can see it now," Bob said. "Elderly man accomplishes a *Guinness World Book* record for the fastest and most creative use of a rolling chair."

"Darn right," Mr. Harty said. "At least I'd be remembered for something."

On the first floor, the young woman stopped and pushed the lever to lock Mr. Harty's wheelchair in place. "Can you two mind him a moment so I can step out the door? I need to flag the attention of the van driver so he can pull up the vehicle."

"Sure," Annabel said.

Mr. Harty began fastening the snaps on his jacket and continued. "And even though I'm in assisted living, there isn't much I can depend on being assisted with. The caregivers, the CNA's, are overworked and underpaid just like the nursing staff. I don't like leaving my designated wing to get someone from over in the nursing home section. I walked through there the other day when residents were crying and a family member was yelling at the nursing staff. The nurses can't help the fact that the place is short staffed."

Mr. Harty looked back up at them and let out a big sigh. "I could tell story after story," he said. "The other day, there was a woman over there who wet herself. Staff tried to change her but she was pounding her fists at them like you'd swear she used to be a sport's fighter. So mean and nasty, but what does that woman know? Her mind is completely gone. It took a whole team of CNAs and nurses away from their other duties to try and distract her so they could put clean clothes on her.

"But what's the point in living when this sorry existence is all these residents have left?" he asked.

"Those are tough questions," Annabel said. "My grandpa slipped into dementia in the end and I counted on and was blessed by his wisdom for years before that. He's in here," she said, putting her hand over her heart. "We hated for him to not be the person he always was in the end. And where a person should receive their care in the end is a real dilemma for the elderly person or patient and the family."

Outside the revolving doors, the aide spoke with a man in a uniform and then he hurried across the salted parking lot.

"The two of you are probably too naïve to realize that the primary purpose of the facility where I live or others like it is to make a profit. It makes for an easy, profitable business. Build cheap buildings with paper thin walls and no extra space, stock it with residents who pay triple the monthly fee of a nice rental unit, stick in a couple of overworked staff, and watch the bank account soar."

"Were you a businessman before you retired?" Bob asked.

"For years, I was in one of the top four positions of a major corporation and then, after I retired, I stayed on as a consultant to the board. My medical problems and transfer to assisted living has changed all of that."

"That must have been a huge and sad change for you," Annabel said.

The van pulled up outside the door, the driver hopped out, and the aide came in. She unlocked the wheelchair and they headed for the door.

"You two did good work," Mr. Harty said as Annabel and Bob took a few steps alongside him. "Thank you and keep it up."

The man from the van helped Mr. Harty up from the chair and took the case Bob was holding. Annabel and Bob watched as they went out and climbed into the vehicle.

Annabel and Bob poured coffee, paid at the register, and sat down. A man in a suit sat at the adjacent table and the cafeteria was peppered with visitors and hospital staff. The breakfast selections were slim; people were drinking coffee or eating scrambled eggs, grits, or bagels.

"I still find it amazing that Mr. Harty is eighty-seven years old," Annabel said.

"He sure is smart," Bob said, "and loves mental stimulation. I bet he has a thousand tales to tell."

As Annabel dumped a creamer into her cup, she realized the man next to them was on his cell phone and she had a beef with hearing other people's private conversations. "Too bad we can't listen to a few of his stories," she said. She leaned over for a spoon wrapped in a napkin and began stirring her coffee. The man beside her was not aware of his voice carrying over to her as he talked.

"All those plans are in place," the man said. "The marketing people I hired are used to recruiting admissions into assisted living facilities."

Bob borrowed Annabel's spoon as she peeked over to the man. Middle-aged and tan ... maybe from a winter tanning bed, she thought.

"What I had to drill into them in no unsubtle terms," the man said, "was that I want to stock the facility with retard women. It's easy to pick women out like that during the application process and interviews. Then all we do is add horny retard men; the two sexes can keep busy amongst themselves and no one will be the wiser. Keep staff to a minimum and if problems develop with residents complaining about anything to outsiders, who's going to believe a bunch of daft old-timers anyway?"

Annabel's jaw dropped as the man tapped a knife on the table and stared off, listening to the other party on the line. She gazed at Bob, who furrowed his brow, and she leaned closer.

"Did you hear any of that?" she asked.

"I missed the beginning," he whispered, "but I heard enough."

"Yeah," the man said, "if you look at my financial schematic, it's a win-win situation. I'll need another dependable administrator if and when I open up the second one on the other side of town. Think about it."

A text dinged on Annabel's phone. Hoping it was Robby Burk, she picked it up immediately. "It's Dr. Watts," Annabel said. "Dr. Schott is back and they're ready for rounds."

"Good," Bob said, pushing back from the table. "Sitting here, we overheard more than we were supposed to or wanted to."

Annabel mustered up a critical frown and glared at the man while Bob placed his half cup of coffee on the edge of his table and tipped it over. With an "oops" and a "sorry," they kept walking.

The brown van pulled into the circular drive under the awning of "Winchester's Cove." The nursing home and assisted living facility received its name from a negligible inlet on the Ohio; the name based more on an idea rather than a reality. The driver helped Mr. Harty out and the woman went with him inside where she handed over the hospital discharge papers to a woman in the front office.

"Mr. Harty," the woman supervisor, Dale, said, "I'll pass along your updated medicine list to the nurse coordinator. I hope you haven't lost all your strength and there are no more GI bleeds."

"Me too," he said, admiring the fresh flowers on her desk. He leaned over and took a sniff at the most natural thing he'd seen in days.

"Would you like one of us to walk you back to your room with that bag?"

"No thank you," he said, knowing she only wanted to get rid of him. He stepped outside her door and fidgeted to open the snaps on his winter coat and ambled down the hallway with his trusty suitcase.

A woman with bright white hair pushed a walker along the carpet as she mumbled something and looked straight ahead, not making eye contact with him. Her room was two doors down from his, but she had never said a word to him. He started to say good morning but decided instead not to waste his breath.

Mr. Harty fumbled in the deep pocket of his jacket for his room key. The facility always locked the room of a resident who was away, but he laughed at that. He knew most of the stealing was done by people who worked there and if a resident stole something from someone, what were they going to do with it? And if an old person did steal, they were either one of the nasty ones or clueless as to what they were doing.

He unlocked his door and stepped into the single big room that functioned as his entire home. A baby refrigerator and a sink with a few cabinets was on the left, a bathroom on the right, and the rest of the single space functioned as a bedroom and a place for a chair. His wonderful drop-table was to the side and his computer still sat on top.

On his dresser, there were only a handful of knickknacks. After holding on to a lifetime of a few precious items of sentimental value, he had none of them. Since space was limited, the facility let him know that collectibles must be limited if not extinct. "No space, or they could get damaged by housekeeping or disappear" was what they told him. He chuckled again at the housekeeping part. If they referred to housekeeping as waving a square cloth around his room once or twice a month as dusting or cleaning other than vacuuming, then he and his wife had done it wrong their whole life.

He opened his double-door closet. Inside, the space now held almost every single physical thing left from his life … like a stack of pictures in a box. Pathetic, he thought, because "they" put a limit on how many pictures he could hang on the wall because of the nail holes they would make. That meant when he died and the room went to the next person to die in, they would have to repair the holes. He hung up his jacket and closed the squeaky door.

When he turned to his computer table, he realized his throw rug underneath was not there. Strange, he thought. The colorful piece had belonged to his parents and he cherished it; they had brought it back from a trip to Europe at least sixty years ago.

Mr. Harty wanted to sit in his recliner for a short rest before the mid-day "dinner" meal but instead walked back up to the office. Every door along the hallway was open and several rooms away he witnessed a man on the floor, a cane on the tile floor next to him. "Help," the man inside said slowly several times.

Kevin kept walking. A CNA walked the other way and he waved ahead for her to stop. "Mr. Riggs fell again," he said. "He's on the floor."

The woman heard him but disappeared into the doorway next to her. "Mrs. Underwood, you need to turn the TV down to a hospitable volume," she said loudly in the room. "And you knocked your milk container on the floor."

Mr. Harty continued on, but the administrator wasn't in the office. He guessed where to find her through the double doors into the nursing section where she most likely was talking to the head honcho of the entire place. Walking through the doors, a new, yet familiar, odor hit his nostrils - the pungent mixture of urine and potent cleaning liquids.

The woman he needed to speak to was headed his way. He waited outside the doorway of Mrs. Trindle, a woman who, years ago, was way ahead of her time. She had started and owned an interior design company and had furnished upscale hotels and businesses with their decorating plans; her husband being her assistant. Her vast wealth was now left to her only survivor – a lucky niece – who rarely and only came to see her to make sure that no one was showering attention on the woman with the motive to somehow hone in on her wealth.

Mr. Harty frowned because now Mrs. Trindle was a demented old lady notorious for peeing and pooping everywhere. He poked his head in because he didn't see her, but he could smell her. Around the bend, she was in the bathroom on all fours smearing poop on the wall. What irony, he thought, the transition from what she was to what she has become; and from being an intelligent woman running a business, now someone needed to wipe her butt. He grimaced and almost missed the administrator who rushed to flee the odors before they permeated into her clothes.

"Dale," he said.

"What is it?"

He lagged as she pulled ahead of him to the double doors. "My throw rug that means a lot to me is not in my room. Maybe one of the staff accidently put it back in my closet, but I don't see it." He carefully chose his words. If it seemed like he was complaining about staff and they heard about it, they would inflict repercussions on him. They would pay him back because they got in trouble. Their deeds would be crafty and nasty or they'd neglect to answer his calls for help in the middle of the night. And then he would have to keep his mouth shut about that too, or he'd suffer worse.

"Mr. Harty, we've told you before that throw rugs are tripping hazards. Before, I was nice enough to ask the maintenance man to store it in your closet, but you retrieved it. One of your doctors said we can't have you falling, so I had the piece removed." She opened one of the doors and held it for him. "Don't be late for lunch," she said and turned into her office.

CHAPTER 9

Annabel and Bob turned into the office where Dr. Schott lounged on the sofa with a *USA Today* obscuring his face. Melody swung her feet while sitting on the desk and Chineka's head was buried in a textbook. Jordan and Stuart snuck glances at their index cards.

"Scientists announced that Antarctica registered the warmest temperature ever recorded," Donn said from behind his newspaper. "Sixty-eight degrees. Time to buy land in Alabama because that will become Gulf-front property someday, particularly for our heirs." He folded the paper and made eye contact around the room.

"Dr. Burg and Dr. Tilson," he said, standing up and pointing to the white board. "We're going to see your patient, May Oliver, first. She is scheduled for her bronchoscopy and I'm encouraging Annabel to go along with her and see the procedure. Nothing like having a bird's eye view of travelling down the upper airway."

Annabel smiled. "Thanks, Dr. Schott. That will be amazing. Not like dissecting a lung in gross anatomy."

"So true. Also, I believe your presence will be supportive and beneficial for Mrs. Oliver."

Donn led them out the room and, with chart in hand, they soon stood inside May's room. The bathroom door was open and she leaned over the sink.

"More coughing up blood," she said out the door. "On top of this, you all disallowed me from eating breakfast."

"You can't have anything in your stomach for the procedure," Dr. Schott said. "You will be sedated and we don't want food passively coming up and accidentally going into your lungs or hindering the process. Is anyone here with you this morning?"

"No. My boyfriend, Jeff, is working."

"Dr. Tilson is going along. She'll show up in the procedure room."

May walked out, her hospital gown hanging loosely off her shoulders; Annabel could swear she'd lost weight since her admission.

"I would appreciate that," she said. "Besides the depression of losing Misty, I'm feeling lousier by the day. What's wrong with me anyway?"

"We're aiming to find out," Dr. Schott said.

Annabel volunteered to start May's IV so she could practice that skill and slid a narrow-gauge catheter into May's hand. The pulmonologist, Dr. Cantrell, ordered Versed immediately and the RN in the procedure room slipped one cc into the IV. Next, the doctor squirted local anesthetic into May's nose and throat; she sneezed, coughed, and then settled her head again against the back of the stretcher. The doctor looked again at her chest x-ray while waiting for the numbness to take effect from the spray.

"My lawyer thinks the dog kennel with the day care isn't going to want the publicity of my lawsuit," May sputtered to Annabel. "He thinks they are going to settle out of court. Maybe they'll pay me so much that it covers all my medical bills." The sedation fully kicked in, she closed her eyes, and her hand relaxed on her abdomen.

"Don't worry about a thing," Annabel said softly. "It sounds like you have a dependable attorney and your lung doctor here is going to make your procedure seem effortless."

Dr. Cantrell inserted the flexible fiber-optic scope through May's nose. Adequately drowsy, they also had her hooked up to oxygen. At the tip of the scope was a light and as the doctor began threading the device down May's throat, the view was seen on the camera at the upper end. Annabel stood against the stretcher and the nurse gave one more dose of Versed when May reacted to the passage of the tube through her vocal cords. They viewed the progress down the cartilaginous and membranous trachea or windpipe.

"Can you guess the age group I do the most frequent emergency bronchoscopies on?" Dr. Cantrell asked.

Not knowing the answer, Annabel shrugged her shoulders. She was not out that long from the first two years of medical school bookwork to know. "No," she said. "I wouldn't guess that many are done."

"Pediatric patients," Dr. Cantrell said. "Kids. They put the craziest things in their mouths, they choke, and then whatever it is gets aspirated into their lungs. The biggest thing I've retrieved so far was a bracelet."

"Jeez," Annabel said.

"Really. Aspiration of foreign objects surprises me half the time too." She infused a warm saline solution down the scope to help clean May's airway, allowing better visualization, and also to collect some of that fluid back through the scope to be used as pathology samples.

They watched as the scope came upon the carina where the trachea divides or bifurcates into two separate smaller airways called bronchi, one going into each lung.

"Based on the respiratory tract's anatomy," the pulmonologist said, "if someone aspirates a foreign object, which path would the object most likely take? The right or left bronchi?"

Annabel thought about her gross anatomy class. The bronchus going to the left lung was longer and the right bronchus was shorter. Maybe more important, she thought, was that the left bronchus took an abrupt angle, making it easier for food or an item to take the less resistant path along the right. "I suspect the right side," she said.

"Correct. And here we are going off to the right, which, as you can tell, is a more effortless path for the scope. We're heading this way because Oliver's area of suspicion is in the right lung."

Stemming from the bronchus were smaller bronchial tubes; Dr. Cantrell guided the scope with the necessary attachment down a main one and then snagged a tissue sample of the questionable area. After she finished examining May's lungs and procuring the biopsies, Dr. Cantrell removed the bronchoscope.

"I'll follow Mrs. Oliver after the procedure," she said, "but you will also be taking care of her. What were the risks of the procedure and what should you monitor her for?"

"Bleeding and infection," Annabel said, "which seems to be a common risk for many procedures. Also, breathing difficulties and hypoxemia, even though May tolerated the procedure well with the oxygen that you delivered. Now, I'll watch her for a fever which could signify an infection, monitor if her hemoptysis becomes worse; and, also, if her lung was accidentally punctured, we could be dealing with a collapsed lung. I mean a pneumothorax."

Dr. Cantrell listened and gave Annabel a thumbs-up.

"Thanks for letting me be a part of the procedure," Annabel said.

"It's part of your journey," Dr. Cantrell commented. She studied May's vital signs on the monitors and patted her shoulder. "Mrs. Oliver, the procedure went fine and we are finished."

May's eyes opened and closed and she nodded as best she could

"You'll still be groggy, but you can rest for a few hours," Dr. Cantrell said. "You can't eat or drink for a while anyway because your throat is numb. Then for a day or two it may be hoarse."

May grunted an "okay" and squeezed Annabel's hand.

"I'm going to go peer over the pathologist's work," Dr. Cantrell said, "and let you all know as soon as we have Mrs. Oliver's tissue diagnosis."

Mr. Harty dozed in his recliner, but he startled from a noise outside his window. A maintenance man stood on a ladder in his winter work clothes clipping a tree limb which had caught on the gutter. The place used him for just about anything and he wondered how much longer the man would continue to work at the facility.

A woman appeared outside the doorway with a therapy dog named Rusty. She visited once a week with her trusted companion, who caused many residents to smile when they saw and petted the dog. Kevin was particularly fond of animals and looked forward to and appreciated the visit more than most. He pushed out of his chair and made his way out to the hallway.

The young woman smiled and waited with the furry American Eskimo dog for Mr. Harty. The dog's tail whipped around and it pranced in its place with anticipation of greeting the old man and being petted. When Kevin stood at the doorway, another resident named Mrs. Potter reached them with her walker leading the way. She wore a loose-fitting top and flared-out knit pants, which sometimes doubled as pajamas. Her skinny fingers un-gripped the top brace pipe and her index finger waved at the woman with the dog.

"Get that dog out of here," she said.

"Mrs. Potter," the woman said, "Rusty is a certified therapy dog and is allowed to visit the residents here."

"Get that dirty dog out of here."

"She's not dirty, Ma'am."

"All dogs are dirty. I know what they do."

The therapy dog woman hesitated and stole a glance at Kevin.

Mrs. Potter waited a second; she tensed her lips in anger because her complaint was not being heeded. "I'm allergic to dogs," she added. "Get the damn thing out of my way."

The therapy dog woman frowned. "Sorry, Mr. Harty," she said and turned. With the dog taking backward glances, she trotted him back to the entrance and headed over towards the nursing section.

Mrs. Potter put her hand back on her walker, huffed, and slowly resumed her way. A satisfied grin spread over her face.

Kevin walked back into his room, his shoulders sagging. If only he had run his fingers through the dog's soft fur and received a wet, sloppy kiss on his hand. Mrs. Potter was a bitter old lady, he thought, knowing the place was half-full of them.

He nestled into his chair again, too tired to poke around on his computer before dinner. He knew it would take weeks to regain his strength after his GI bleed; however, this time, he doubted it would happen. He sensed he was facing one big bleed after the other.

In a half hour, a woman came in with a tiny cup of meds and tapped her foot while Kevin slid them down his throat with some water. "Time to go for dinner," she said when she left.

Mr. Harty took off his non-skid slippers, slipped into presentable shoes, and went up the hallway to the dining area. Totally hungry, he sat at his usual table; he had balked at the lunch or main meal in the middle of the day and had gotten up and left. Now he absolutely needed the nutrition and calories. What they served would be vitally important.

Two other usual residents came over and sat at his table; the three of them resigned to little chit-chat at meal times. The only huge news ever to befall any of them was if a family member was due to visit, especially grandkids. Their visit would practically give a resident a stroke, such was his or her excitement. Kevin nodded at both of them but was in no mood for small talk about his hospitalization. It was done and over with and discussing blood per rectum was not a fit discussion during their meal.

Two women with aprons on came out of the adjoining kitchen wheeling two aluminum carts. They placed dinner plates down for each resident. Mr. Harty stared in front of him: a round mound of macaroni and cheese, a couple of French fries, and a slice of dried meat loaf. The bread basket was filled with dense rolls and butter packets. Amazing, he thought, no hockey-puck chicken tenders, but the meat loaf and the rest of the crap was no better. He pushed away from the table and ambled over to the kitchen door.

"Helen," he said to the older woman inside. "Can you serve me something else to eat? Honestly, I cannot and better not eat anything on that plate."

"Why?" the woman asked with a shake of her head.

"There is no fiber, vegetables, or greens to make my intestines work the way they are supposed to. Why bother with the three items, anyway? Just serve us bread and potatoes and be done with it. That plate is filled with starch, loaded with calories, and it gives me severe constipation, which makes me have to strain when I go to the bathroom. My doctor calls it a Valsalva movement. Some of my GI bleeds have erupted after I needed to do that." He tried not to glare at her. "We've been through this before, but you asked me 'why,' and forced me to give you the real, unadulterated answer."

The woman squirmed.

"Again," he said, adding more to make his point, "you asked me, which made me spell it out for you. I will end up in the hospital again soon if I keep eating this institutionalized food not even fit for Rusty."

"I don't have control over the menu or the purchase of food like you think I do," Helen said. "But, in any case, aren't most of you on handfuls of laxatives?"

"Yes, precisely, and a variety of them. Which tells you how bad the situation really is. Even they can't make proper waste of the poison you feed us."

"All I can tell you is that I will relay your concern at the next meeting between kitchen services and administration." She stood over the sink with an unused plate of food for a resident who didn't show for dinner and scraped it down the garbage disposal.

"That's exactly where it belongs," Mr. Harty said. "And you can add mine to it." He turned and walked by the residents at the tables with ceramic ornaments in the center and kept his focus on the floor.

Back in his room, he took out a slim album of photographs and thumbed through them until the sun was long set and the facility's outdoor lights came on outside his window. So many memories in one single book, he thought. Snapshots of being a youngster with bony knees and a fishing pole, photos with his wife while they toured New York City, color snaps of a him giving a presentation to business people in a conference room. He had been successful and esteemed and had forged some loving relationships. What a pity that many of those people were gone. It was better not to hang on like a spent fish at the end of a line when all the odds were against him. If he couldn't stand it now, what made him optimistic that things would be better in six months or a year? By then, the severity of his problems would escalate to such depths that they would be total hell-on-earth.

Kevin placed the album with loving respect on his bureau and closed the blinds of his window. There was not a peep now coming from the hallway, only one loud television blaring from some resident's room. He went to the doorway and looked up and down the hall and noted doors either open or closed. The bulk of the old timers were either fast asleep in bed or half-passed out in chairs. The few staff working the overnight shift had barricaded themselves somewhere where they weren't seen; being out of sight was a ploy so residents didn't ask them for assistance.

He closed the door and padded back into the room in his trusty slippers; he wouldn't worry anymore about storing two pairs of them. In essence, he wouldn't have to worry about or put up with anything anymore. Especially his GI bleeds and consequences.

Kevin opened the double doors to his closet. Shirts and trousers lined the hanging bar from left to right. The regularly used clothes, bathrobe, and jacket he kept on the right hand side; less used and good clothes were to the left, although since moving there, he had only used the finer clothes for funeral services. At the very end of the left side, he took down a hanger with a pair of clean, pressed trousers that he'd never worn. He undid the button on the back right pocket and pulled out a plastic baggie meant for sandwiches.

Before he moved into the facility, he had saved unused narcotic prescription drugs. If ever the need arose that life was not worth living or he needed Kevorkian action to be taken, he would have a plan and a method in place. He had plotted adequately for most things in his life; it made sense to do the same for the terminal end of living as well. His current situation deserved and demanded the enactment of his strategy.

He carried the baggie with him, poured a glass of water, and sat back down in his only chair. The bag contained mostly oxycodone pills and he poured all of them into his hand. One by one, he put them in his mouth and took a sip of water. They went down smoothly and he continued the process, making sure he didn't drink too much liquid that he became full. With all of the contents of the bag gone, he stepped over to his bed, slid under the covers, and rested his head on the pillow.

For the first time ever, he gloated over the fact that the place was theoretically unattended and no one would find him until the morning when perhaps a CNA poked her head in to remind him of breakfast. He closed his eyes and thought back through his life, picking out the beautiful scenery he'd witnessed, the people he'd loved, and the one and only dog that had meant the world to him. He had been caring and supportive to people and causes, as well as an intelligent and successful man. His euthanasia also reflected his unselfish ability to not hinder any more people with his management; he would not tolerate the continuance of the absurd medical problems and living condition he was presently imprisoned in.

Simply, he was desperate to die, and his death proceeded with ease and serenity.

CHAPTER 10

On the next day's morning rounds, Dr. Mejia showed up unannounced. Jordan Maldonado finished presenting his newest patient to the group and wrapped up his student H&P.

"This young female patient has persistent nosebleeds, so our job is to differentiate if it is from a systemic disease or just an isolated epistaxis." Jordan took a subtle step to the side, his shoulder impolitely putting Donn behind him as he tried to impress the attending. "The plan is to work her up and consider all bleeding disorders."

"When and if you go into cardiothoracic surgery," Dr. Mejia said, "bleeding problems will be your nemesis. Even I get into trouble threading stents up people's major blood vessels into the heart when they have undiagnosed abnormal bleeding. In your first two years of med school, you learned that platelets circulate in the blood stream and assist in blood clotting. They do that by adhering to each other and damaged epithelium in blood vessels." He opened the patient's chart in his hands, looking for Jordan's H&P, and continued, "Since you read up on your patient, you may tell your fellow students the name of, and the official number of, a low platelet count."

Jordan faced Annabel, Bob, and Stuart. "Thrombocytopenia is the term for a platelet count that's below normal; a count of less than 150,000, but some definitions use a count of 100,000." He glanced from one to the other and spoke slowly as if teaching children.

"But," the student said emphatically and gloated, "the most serious risk for life-threatening bleeding comes with a count less than 10,000."

Annabel wished Dr. Schott was in front and could see the smirk on Jordan's face.

"A count that wimpy has dire consequences," Dr. Mejia said. "Knowing your patient's sex and age already gives us a high suspicion that she has ITP, or idiopathic thrombocytopenia. Which means we won't find the cause; it's spontaneous and the etiology is obscure. But, of course, we will do a full work up because it's possible the problem is due to something else." He smiled at Jordan and expected a perfect answer to his next question.

"Pertinent to this day and age, what would be a strong possibility of a secondary cause to your patient's low platelet count?"

"Hepatitis C or autoimmune hemolytic anemia," Jordan said.

"Good, and ..." Dr. Mejia furrowed his forehead and waited. Without an answer, he focused on more possibilities from the other students.

"We heard a convincing patient case history at grand rounds this week," Bob said. "It made an impression on all the students who attended about the effects of thrombocytopenia."

"I remember seeing the topic posted on the internal medicine bulletin board." Dr. Mejia stared back at Jordan while Bob stole a glance at Annabel. She parted her lips and held back a full smile.

"Give us a summary," Dr. Mejia said to Jordan.

"I had family concerns that day. I had to skip the lecture."

"Family concerns? Right after you were sprung from the wards and supposed to be on the medical campus?"

"The timing wasn't perfect. I didn't want to ask Dr. Schott if I could leave early." He began rubbing one thumb over his other hand.

"We know Dr. Palmer was there," Dr. Mejia said. "Annabel, tell us the gist of the lecture."

"A patient presented with thrombocytopenia and an interesting, sudden mononucleosis-like illness. One thing the team thought was that he had ITP or idiopathic thrombocytopenia, but when they did laboratory testing to search for a secondary cause, they discovered he had HIV. The lecture was all about human immunodeficiency virus."

Dr. Mejia nodded, fell silent, and narrowed his eyes at Stuart. "What about you?"

"We learned that PJP is the most common opportunistic infection affecting AIDS patients, sir, and very difficult to diagnose."

"Tell your fellow class-cutter what that stands for."

"Pneumocystis jirovecii pneumonia."

Dr. Mejia pointed down the hallway, ready to resume seeing patients. He ignored looking again at Jordan as they turned and walked alongside Dr. Schott. "You have a quiet, smart student and an arrogant young man who later on will probably give doctors a bad reputation."

Annabel and Bob were directly behind them and couldn't believe their attending spoke without discretion; they wondered if Jordan and Stuart overheard him.

"There are also two fine students who work synergistically with each other," Dr. Mejia added.

Annabel and Bob glanced at each other and smiled. She dug her fingers into the espresso bean's box in her white coat, pulled out a few, and shared them with Bob.

"Did anyone talk to the pulmonologist about May Oliver's bronchoscopy results from yesterday?" Dr. Schott asked as they rounded the bend to the nurse's station.

"They were still working on slides yesterday afternoon," Melody said.

Up ahead, the lung doctor sat hunched over May's chart and looked up at them with a glum face.

"Uh-oh," Annabel said for all to hear. Earlier, she had no biopsy news and tactfully told May that pathology results often take time. Now she dreaded hearing what Dr. Cantrell had to say.

The team reached the counter and Dr. Schott sat beside her while the others huddled around them.

"I retrieved good lung samples yesterday," Dr. Cantrell said, "and the pathologist's findings are crystal clear. Mrs. Oliver has cancer; which is no surprise. Unfortunately, it is adenocarcinoma."

A shudder ran through Annabel. Because of her reading and studying so far on the topic, she wished May had one of the other types of lung cancer. This was dire news for the young woman.

"We were afraid of that," Dr. Schott said. "She fits the profile; young and never smoked." His eyes glossed over as if he had received bad news himself.

"Too bad," Dr. Mejia said. "We will continue to need your assistance with the case. Any input for our patients' treatments will be appreciated. This diagnosis, however, now turns our attention to the fact that she may have metastases. Before we start doing anything invasive on her lung or getting into chemotherapy or radiation, Dr. Burg and Dr. Tilson need to start looking at other organ systems."

"I agree," Dr. Cantrell said. "Before I make recommendations, we will need to find out what she wants to do and if her disease has spread. I haven't told her anything yet."

"We'll inform her of her diagnosis right now," Dr. Schott said.

The pulmonologist nodded, handed him May's chart, and the team headed to May's room.

May had positioned the bedside chair facing the window and she sat with her feet propped on the heating duct, staring out the window. Clouds swept along the sky and the sun intermittently shone on the scarce amount of snow on the grassy sections of the parking lot. She didn't move when they gathered beside her bed; she only turned her head to the side.

"Mrs. Oliver," Dr. Mejia said, "Dr. Schott discussed your case with the pulmonologist."

"I figure if it was okay news, you all would have told me already," she said glumly. She wore a sweatshirt and sweat pants and shuddered beneath them with a chill.

"May," Dr. Schott said, "I'm afraid the lung tissue biopsy that Dr. Cantrell took is significant for lung cancer."

May went back to focusing out the window. "Strange," she said after a prolonged silence. "I sensed bad news. What did I do, health wise or otherwise, to deserve this?"

"More than likely, nothing at all," Donn said. "Your type of cancer does not need a precursor of bad habits."

"It figures. What's it called anyway?"

"Adenocarcinoma."

"I've heard of that. So, where do I go from here?"

"We need to know the extent of it. In other words, has it traveled to other parts of your body?"

She turned her head and opened her eyes wider. "It may not only be lung cancer? It could be other places? That's a horrific idea. I'm shocked enough with being told what I suspected. I don't understand how I'm going to wrap my head around that."

"You have a lot to think about. Dr. Burg and Dr. Tilson will be ordering some tests, however, which will let us evaluate other areas of your body. Is that okay?"

May closed her eyes and nodded. The team retreated in silence but, outside the door, Annabel touched her chief resident's sleeve. "Do you mind if I spend a moment with her? I'll catch up."

"Go ahead," he said. "We're going to Darlene Pratt's room and you can meet us there."

Annabel walked back in and squatted next to May's chair. "I believe I know what you're feeling," Annabel said. "Shock, despair, anger that it happened to you, maybe even some denial. Absolute sadness that your own body is a host to cancer."

With skepticism, May turned towards Annabel. "Yes, but on top of it, I'm too damn young."

"So am I."

May narrowed her eyes and tilted her head.

"I was diagnosed with malignant melanoma a few months ago," Annabel said. "I experienced all those emotions: rage, disbelief, despair, etc. You believe the universe signaled you out and dealt a death card."

May leaned closer to Annabel. "What did you do? Do you still have the same diagnosis?"

"I had surgery. The lesion was fully removed. Although I have a clean bill of health, the threat will always be in the back of my mind. However, now I appreciate life in a more spiritual and potent way."

May swallowed and took Annabel's hand. "Thanks. I hope I turn out as lucky as you."

Annabel patted her hand. "You're welcome. Be optimistic, May, and we'll keep our fingers crossed."

When Annabel hurried back to her team, her insides twisted in a knot. May looked too terrible to simply be harboring the single lesion in her lung. Sometimes it didn't take a big "workup" to figure out when someone was not well at all.

Inside Darlene Pratt's room, the elderly woman pushed her daughter's hand off of her hair. Annabel watched from the side as her agitation grew worse and she began hitting into the air, aiming at her daughter.

"Mama, stop it," Gloria said. "All I'm trying to do is brush your hair." She put the brush on the bed and turned to the team. "This kind of behavior from her is escalating."

"Let's address that," Dr. Schott said. "In the meantime, Dr. Tilson can give us an update."

Annabel stepped between Bob and Jordan. "Mrs. Pratt has been afebrile for forty-eight hours and her IV course of antibiotics ends today. The results this morning of yesterday's urine sample appear to be clear of a UTI. When I examined her this morning and palpated her lower abdomen, she had no guarding. All her other lab work appears normal and her dose of carbidopa/levodopa seems to be well tolerated; the efficacy of her medication is not declining."

"Which would be a problem if it were," Donn said and turned to Gloria. "Mrs. Pratt, do you believe your mother's cognitive function is growing worse?"

"Her mental status deteriorated the last few years but, yes, now it's jumped to another level. Sometimes I think she's gone crazy over and above her disease."

"She's back to baseline as far as why she came to the hospital and we can prepare to send her home. However, why don't we have psychiatry come by and evaluate her again? They saw her in the past; they'll be able to judge her progression and offer suggestions."

"Sure, send them on. The sooner the better so I can get Mom home and we get back to a routine. I need to work, you know."

"Consider it done," Dr. Mejia added.

With the day behind them, Stuart picked up his things from the office right after Jordan left. "Good night," he said. "See you both tomorrow."

"Later," Bob said and reached over and grabbed Annabel's bag.

"We're getting out at a decent time," he said. "How about getting a bite to eat together?"

"Sure. Do you mind if we go to my neighborhood coffee shop? They sell sandwiches and salads and the place is close to home for me and not out of the way for you."

"All right," he said. They took the stairs and they both rushed in the cold air to their cars. "See you there," Bob said.

Annabel parked two streets over from her apartment and trudged up the hill to the corner coffee shop. She pulled her warm hat further over her ears and smiled at the cloudy condensation from her breath. At the corner, Bob came from a different direction and they went in, giggling as they hurried into the warmth of the shop.

They piled their things against the wall and, after sitting at the nearest wooden table, Annabel handed him a single-page menu. "Here," she said. "And there are other items listed on the blackboard. But we order up there."

The young manager Annabel knew from before smiled from behind the counter as they approached.

"So your first date obviously went well," the young man said.

"Huh?" Bob said.

"Oh, no," Annabel said. "The date got mixed up and we never met."

"That's too bad. Maybe it was a blessing in disguise. Well then, this must be your fine friend that you bought the special purchases for."

Annabel laughed. "Yes, you have a good memory."

"Special items?" Bob asked.

Annabel laughed again and pointed below to the wooden cubbyholes at the counter filled with snacks. "He sells our espresso beans and blueberries."

Bob smiled. "Then it's my turn to stock up. We thrive on these when we're in the hospital. Between us, it is an expression of friendship."

"Quite a friendship."

Although she didn't know why, Annabel felt her cheeks reddening. "Are you still serving some soup?" she asked.

"Broccoli cheddar. And with a grilled cheese Panera, you'll be ready to study tonight together."

"I'll take the soup and sandwich," she said.

"And make that two," Bob added, "with a hot chocolate."

"I'll take a hot tea," Annabel said.

Bob insisted on paying. "Not a big deal," he said. "You stashed us with snacks so forget about it."

Annabel shrugged. "Thank you."

They went back to the table and Annabel made herself ignore her cell phone. Robby had still not contacted her since their failed date and she had likewise kept from contacting him.

CHAPTER 11

"We could do what the manager suggested," Bob said while shaking salt and pepper on the broccoli soup.

"What's that?" Annabel asked.

"Study together tonight. You're right down the block and we both have our books."

"We could, but you've never been to my small place. All I have is one comfortable chair, a desk chair, and two kitchen stools to sit on. But besides that, I hesitate because of what Karla might think of us studying in my apartment."

"When it comes to our training, she's been under similar circumstances. The sexes merge when it comes to call rooms and study habits. In any case, she's so busy these days, we're lucky if we get together once a week."

Annabel picked up her sandwich and took a bite. "How can such a simple grilled cheese taste this special?" she asked.

"Because you've hungry and it's damn good."

She nodded in agreement and steeped the tea bag. "Is there still a spark between the two of you?"

"I don't know. You posed a thought-provoking question. But as far as studying, I don't mind sitting on your desk chair for an hour."

"Not tonight. I just want to kick back on my bed and do some reading there. And by the way, that was brilliant what you did on rounds."

"What did I do?"

"You finagled the subject of this week's grand rounds into the discussion without mentioning the topic. You ensnarled Jordan with Dr. Mejia because of his lack of attendance. I can't think of any student more deserving to be tripped up."

"He embarrassed himself and got what he deserved. Maybe he'll stop being intellectually arrogant."

"I doubt it. His God-syndrome is probably going to grow worse."

"Dr. Mejia made a revealing discovery, however, which I never thought about. His comment bodes well for us studying together too."

Annabel arched her eyebrows.

"He diagnosed how we work together. He didn't say we're symbiotic, which is a cooperative relationship, but he told Dr. Schott that we work together synergistically. We produce an effect together greater than the sum of our individual contributions. Can you believe it?"

Annabel poised her soup spoon. "I heard that and couldn't discard it like he was simply making conversation. We've spent so much time together on rotations, we're becoming like intuitive twins."

"Not just time on rotations. We've been through some harrowing situations and have dealt with, and consoled each other, over a number of patients. Even an attending." Bob frowned and handed Annabel a napkin from the dispenser.

"So true." She stared out the window a moment and added, "My dad never told me medicine would be this gut-wrenching. No wonder doctors are accused of being unsympathetic. They have to become cold to all the emotional trauma or they themselves would become basket cases and unable to treat patients and remain objectively neutral."

"We've kept empathy, Annabel. The key must be to hold on to some of it … not too much and not too little."

She nodded. "I agree. And to think of all the years we still have in front of us. I could write a book already on everything we've been through."

The manager walked over to their table. "How is everything?" he asked. "I waited to come over; you two are absorbed in conversation."

"This is better than a five-star meal right now," Annabel said. "By the way, what is your name?"

"Pete."

"Thanks, Pete," she said. "I'm fortunate your place is so close to me."

"I won't hesitate to order both of these again," Bob said, "because I'll try and come back with Annabel if she doesn't mind."

Pete gave them both a wide smile. "More water for your tea?" he asked.

Annabel acknowledged another refill and Pete went back to the counter as the bell on the top of the door sounded and another couple came in.

Annabel and Bob finished and dressed back warmly in their jackets and caps. With book gear in tow, they both left and huddled into the wind in two separate directions.

In pajamas and sprawled on her bed an hour later, Annabel focused on reading about adenocarcinoma of the lung. She had read before, in general, about lung cancer, but now she was reading more about May Oliver's specific type and how it metastasizes early. Since it was known to travel to the central nervous system, bones, and adrenal glands, they had ordered May specific tests for the next day - a bone scan and CTs of her head and abdomen. A shudder ran through her as she contemplated what the results may show.

In another hour, Annabel's book slipped from her hand to the bedspread as she accidentally dozed off. She opened her eyes and padded over to the desk to set aside her textbook. On her way back from the bathroom, her cell phone rang and she gasped with excitement at the caller's name: Robby Burk.

She sat cross-legged on the bed, took a deep breath, and answered.

"Annabel, hi. It's Robby. I hope I'm not calling too late. You're not in the hospital on call, are you? Otherwise, I can ring back tomorrow."

"I'm home and wrapping up reading for the night."

"I meant to call a few days earlier, but I was in San Diego for a conference."

"I bet the weather was warmer than here." She glanced out the front window and snow flurries had begun, twirling around outside like angel dust.

"It was beautiful but, as you'll find out in the future, you don't enjoy the weather when you go to a conference. Your days are spent sitting for hours in a large room trying to maintain your concentration on slides and a speaker who may or may not hold your interest. The highlight of each day is lunchtime and strolls to the bathroom."

"I'll remember that."

"I also gave two of the lectures. Unfortunately these days, there are many attendees that sit in the back on their iPads checking emails and googling, which is distracting and disheartening to a speaker."

"I'm sure that does not reflect on anything you said or did. If your teaching as a chief resident is any indication, your presentations must be awesome."

"Thanks for saying so. I like teaching as much as the clinical aspect of doing surgery. But enough about me. We can talk more about you if we can arrange another date that doesn't end up like the last time."

Annabel's heart raced and she held her breath. "You did promise me a dinner," she said cheerfully.

"How about the day after tomorrow, which at least falls on the weekend? I'm on call tomorrow."

"So am I," she said. "That would work."

"How about a diversion from medicine? Let's grab an early evening movie and then go for a bite to eat."

"That sounds fine. I'll dress casual."

"I'll find out the movie times and I'll pick you up at your place this time. I'll be by at 5:30."

After giving him directions to her apartment and hanging up, Annabel wrapped her arms around her knees and gave them a squeeze. How would she concentrate on the wards tomorrow after he had called her and they were set again to go out? She let go of her legs and slumped back on her pillow, creating visions of him in her mind. His chocolate eyes and hair; his height and toned, tall physique; and his preppy dressing drove her crazy. As she drifted off to sleep, she realized she couldn't wait to tell Bob that a date with Robby was imminent.

The sports section of *USA Today* covered Dr. Schott's face as the students and residents gathered in the office. "I sure am overdue," he said, "to visit a sport's bar for a couple of beers and a triad of screens showing football and basketball at the same time."

"I'll second that," Bob said. "What's more fun? The Super Bowl or the Final Four?"

"Both," Donn said and folded the paper. "And for living here, the University of Cincinnati isn't too shabby as far as basketball."

"I won't discuss teams with any doctor somewhat in charge of my grade," Bob said.

"I will," Annabel said. "I must be loyal to my hometown Vanderbilt."

"Hmm," Donn said. "She's got more guts than you do." He stood and went straight to the blackboard. "This patient list is going to grow today since we're on call, but a nice afternoon break will be the outpatient clinic. We're due downstairs at 1 p.m. If we're not too swamped, you students can do preliminary visits with the patients and present them to Dr. Burg and Dr. Watts. Otherwise, just follow us around."

"Outpatients aren't as interesting as inpatients," Jordan said.

"They are our success stories after we care for some of them in the hospital," Dr. Schott said. "So, no, they are as interesting. And they still can present with an insidious problem that requires us to admit them for observance or treatment. Now then, let's get going and see our patients. Annabel, May Oliver needs her workup today, so we won't spend much time with her. Let's go see what psychiatry said about Darlene Pratt."

"I saw the psychiatrist headed into her room after I saw her," Annabel said. "Her daughter, Gloria, was in there as usual." Donn walked faster and Annabel decided to tell Bob later about her date with Robby Burk.

Darlene Pratt was bolstered up in the chair, trying to grab the string hanging off her personal nightgown. The psychiatrist, Dr. Amin, was a long, lanky, older physician wearing a red bow tie on a white shirt. His lab coat was also bleach white like it came straight from the cleaners.

"Come in, come in," Dr. Amin said to the team. "You should all hear this too."

"Thanks for being so prompt," Donn said.

"No problem," he said. "I'm explaining to Mrs. Pratt about her mother's progressive decline in cognitive function. She understands, but the students should know ... her downward spiral consists of diminished thinking, organizing, planning, and problem solving. All the fundamentals comprising dementia. She is so much worse than the last time we evaluated her; she is not capable of any of those normal behaviors."

Gloria nodded with understanding and Dr. Amin continued with a steady, slow pace. "The new behavior, which is another game changer, is that Mrs. Pratt has developed a psychosis. This predicts a very poor prognosis. I'm afraid, Mrs. Pratt, this increases your mother's need for nursing home placement as well as the likelihood of an early mortality."

Gloria peeked at her mother, who had slumped to the side, her resting limb active with a hand tremor; her legs hanging; her feet unsupported.

"Dr. Amin," Gloria said, "you all give out advice like you know what goes on outside of these hospital walls. I live with my mother and take care of her better than any facility can. Our home is set up like a nursing home and she has 24/7 care. I am way ahead of your needs analysis."

"I commend you for that. You are more diligent than most family members, so I apologize for thinking otherwise."

"That's okay," she said.

He took a step back and addressed them all. "In my note, I suggested another medication, clozapine, to help with the psychoses. It may or may not help but feel free to give it a try."

"Thanks for your help," Dr. Schott said.

Dr. Amin leaned forward and patted Gloria on the arm. "All the best with your mom."

With Dr. Amin gone, Gloria plodded over to the chair in her thick shoes. "One of you help me move my mom back to the bed for a midmorning nap," she said.

Annabel and Bob obliged and gave Darlene support in her armpits. The woman took one step and stopped as if she would take a fall; she repeated the same movement with the other foot. When they situated her in the bed, Gloria thanked them.

"We'll write up your mom's discharge papers," Dr. Schott said. "I think we've done all we can for her. Would you be able to bring her back to clinic in about two weeks?"

"Of course," Gloria said. "If my mother could, she would thank you too." She turned to the sink and squirted hand sanitizer in her palms as they left.

The team reconvened near the nurses' station. "That was the first time you students probably witnessed a Parkinson's patient with what's called a freezing gait. They experience a sense of falling every time they lift a foot off the floor. If you noticed, each step Mrs. Pratt took resembled a controlled fall. Unfortunately, that gait appears late in the course of Parkinson's."

"What a terrible disease," Annabel said. "I'm grateful we had her as a patient. I had no idea."

"Are you and Dr. Watts satisfied that we've done the best we could?"

"We took care of her UTI," Dr. Watts said, "and helped clarify the end-stage of her disease."

"And," Annabel commented, "we are sending her home in good hands."

Annabel unzipped her thermal bag from home and pulled out a yogurt, sandwich crackers, and fruit which she'd packed that morning to bring in because of call. It was one thing to eat a single meal from the cafeteria later on, but she couldn't force herself to do it for lunch too. She peeled off the paper lid and dipped her spoon into a strawberry Greek yogurt.

Everyone was off somewhere else, but she knew they'd burst in soon because they were all due soon in clinic. Dr. Schott's newspaper was at the other corner of the couch so she reached over and flipped to the Life section.

As she savored another mouthful, Bob came breezing in and went straight to his bag. "I don't have much time, but I brought a sandwich," he said, opening a baggie. "You can't seriously be reading that newspaper."

"Why? I can't eliminate all life outside of medicine. I have a Robby Burk update and that's why I'm glancing through here."

"Is his picture in the newspaper? I suppose you'd never forget him then." He moved the paper a bit and sat down. "I'm just giving you grief," he added and took a bite.

"No. He's not in the paper. A local paper I could understand, but not a national paper." She thumped his elbow.

"I make the best sandwiches," he said, "but I digress. What's your update?"

"After I went home last night … after we met at the café, he called."

Bob raised an eyebrow and chased down his bite with a gulp of water from a bottle.

"We're going out tomorrow," she said, excited. "After we get a twenty-four or thirty-six hour call behind us."

"Congratulations. I hope you both figured out ahead of time the correct name of the restaurant to meet at."

"No, we're driving wherever together. I'm flipping through the paper to check what's playing because we're going to the movies and then to eat. But stupid me just realized they don't list local movie theatres."

"That sounds like fun. A real date. Finally. I'm happy for you." He took another bite to camouflage the lack of a smile.

"Have you heard of any good flicks playing now?"

"I bet you would appreciate the new blockbuster comedy, which has a decent cast and isn't too goofy."

"Sounds like the perfect escape," she said and then thought that sitting next to Robby in a theater would be the best part about it.

CHAPTER 12

"We're going to see all these patients?!" Jordan exclaimed after the students walked single file through the outpatient waiting room and into the office area. "Almost all the chairs are taken out there and some men are standing."

"I bet you can handle it," Bob said.

"Even all by yourself," Stuart added.

Annabel smiled at Bob. For the first time, Stuart added a smart quip relative to Jordan's behavior.

"You all forget," Jordan said. "We go back to the hospital after this for an all-nighter. We'll be dead tired after dealing with all those patients."

"Maybe you should take a Viagra," Bob said, his face serious. "That'll perk you up in more ways than one."

Jordan narrowed his eyes. "I don't think I appreciate your comment."

Bob shrugged his shoulders. "I'm just trying to help."

"Two of you come over here to Dr. Burg," Donn waved as he saw them approach, "and whoever's left go over to Dr. Watts."

Bob walked towards Chineka and Annabel followed. She tugged his sleeve and leaned into him and laughed. "I can't believe you said that to him. That was the best."

"You two look like you're having way too much fun," Chineka said, handing them each a sheet. "I made copies of the patient list for today, which also has their diagnosis and indication for the visit. Use it as a helpful summary before grabbing their charts from the plastic boxes outside the exam rooms. Annabel, come in the first patient's room with me while Bob does a preliminary evaluation of the next patient."

Chineka grabbed the first patient's folder and thumbed through it in the hallway. "This woman is a veteran's spouse and I remember seeing her two weeks ago because of high blood pressure. Sometimes patients are given the label of being hypertensive without the adequate initial clinical approach. Patients' blood pressures must be measured on two or more separate occasions before hypertension can be diagnosed."

"Makes sense," Annabel said. "I'll be sure to tell Bob in case he doesn't know. It also sounds like a good question for an exam."

"Her last name is Picks," Chineka said, knocking on the door.

Inside, a woman with matching pants and a blouse crossed her legs over the side of the exam table. She was average height and weight, which caused Annabel to discount obesity as a risk factor for hypertension.

"Hello, Mrs. Picks," Dr. Watts said. "This is Dr. Tilson, one of our medical school students on rotation."

"Nice to meet you."

"The clinic CNA recorded another high pressure today," Chineka said. "134/90."

"I told this to Dr. Watts last time," Mrs. Picks said to Annabel. "I used one of those supermarket blood pressure machines and found out I am above normal. I want to get pregnant soon and want to be as healthy as possible if I'm going to be carrying a baby around."

"Smart planning," Annabel said.

"As you'll find out on your ob/gyn rotation," Dr. Watts said to Annabel, "hypertension during pregnancy is not without its risks to mother and baby."

"Should we check Mrs. Picks' pressure again?" Annabel asked.

"Yes. Don't use the automated machine." Chineka handed Annabel the cuff from the counter and Annabel pulled her stethoscope off from around her neck. She took Mrs. Picks arm and listened to the sounds corresponding to her systolic and diastolic measurements as the cuff deflated. "132/90."

"Which means we have reproduced her high blood pressure numbers several times," Dr. Watts said. She leaned in and said, "Last time, I gave you a thorough exam and we determined there are no apparent complications from your pressure. Your hypertension is considered stage one and I'll note that in your record. Now comes our decision for treatment."

Chineka grasped her hands in front of her mouth and then put them down. "There is a multitude of high blood pressure medications and reasons to use one or two over the others. In your case, our consideration rests on your possible impending pregnancy. However, most of the drugs are contraindicated for all nine months or all stages. We do possess a tried-and-true safe class of drugs for pregnant women called beta-blockers; the one most widely used is labetalol."

A look of relief washed over Mrs. Picks face and she smiled.

"I'll send you home with a prescription and we'll see you back here in two weeks. Call sooner if you experience unpleasant side effects such as lightheadedness, dizziness, or excessive fatigue."

Mrs. Picks placed her feet on the step of the exam table and stepped down. "I can't thank you enough. I'll make sure the medication is working before my husband and I start our family."

Annabel and Chineka went back to the central desk where the resident did her paperwork. "If all women were as thorough as her, there would be less obstetric complications," Chineka said and pulled out their patient list. "Mr. Harty is next. Back after his recent hospitalization."

A nurse assistant passed in front of them as she escorted a patient to a room. "Mr. Harty hasn't shown up," she commented after overhearing them.

"Maybe he's just late," Dr. Watts said. "Annabel, why don't you call his assisted care facility to check if they are on their way while I go into the next room where Bob is with a patient?"

"Sure thing."

Dr. Watts went off and Annabel rummaged through the pending patient file folders for his number. She dialed and when she had no answer from Mr. Harty's room, she called the main number for assisted living.

"Hello," Annabel said after someone in the front office picked up. "This is one of the medical students at Mr. Harty's outpatient clinic. He is late for his appointment. We're wondering if the van is on its way with him."

A silence ensued. "No, it's not," a woman finally said. "Mr. Harty passed away. He committed suicide."

Annabel gasped. At first, she couldn't think of what to say. His action made no sense; he was too smart to do something like that. Bob's patient was one of the sharpest elderly patients she had come across. How does an old person commit suicide in a place that has employees checking on them anyway?

"How?" she asked.

"We didn't know," the woman said defensively. "We can't monitor every little thing."

"Know what?"

"That he previously hoarded, saved, and hid narcotic pills for pain and then took enough to accomplish his goal."

"Thank you for telling me. I'll inform the other doctors who helped take care of him. We all liked him a lot."

Annabel hung up and stared at the chart with a heavy heart. She wasn't exaggerating when she said they all liked him, especially her. But the more she sat undisturbed in the temporary quiet, the more she remembered the things he had said and the more she accepted what he had chosen for himself.

Bob and Dr. Watts both came out of a room and headed Annabel's way. "If you go into internal medicine," Dr. Watts said when they stopped, "you will see so much COPD in your residency, diagnosis and treatment will become second nature. They become more of a challenge when they land in the hospital. Any time someone has that much difficulty breathing, I end up with butterflies in my stomach. I have a low tolerance for calling anesthesia to come intubate them."

Chineka stopped her medical discussion and noticed Annabel with a forlorn expression.

"I called like you asked me to, but you're both not going to like this. Mr. Harty committed suicide."

"No," Bob said. "He lived in a supervised environment."

"But when a person is determined enough ..."

Bob shook his head.

"That's terrible," Chineka said. "Chances are he could have lived another year."

"Not the way he wanted," Annabel said softly.

"Human beings performing euthanasia on themselves is not acceptable," Chineka said. "He shouldn't have done that," she added with more annoyance in her tone. "What a waste."

She frowned at the protruding charts from all the doorways. "We better start hustling because our patients are accumulating. No more of our patients better pull a stunt like that in the foreseeable future."

A half hour later than expected, the team saw their last outpatient while Dr. Schott's pager beeped regarding their first admission.

"I'm going over to the ER," Donn said, "and taking Dr. Watts with me. I want all of you students to go grab dinner first before showing back up on the wards."

Thankful for the definitive break, the medical students disappeared fast; one by one, they slid through the hot food line and sat in the cafeteria.

"My patient, Mr. Harty, didn't show up in clinic today," Bob informed Jordan and Stuart, "because he was found dead from an overdose."

"I wonder how rare that is," Jordan said. "I never hear about old people doing themselves in with drugs."

"Maybe geriatric suicide is carried out more than you think," Stuart said, "especially if they leave no trace. No one would think to question an elderly person's death if it was feasible they died from a heart attack or just quit breathing due to old and slightly diseased lungs."

"I am feeling a bit guilty," Bob said, "wondering if we missed any tell-tale signs." He scraped gravy off the meat loaf he'd bought and took a bite.

"I'm sorting all of that out too," Annabel said.

"What, like he was clinically depressed and shouldn't have been discharged?" Stuart asked.

She nodded and tugged at the lopsided stethoscope around her neck.

"We recently took psychiatry," Bob said. "We were sure he showed no signs or symptoms of a real clinical depression. He was rational about his age and his medical problems and the fact that he was only getting worse."

"He lived a good life," Annabel said, "and didn't want to be caged in a facility without the ability to take care of his own needs. The situation was deplorable to his dignity and pride. He tried his damnedest to prevent further medical problems, but the odds and circumstances living there were stacked against him. How many of us would feel the same way? Would we make the same decision?"

"Unless I was exactly in his shoes," Jordan said, "you pose a hypothetical question I don't think I can answer."

"My opinion," Stuart said, "is that most geriatric patients would not think about the issue as deeply as Mr. Harty did. They are passengers along for the ride and are not responsible for what can and does happen to them."

"Do you empathize with Mr. Harty's thought process and not negatively judge him for what he did?" Annabel asked and waited for an answer.

"Yes, I felt strongly for the issues he spoke about and I can't fault him for what he did. Society doesn't condone taking one's life, but the public tide of approval for tricky subjects sometimes takes time. Look at Dr.

Kevorkian. There is more acceptance of his philosophy now than before."

"Patients used to seek him out," Bob said. "They used to leave their home state and travel great distances to be put under his care; his terminal care."

Bob turned to Annabel. "Would you do what Mr. Harty did?"

"It is too difficult a question to answer with certainty. But, I believe I would. I also think what he wanted us to understand was that, in the end, his quality of life mattered more to him than extending the duration. Of course, at that age, it takes foresight to prepare the way he did and, most likely, the circumstances might not always work out. I, however, could not commit suicide with some kind of drastic measure."

"Like what?" Jordan asked.

"Any kind of violence. Such as a knife or a gun."

"But what if you were desperate? Maybe the only possibility would be to slit a wrist."

Annabel took a heavy sigh. "So true," she said. "Goes to show ..."

"What?" Bob asked.

"If we're having this much trouble figuring it out at our age, imagine how difficult it would be fifty or sixty years from now."

"Let's change the subject," Bob said, "and silently say a prayer for Mr. Harty. If there is a God, I hope Mr. Harty is in his graces and found a spot at the pearly gate."

"However, that's another part of the discussion," Stuart said. "The religious and spiritual aspect of what he did."

"My goodness," Annabel said. "I didn't know this topic would become so involved."

"We owe it to you," Bob said. "We're having this conversation because we're becoming thoughtful medical thinkers and not just students cramming stuff into our brains and spitting it back out."

Gloria Pratt gathered all her mother's discharge papers into her bag and then went to the pharmacy to fill the new prescriptions. Meanwhile, a nursing assistant wheeled Darlene to the front door of the hospital. With new medications in tow, Gloria brought her car to the front of the building, and with assistance also from the doorman, they loaded Darlene into the front seat of the SUV. Her help left and she struggled with the wind at her back to fasten the seatbelt past her mother's bulky winter coat.

"Mama, we're going home," Gloria said as she left the secondary roads and proceeded onto I-75. "Back to the surroundings you're familiar with. Your own bed, your own house, and special food prepared for you. I'll even put on your favorite show."

Darlene stared with an empty expression out the front window while Gloria turned the wipers on slow-speed for the slushy precipitation that had just begun.

"I don't mean a TV show that is your favorite now," Gloria said, "because we both don't have a clue what that would be. We'll stick with what you loved before Parkinson's changed you into a different human being ... as if you were dropped off from outer space. I don't mean that to sound nasty, Mama. You were dealt a nasty card and it's not your fault."

Gloria hummed for the rest of the trip home as if to keep company with herself. She pulled the vehicle into the garage of the small two-story home and twice plodded back and forth into the house to unload her mother's things. Lastly, she began the arduous task of getting Darlene into the house and getting her situated into bed for a midday nap.

Having worked up a sweat, Gloria put the guard rails up on her mother's bed and massaged hand sanitizer into the palm of her hands alongside the bed. She'd neglected her own needs for hours and then ran to the bathroom because she thought her bladder would burst.

CHAPTER 13

Gloria woke up and, in her normal fashion, listened for any sounds coming from her mother downstairs. All was quiet. She grabbed clean clothes, went to the window, and noticed the frost on the trees and the grass outside before hurrying to the bathroom. It took only a few minutes to wash her face, brush her teeth, and change. She grasped the handrail and swiftly went down the staircase.

Gloria first eyed her mother in bed, her chest rising, her mouth making smacking noises. She prepared a pan of warm water and a washcloth and placed it where she needed it.

"Mama," Gloria said, putting her hands on Darlene's shoulders. The woman sleepily glared at her daughter and pushed one of her hands away. Gloria raised the back of the bed, and with efficiency, slinked her mother to the edge of the mattress and got her up. With one arm around her waist and the other holding Darlene's arm around her own shoulder, she grappled with walking her a few steps and setting her on the portable toilet chair. She always sat her on it once or twice a day. It got her blood moving and it made it easier to discard her overnight adult diaper and then apply a fresh one.

Not too much urine trickled into the pot. Gloria swished the cloth into the pan of water and, while holding Darlene up, washed her private parts as best she could. She applied a fresh diaper, propped her up in the wide nearby chair and fought to pull up a pair of loose pants with an elastic waistband and a flannel shirt with wide buttons.

On the kitchen counter, first Gloria rubbed a handful of hand sanitizer into her skin. She proceeded to line up all of her mother's medicine bottles and opened the lids of a blue pill container labelled from Sunday to Saturday. Starting with the most important one, carbidopa/levodopa, she counted out each medicine seven times and dropped them into the plastic slots. With the drugs ready for the next week, she took the morning pills over to Darlene and spent five minutes making sure the woman swallowed each one with a teaspoon of apple sauce, which Gloria craftily sneaked into her mouth.

Gloria fed Darlene oatmeal with honey over the next hour, started laundry, and turned on the TV as she folded the wash and sipped her first cup of coffee. Then it was already time to situate Darlene back in bed. Usually, she would fall asleep for a nap.

After she trudged over to the kitchen counter, Gloria fixed another cup of coffee, and spooned oatmeal into a bowl for herself. As she ate at the round kitchen table, she intermittently peered over at Darlene. Her mother had done an excellent job of continuing to raise her in her teen years after her father had died early from a heart attack. She had been a clerical worker in the very hospital she just came from, having continued the tradition of her husband - to work somehow for the men and women who had served in the military.

She thought back to the day her mother received the news of her diagnosis. Darlene read the literature she received from the doctor in one afternoon, continued to study about the disease, and finally sat down with Gloria a month later to express her concerns.

"I'm going to do everything I can to beat this disease," Darlene said. "However, I hope to never, ever become a burden to anyone, especially to you."

"Mom, please don't say that," Gloria had said. "A mother can never be a burden."

"I'll put it another way. If I can't maintain caring for my home, my loving relationships and roles, and my own self-care such as eating and dressing, I don't want to exist."

"Stop talking like that."

"No. I must finish. I am entitled to go downhill mentally; however, if the situation becomes deplorable, if I can't communicate sensibly, if I don't understand half of what's going on, and I can barely function in a few daily activities, then I don't want to be alive. I don't know what it'll take, because at that stage, I don't think I'll be capable enough to smother myself with my own pillow."

"Ma!" Gloria shouted.

"Oh, hush."

In the next few weeks, Darlene visited an attorney and had him draw up her will, power of attorney, and medical directives. All monies as well as all decisions would go to Gloria. She directed the attorney to make a non-standard "do not resuscitate" order if her Parkinson's was in its advanced stage and asked for no life saving measures under any medical emergency. If they could even let her wither away and die, she would prefer it.

After that, her life turned into the key components of Parkinson's management: education, physical therapy, and eventually speech therapy and occupational therapy, and her signs and symptoms progressed eventually to her present state.

Gloria looked over at her mother, who still hadn't closed her eyes. Her hand beat up and down on the blanket and she sputtered out the first sensible word of the day. Gloria poured part of a nutrition drink into a cup and assisted Darlene in drinking one sip.

She finished her own oatmeal, grateful that her mother would soon close her eyes. Gloria glanced at the time. Her hired help would be at the house in an hour to fill in for her because of a job interview at the same government hospital. She wanted the job badly; she'd make a little bit more money. It was important, however, to still keep her schedule at three ten-hour shifts.

She began packing her purse with her CV and other essentials but couldn't shake the feeling that had been growing in her the last several months. The guilt was worse now since the doctors at the hospital had confirmed her mother's condition and godforsaken prognosis. Her mother never wanted to get to the stage she was in now, let alone get worse. Gloria would do anything to care for her, however, the very things she was doing were in contrast to the care her mother wanted. Her mother didn't want any care!

Darlene Pratt, if she could make sense right now, would smother herself with her own pillow or reprimand Gloria for going against her wishes and not letting her go. Gloria swallowed hard, doused her hands with hand cleaner, and prepared for her job interview.

"You're all sprung for the weekend," Dr. Schott said to the students after rounds the next morning. "You all lucked out with a quiet night. Go study this weekend and the residents and I will do rounds on Sunday morning and then check our patients out to the call team."

Annabel, Bob, Stuart, and Jordan glanced at each other with surprise, turned before Donn changed his mind, and echoed their thanks.

With the ringer still off, Annabel felt the vibration of her cell phone on her waist as they headed to the call rooms. "A family member is calling from home," she said with concern, glancing at Bob.

"Hello," she said.

"Annabel, it's Mom. Can we talk a moment?"

"Sure," she said, picking up on Sara's anguished tone.

"We didn't tell you something because we've been handling the situation and didn't want to upset you, but now we're at cross roads and need to make a family decision."

Annabel slowed her pace as she kept her head down, focused on the tile floor. She gave Bob a tentative wave to go ahead, but he hung by her side.

"What's going on there? Tell me what?"

Her mother, Sara, breathed a heavy sigh. "After you visited us during your surgery rotation, Dakota had a stroke."

Annabel's eyes widened and the words "Dakota" and "stroke" echoed in her brain. Dakota was their one and only pet, a Chesapeake Bay retriever, with intelligence that, in her mind, surpassed at least half the human beings on the planet.

"A stroke? What does that mean? He's like incapacitated or something and you didn't tell me?"

"Sweetheart, for three days, we all took turns at his side 24/7 and we made some progress. He had no control with his housetraining, slept almost the whole time, and didn't eat. We managed to keep him hydrated and then the next two weeks things perked up … a little bit. We took turns figuring out what he would and could eat and finally he started eating half cans of chicken with rice." Sara gulped a sigh and stopped.

"I'm listening, Mom." Annabel finally glanced at Bob with a frown and shook her head.

"Anyway, his situation improved, he had no adverse mental sequela, but his GI tract took a toll. We have been taking him out basically every three hours ever since then, even during the night. And he's so good not to have an accident in the house; he breaks our hearts when he sincerely nudges us in the middle of the night to go out. It hasn't been easy on us, but it's worse for Dakota. Your father put him on Pedialyte to replenish his electrolytes because of all the diarrhea.

"Besides this situation, his joints are degenerating by the day. His arthritis is so painful, we hate to watch him follow us around. He wants to be by our side because he loves us, but we agonize when he has to reposition himself with difficulty and lay down again."

"You should have told me," Annabel said sternly. "I would have made a quick visit to help and offer him my comfort. But this is just the preliminary set-up, isn't it?" Annabel tried to keep her heart from thumping in her chest. "What's the caveat, Mom?"

"The last few days, Dakota developed stridor; your father and Casey told us that's the official name for it."

Annabel thought of the combined medical knowledge between her father being a neurosurgeon and his best friend and brother-in-law, Casey, who was a paramedic. They would know what to call practically anything medical related. She thought of the word and only now knew its meaning because of her medicine rotation. Dakota must be breathing noisily with a harsh vibrating sound which occurs during inspiration. Besides a possible obstruction in the respiratory tract or upper airway, there were many other potential causes.

"Do they know why?" Annabel said.

"Since there is no obvious obstruction and Dakota has no respiratory disease, your father thinks it's central in origin. In other words, like his stroke, a neurologic insult is the key factor. Perhaps a tiny mini-stroke in the brain or brainstem. And by the way, Dakota's been on a baby aspirin as a stroke preventative, but there is only so much we can do."

"So are you all imminently worried?"

"Yes, sweetheart. As of yesterday the breathing problem which affects his jowls is making it difficult for him to eat and you know how much he loves to eat. This morning, he could hardly scarf anything down, and the little he did had to be choked down."

Annabel fought the emotion welling in her eyes and her throat and her heart. A silence engulfed both of them.

"We are making a family decision today. We believe the time has come to put him to sleep. As difficult as it would be to euthanize him, the next week or two may be hell for him and purgatory for us to watch. The whole problem with all of this is that he hasn't lost his spirit, still wags his tail, and is following us around with all his usual loyalty. We feel you must voice your opinion. It may be impossible because of your schedule, but you may be able to come say hello or good-bye to him. However, we may absolutely need to put him to sleep today. Dakota's regular doctor is the vet on-call tonight, so we would spare Dakota another night and day of all these complications."

Annabel now couldn't hold back the tear hanging off the inside of her eye. It rolled over her cheek and spun away as Bob walked much slower with her. With a slight touch, he directed her closer along the wall to leave room for a medical student coming the other way.

"I'm coming down," Annabel said. "I'm wrapping up a night on call and I'll be there as soon as I can. Don't do anything without me, Mom."

"Besides everyone else, I'll tell Dakota you're coming."

Annabel ended the call, shoved the phone in her pocket, and immediately looked at Bob. "Our family dog is really sick, Bob. I have to go to Nashville because they may put him to sleep today. I have a say in the matter, but I can't not see him or say good-bye. God, how I love that dog."

"I'm sorry, Annabel," he said, trying to further examine her features and her sorrow. "Don't get mad at me for saying so, but I don't think you should take the drive yourself, especially if you lose him and drive home. Plus, the weather has made for less desirable road conditions in the last few days. Why don't I take you? Do your folks have an extra couch I can crash on?"

"I would hate for you to do that," she said but nodded at the same time.

"Then it's settled. Let me go home first to repack and cancel an appointment and I'll be right back over to your place. I'll wait on you if need be."

"You won't have to wait on me."

After grabbing their books and overnight bags, both of them left to prepare for a weekend emergency trip to the Music City.

Bob rapped on Annabel's door and when she opened it, she shoved a small cooler at him. She turned and grabbed her scantily packed bag and one textbook. "I doubt if we're going to do any reading, but I'm bringing this along just in case." She frowned as she turned and locked the door. "The problem is, we're bound to a six-hour drive each way."

Downstairs, Bob had double parked, so they hastily climbed into his small Honda, keeping the cooler on the floor in front of Annabel.

"I-75 to I-71 to I-65," she sputtered as they pulled away. "Have you ever been to Nashville?"

"I pass by and never spend time there. That goes for the whole state."

"You're missing out on the best there is to offer: the Smoky Mountains, all the state and national parks, lakes, and the activities in the three big cities. And for live music, you can't beat the Music City. It beats Indianapolis."

"You remembered," he said. "Yes, I grew up in Indianapolis and our only claim to fame is an annual fast car race. The state is flat and boring, but maybe I became a good student because of it. I wasn't lured to the great outdoors, an ocean, or a lake. Someday I'm going to make up for the lack of those experiences."

"I don't know," Annabel said. "It's all downhill from here as far as leisure time goes."

"I hope that's not totally true."

Bob soon pulled onto I-71, headed southwest, and cut back on the heat blowing from the vents. As he pulled out his hot coffee from the cup holder, Annabel let out a gasp.

"Oh, no," she said. "I can't believe I forgot tonight's date with Robby Burk."

Bob glanced for a second at her and eased his foot off the accelerator. "Do you want to go back?"

She gulped and closed her eyes. "There's nothing I can do about it. The timing is deplorable for a date, but I wouldn't miss going home where I'm needed. If I theoretically think it through, Robby Burk isn't going anywhere, but the most special dog in my life is."

She frowned. "I guess I need to call our old chief resident."

CHAPTER 14

The clouds above thinned and parted for a few minutes, allowing the sun to bathe the Honda Fit as Bob and Annabel sped along in the right lane with little traffic. The sunshine gave them the illusion it was seventy degrees outside the car.

With the phone still in her hands, Annabel contemplated what she would say to Robby Burk, especially if she was forced to leave a voicemail message. She would hate doing that. Leaving a message was a cold way to break a date ... only one step better than standing someone up.

As she dialed his number, she bit her lip. Maybe he was sleeping after his call.

"Annabel, I'm glad you called," Robby said right away. "I'm home after a hectic night and surgery. I just checked the online schedule and found us a movie for tonight. It features a new crime detective team with lots of action. But, of course, I'm looking forward to seeing you over dinner and hearing about your rotation."

She hated to burst his bubble but plunged ahead. "I learned terrible news from my family this morning, Robby. Our geriatric dog is at the end of his life span. I am heading home now. An important family decision needs to be made together and we may need to put him to sleep."

"Home is Nashville, isn't it?"

"Yes."

"You are making a long drive for such a short circumstance. That's considerate of you."

"Nothing that you wouldn't do."

"For a person, you're right ..."

She scrunched her forehead. Did that mean he wouldn't do the same thing for a beloved family pet?"

"I'm really sorry that I must break our date for tonight," she said, "particularly since we fumbled up the first one and synchronizing tonight wasn't easy."

More than that, she thought, she had the hots for him and couldn't wait to finally be on a real date with him - a one-on-one dinner sitting across from him. A date that could end up with a good night kiss or more. His lips, she bet, would taste better than any dreaming about them. She gulped some air and snapped back to their conversation.

"I'm sorry too," he said. "Perhaps we can rearrange something at a later date. You get on with your driving. Why don't you give me a call in a week or two after you figure out your dog?"

"Okay," she said. "Thanks for understanding."

"No problem."

They both hung up and Annabel stared a moment at her phone.

"Annabel," Bob said, breaking into her thoughts. "One of these nights if you're feeling depressed, we can go to that comedy to pick up your spirits … the movie we talked about and you were going to see tonight with Robby."

She blinked a few times. "Yeah, maybe. I didn't seem to have a say in that movie because he said we were going to a detective action film."

Bob didn't comment; they continued on in silence in northern Kentucky and drove straight through Louisville.

Gloria fussed about leaving her mother alone with the caretaker because it was not a normal day to do so. She stayed committed to the house and her mother except for the three long days she worked. After leaving unnecessary redundant requests for the aide, she finally left and headed for her interview.

She dispelled any nervousness as she sat in front of the personnel manager. The middle-aged stout woman gave Gloria the benefit of the doubt why she didn't work a forty-hour week; in essence, she worked about a hundred hours a week between her mother and her employer. "You are a saint," the woman said. "A Mother Theresa in Southern Ohio. I would love to snatch you from your present job and bring you on board here."

Gloria rubbed her hands. She could practically smell the sanitizer because of her massaging it deep through the epidermis. "Does that mean I can give them notice and I'm hired?"

The woman smiled and rose. Extending her hand into Gloria's, she nodded and said, "The need for medical assistants in our hospital, as well as everywhere else, keeps growing. Yes, you are hired. Let me know when you can start and come by soon to sign the paperwork. And continued good luck with your mother's care."

Gloria put her hands on the side of her head with enthusiasm and pulled at her golden honey hair. "Thank you so much. Rending care in a military hospital is what my family was all about." She put on her jacket in the hallway and forced herself to put the news aside. A new thought-provoking decision was at hand and it was her duty to prepare. Implementing the needed actions, however, was a different story; she didn't need to commit herself to any uncomfortable deeds ... yet.

She left the medical campus as the clouds thinned out and a fraction of warmth penetrated the inside of her car. It warmed her body and her soul and being the religious and superstitious person that she was, she felt a spiritual angel had nodded his or her approval at her considerations.

The aide would still be at the house minding Darlene, so Gloria had plenty of time to go to the home improvement store where the rows and rows of stocked items on steel shelves out-supplied what she had viewed online. Besides, she would avoid making a record of her purchase online and she had thought ahead about today's purchase as well. At the register, she'd use cash and not a credit card, and she'd also buy plenty of what she needed in only one large size. She got out of her car, trudged her way along the salted asphalt parking lot to the automatic doors, and disappeared inside.

Darkness settled on the roads as the sun slipped away behind the buildings in Nashville and Bob scanned the skyline. He noted a skyscraper to the right towering above the rest of them. "Those two soaring spires on that building make it look like Batman," he said.

"That's the AT&T building or, like you say, the Batman building. More importantly, below it is Broadway and the makings of the best bars and music joints anywhere. You can spend night after night walking in and out of them and listening to live performers. Of course, you sip some moonshine along the way."

"Sounds like fun. We should do it sometime."

"Before we go our separate ways on rotations," she said, "or because of residencies."

"I have never tried moonshine."

"It's such a kick ... like starting an IV and mainlining booze."

"That bad, huh?"

She laughed. "Not only that, you'll want to taste-test a couple of flavors. Everything from coffee to blackberry. You can end up on your ass before you know it."

"I'm glad to hear you laugh, because in a little while, nothing at your home will be very funny."

"Speaking of which, I need to fill you in about my family. You're aware of my dad being a doctor. There's a lot to take in about the rest of the family and, if I've told you anything about them before, you probably don't remember."

"Please tell me. I can't crash on a couch where I don't even know everyone's names."

"You're not sleeping on a couch. The house is huge. My mom and dad live in the basement with their own separate entrance. The place is big and spacious and how they ended up there is a long story. In addition, they aren't married."

"What?" Bob asked, wanting clarification.

"They divorced because of an affair my dad had, but then they got back together again. I have a half-sister, Julia, from my dad's indiscretion. Not only that, but Dakota was originally the 'other woman's' dog. She was, and probably still is, the most diabolical human being to ever come into our family's life or anyone else's life for that matter."

"Annabel, she sounds like a loser."

"I summarized all that, but the saga is much more harrowing than it sounds. Anyway, the big house belonged to my grandparents. My father's only sibling, my Aunt Mary, was bequeathed the home. She married my father's best friend who is a paramedic. His name is Casey and he's the coolest guy. They live in the upstairs, but everyone kind-of always gathers on the main floor and out in the yard during the summer. In addition, they have young twins named Tommy and Melissa."

"What about the sister you mentioned?"

"Nancy's younger than me and graduates from college this spring, but she doesn't know what she wants to do. You may remember me telling you I had another sister who wanted to go to medical school. She died," Annabel said with sorrow. "That was rough on all of us and I still miss her. My aunt and uncle named their female twin, my cousin, after her."

"It sounds like your family is very close to each other. That's remarkable everyone lives under the same roof because extended families living together is a thing of the past."

"Except for my half-sister, who is with her mother, we are all bound to each other and almost inseparable. It has been that way for as long as I can remember and I wouldn't want it any other way."

"Thanks for the family history lesson. Now I won't feel like such a dork when I meet them all."

After Annabel pointed to an exit off of I-65, Bob later entered a spacious subdivision, drove down a long street occasionally dotted by a mega-home, and pulled into a driveway.

Due to security cameras installed on the edges and entryway of the house, Danny watched the Honda pull up to the garage. He opened the front door as Annabel was about to grasp the door knob.

Annabel fell into her father's arms and he gave her a tight squeeze. "Dakota and all of us are glad you made the trip," he said. "I hope the inconvenience isn't going to disrupt your clinical duties."

She bobbed her head back and forth and continued to hold on to him from the side. "Dad, this is Bob. So far this third year, we've been through every rotation together. Bob drove me here and maybe tonight he can sleep in Melissa's old bedroom."

Danny extended his hand with a smile. "Nice to meet you."

"Likewise, sir."

"I'm sorry the circumstances aren't better, but welcome to our home."

"Thank you. I won't be an imposition."

"No friend of my daughter's is an imposition. Do you have anything to bring in from the car?"

"Not much, Dad."

"I'll go fetch our belongings," Bob said.

Danny stepped out and followed Bob while Annabel walked through the corridor to the rear of the house. She scanned the kitchen and great room to see family members, but her eyes settled on Dakota on the floor. He awkwardly rose, his tail acknowledged her, and he limped over to greet her.

"Dakota," she said and kneeled on the floor. He leaned against her and her arm wrapped around his belly. She sidled her head against his, kissed him, and smelled the familiarity of his coat. Her hand came out from under him and she rubbed her palms back and forth into his neck and his sorrel fur. She leaned her head in and kissed his forehead and his snout. "Look at you, boy. I missed you. I'm sorry you don't feel well."

Dakota surprised her and stepped over to his toy box and barked. After selecting a plastic bone, he grabbed it in his muzzle, and dropped it beside her.

"You still possess your spirit, don't you, boy?"

Her mother, Sara, waited and then gave her a hug. A long sweater hung to her waist like she was wrapped up for comfort.

Behind Annabel, Danny and Bob now stood behind her.

"Aunt Mary, Uncle Casey, and Nancy, this is my friend, Bob," Annabel said.

Casey leaned over and shook Bob's hand. "Thanks for coming with Annabel," he said.

"Hi," Nancy said.

"I'm glad you came," Mary said. "What can we get the both of you?"

"Just something to drink," Annabel said. "Where are the twins?"

"Upstairs taking an overdue nap," Mary said, stepping to the refrigerator. After Bob also met Sara, Danny motioned them to the couch. Annabel sat cross-legged on the floor in front of the ottoman. Dakota carefully lowered his back hips half way and then gingerly completed the distance to the floor. His front legs slinked down until he nestled near Annabel.

"I can tell by the look on your faces that the decision is made," Annabel said.

Casey took one of the soft drinks from his wife and crouched down to Annabel and handed it to her. Her hand cupped the glass and she searched her uncle's face. He was a handsome paramedic with a happy disposition and a devout gym routine. For as long as she could remember, he had a body that would stop women short. However, she admired his devotion to her aunt. In a way, her aunt and uncle's lives were so unalike. He was an adrenaline junkie out in the field saving lives in nasty trauma accidents or in home medical emergencies while she spent quiet days at home upstairs in her art studio painting landscapes and portraits.

"His condition," Casey said, "has required constant care, which we've carried out with love, but the last two days are pulling at our heart strings."

A high-pitched sound came from Dakota's mouth and the skin around his mouth flapped along with the breathing turbulence. He rested his head back flat between his paws.

"I see ..." she said.

"He can barely choke down his food because of that," Casey said. "This morning, we sadly watched but didn't try to feed him his second meal of the day."

Annabel wiped a tear away before it slid down her cheek and she rested her hand back on Dakota's fur. "I agree with you all," she said, her voice quivering. She couldn't look back up at them. "It's time," she added.

Danny called the animal hospital and informed the staff working late that they would be coming in an hour.

"We have time to give Dakota more hugs," Danny said with a frown. "Who is coming with me?"

"It would be too much for all of us to go," Mary said. "Casey and I will stay. You're the one who brought Dakota into our lives, Danny, so you should be with him in the end."

Casey nodded and rubbed Annabel's shoulder.

"I'll stay," Sara said. "Do you girls want to be there?"

"Even though I may not be able to handle it, I'm going," Nancy said.

"I'm coming, Dad," Annabel chimed in.

A silence ensued until Nancy curled up with Dakota and her sister on the floor. "We love you, Dakota," Nancy said. "We're going to miss you like crazy, but we'll see you later in heaven."

Dakota rolled more to his side into Annabel as they continued to pet him.

"We'll have a bucket load of fond memories," Sara said. "We can take solace in that."

"I think quite often how Dakota may have saved Julia's life," Casey said.

"What happened?" Bob ventured.

"Julia is Danny's other daughter. She was just a baby in the playpen on the back patio. It was our wedding day," he said, pointing to Mary. "We were all running around here like chickens without our heads. The ceremony and reception was scheduled here for later that day.

"Anyway, Dakota was barking his head off out there," Casey said, pointing out the French doors, "trying to get someone's attention." I stepped out where he was minding Julia in her playpen and still didn't know what his fuss was all about. He corralled me over to the other side of the playpen where I couldn't see and there on the ground was a copperhead."

Bob peeled his eyes away from Casey and stared at Dakota. "Wow," he sighed. "That must have been quite a scare. Your dog is a lifesaving hero. I can't begin to grasp how difficult this must be for all of you. And him, too."

"On the bright side," Danny said, "our Chesapeake has had a great life. We can be proud that we gave him back his love in return."

In less than two hours, after Danny lifted Dakota out of his car, Annabel, Nancy, and Danny walked their Chesapeake along the hardwood floor to a secluded back room in the animal hospital. The dog followed his family back in good faith and without hesitation. Danny sat on the leather loveseat and Nancy sat on the floor against the wall. Annabel cuddled next to Dakota, the door opened, and a young woman Annabel's age entered.

"I can take him to the back to start his IV," she said.

"Why can't you do it here?" Annabel asked.

"I may need help."

"He's not going anywhere and we can assist."

The girl relented and planted herself at their level. She took a portable shaver from her pocket and selected fur on Dakota's right foreleg. As soon as she leaned in, he began trembling. Emotion rose in Annabel's throat; Dakota sensed what was coming.

When the tourniquet went around the dog's leg, Annabel pointed out a bulging vein and the technician easily slid the IV in, capped it, and taped it in place. The woman opened the door and left.

"Dad," Annabel said. "I don't know about anyone else, but I feel like a heel bringing him here to do this. With his spirit intact, he is not desperate to die. It's like we are playing God and snuffing his life away from him. Maybe this isn't right. On the other hand, my team just had a patient that was so fed up with his terminal medical problems and the way he was living, that he took his own life. This is all so confusing."

"With our pets," Danny said, "it is unfair when we have to make their final life or death decision. They can't make or carry out a verdict themselves like what your patient decided for himself, whether he was right or wrong. But we are more informed than dogs. We foresee what is going to happen to Dakota in the next few days. Do we want him to suffer over time or do we make death easier for him? Should we let him go further downhill in the house with his family giving him more hugs and love or let him go sooner? If he could talk, what would he tell us? This is a moral dilemma and there is no satisfactory answer to appease our souls. As a neurosurgeon, I have been through this with patients and their families too many times. Mankind doesn't possess a solution. We only have laws relative to the subject and laws are written by men. So we end up back where we started from. In a gray zone."

The tears started to stream down Annabel's face, and with one hand, she pulled a tissue from her pocket and wiped her cheek. Even her father didn't know the answers. She dug her fingers deeper into Dakota's neck and savored the moments before he would take his last breath.

The door opened and Annabel quivered like Dakota. "I was wondering when you all would be back," the vet said. He smiled with understanding; comprehension of a situation he'd been in many times before. Like her father with neurosurgical head cases, she wondered, when do doctors give up on patients and let them go?

"Dakota's stridor and difficulty eating is the last straw," Danny said to the vet, jolting Annabel back to reality.

"I understand, Dr. Tilson," the man said.

The young veterinarian assumed a position on the floor and injected a few cc's of propofol into Dakota's vein. The dog's head slumped further on his front legs with contentment from the sedation. The man wasted no further time. He pulled out the first syringe, inserted the next one, and followed with a lethal dose of barbiturates.

Their beautiful Chesapeake's tongue partially protruded, it drained of oxygen, and turned a deep, dark purple.

CHAPTER 15

"I'll give you all a moment with him," the vet said when Dakota stirred no more. "I'm sorry for your loss."

"Can we leave him here for cremation?" Danny asked.

"Yes. That service is in the separate building in the back. We'll call you in a few days when he's ready."

The vet left and Annabel and Nancy both continued to linger over Dakota. "Dad, I didn't know you were going to do that," Nancy said.

"I never brought the subject up at home because my decision to cremate him was firm; he's going back home where he belongs."

"I like the idea."

"Just know that one of you is going to bury his ashes with me when I go."

Where did her father come up with these ideas? Annabel thought. "I'll do it if Nancy doesn't," she said. "He's been your faithful buddy."

"No matter what time I rolled into the house from some horrendous cranial case in the middle of the night," Danny said, "he was the one who would wake up, greet me, and comfort me in his own way from the traumatizing circumstances I would leave at the hospital."

Danny pushed himself off the couch and covered his eyes with his hands. "Come on, girls. We better let them put him on ice." He stepped over, placed his hand on Dakota's fur, and kissed him good-bye.

"On ice?" Nancy asked.

"Sure," Annabel said, looking back one more time from the door. "You can't believe how fast bodies decompose. Bye, boy," she said blowing over a kiss.

"You all can leave," the woman at the desk said. "We'll bill you when you come back for Dakota."

"Thanks," Danny said. Outside, they piled into Danny's Lexus and turned on the heat.

"This is too difficult," Annabel said, emotion welling up all over again. "We just had him in the car and now he's gone."

Danny pulled away from the building. "I can tell you some insane stories. I don't think I ever told you of the night I spent with Dakota in the beginning when I was being unfaithful to your mother and she kicked me out of the house. I was staying in a rental apartment with him, but I didn't know dogs weren't allowed. Long story short, they tried to contact me to tell me to remove the dog from the premises, but I never received the messages. My hours and life were so complicated, I couldn't see straight."

"You made it more complicated with an affair, Dad," Annabel said.

"Yes, well, I admit I was an idiot. Anyway, it was late at night and the management company had changed the locks on me so I was locked out of my own place. I couldn't find a hotel that would take dogs, Mary was out of town and the big house was locked, so I ended up sleeping in my car with Dakota at the Caney Fork River and still needed to be at work in a few hours." He slowed down his words and continued. "It was one hell of a mess and Dakota was part of the fiasco. When I arrived at the office looking like a homeless person – which, theoretically I was - Dr. Garner put me on leave."

"I never knew all that, Dad," Annabel said. "Nancy and I were aware stuff was going on, but that's pretty bad. I can see you and Dakota now. I'm glad you had his faithful companionship during those trying times. You were messed up; I bet he helped you realize again what was more important in life."

"I don't think I have to worry about you girls in this regard, but never let sex or a hot romance cloud your judgment."

Annabel froze in her seat. She couldn't believe what he said. If he only knew of her indiscretions due to Findar, her social dating app. She had been doing far worse than her father had ever done except that he had gotten ensnarled by a woman wanting to charge him child support. All for a child she wanted to brainwash, raise herself, and keep from him.
The complexities of his situation boggled her mind. She had better learn from him and use more caution in the future, especially if she continued to find men on social media. Of course, however, there was Robby to consider. Her dad would certainly whole-heartedly approve of him.

"Wasn't tonight your date with the heartthrob?" Nancy asked from the back seat, as if reading her sister's mind.

"Heartthrob?" Danny asked.

"I told you about my chief resident during surgery," Annabel said to him. "He asked me out. Unfortunately, this is the second scheduled date we're missing."

"Ouch," Nancy said, leaning forward.

"Hmm," Danny commented.

"Dad, whenever you make that noise," Annabel said, "you know something I don't know."

Danny shrugged. "Perhaps."

"If you don't care," Nancy said, "I think your friend, Bob, is a hunk. Does he have a girl friend or can I somehow keep in contact with him?"

"He has a girlfriend, but he says they're not serious.

Nancy leaned back, satisfied with the answer.

"Has anyone eaten?" Danny asked.

"No," Annabel said. "But I'm not really hungry."

He pulled into a chain pizza place. "Someone else may want a bite," he said. "Even your guest. Let's bring home a pie." They went in and soon continued home with two boxes of piping hot cheese pizzas.

"Dad," Annabel said. "In a way, I'm glad I'm going back to Ohio tomorrow. The emptiness in the house without Dakota is going to be too distressful. It would continue to break my heart if I was living here."

"I can understand," he said. "I'm glad your friend came with you and is supportive. Just be sure to keep focused on the wards next week. Now that you're in medicine, your personal life will continue to have upsets, and you must always do your best to not let it affect your care of others."

"How'd it go?" Sara asked tentatively when Annabel, Nancy, and Danny walked into the house. They put down the pizzas and Nancy grimaced.

"Dakota sensed exactly why he was there," Annabel said. "The situation could not have been any worse than that."

"I'm having him cremated," Danny said.

"Excellent plan. Now let's open these boxes and be hospitable to our guest. Plus, Casey is working the eleven to seven shift and needs to eat. We'll have plenty of time to mourn over Dakota. I only hope I am over it in a year."

"Or two," Danny said.

Nancy rummaged through the pantry for paper plates. She passed them out and turned to Bob. "We hope you like it without toppings. Can I fetch you another soda?"

"Tell me where to find one," he said. "I'm here to help, not be waited on."

"Okay. But since my sister doesn't tell me much, at a later date, maybe you can tell me your perspective of medical school. Like is it worth all the work?"

After dinner, Casey showed Bob where to sleep upstairs and he got ready and left for work. Annabel slept in her regular room in her parents' place downstairs.

For Annabel, the day had been long ... starting out on the wards, the phone call with bad news, and then a long drive culminating with the euthanasia of Dakota. For fifteen minutes, after settling under the covers, she stared in the dark at the ceiling and grabbed the blanket high around her neck. Robby came into her thoughts, but she successfully cleared him away. All she wanted was to purge her mind of everything but Dakota. Her mind relaxed and she went fast asleep.

Annabel startled in the dark. She heard something and glanced at the alarm clock, which said 3:49. Her bedroom door was open to the hallway outside, which had faint light from a night light. She rested her head back on the pillow, but this time, the sound was unmistakable.

Annabel turned to the side to glance out the door. "Dakota?"

No, she said silently to herself. It can't be him. The events of the evening flooded back while she had held Dakota close and he had left this world. But again, she heard a clickety-clack - his toenails on the hardwood floor. She froze and held her breath and then a few more rhythmic clicks sounded from beyond her room.

"Oh, my God," she whispered and tossed off the blankets. She rose, tip toed to the hallway, and strained to see in the dark towards the family room. The hallway was empty and the noise of toenails had stopped. Her hand rubbed over her heart and, because she couldn't stop herself, she walked the corridor and then glanced around in the dim room. Finding nothing, and no explanation for the sounds, she slipped back into bed.

Annabel closed her eyes; memories of Dakota swelled in her mind as she tried to sleep. Unequivocally, she thought, she was sure of what she had heard.

Finally, she went back to sleep knowing that she and Bob had a long trip back to Ohio in a few short hours.

Annabel and her Aunt Mary lingered over the kitchen counter on the main floor of the house. They both sat on stools and leaned forward, stirring creamer into fresh coffee. The twins amused themselves with toys and cartoons on the television in the background.

"This is already the pits," Mary said, "not having Dakota around. By this time, when he would sleep on this floor, I would already be letting him out the back."

"I think he was downstairs last night," Annabel said, thinking of her experience a few hours ago.

Mary scrunched up her forehead and tilted her head.

"No, I haven't lost my mind," Annabel said, "but it's best if I don't talk about it."

Bob cleared his throat as he came down the stairs and showed up in a fresh, form-fitting cotton shirt and his hair groomed in his usual sculpted style. "Good morning," he said and focused on Annabel. "Did you manage to sleep?"

"Enough to make it through the day," she said.

"Coffee?" Mary asked him.

"I'll get it," he said and went to the coffeepot.

A car rolled into the adjoining garage, and in a few moments, the door opened. Casey appeared with a warm smile. "How are the two most beautiful women in the world this morning?"

"We're hanging in there," Mary said, "without our best buddy. How was your night?"

Bob put down his mug and Casey patted him on the shoulder to acknowledge him. He went inside, stooped down, and greeted and hugged his children.

"I'd be taking that rapscallion of a dog out right now," Case said, stepping back in. "My routine with him after an eleven to seven shift. And work was fine; less busy than usual. I think the Arctic blast of cold air kept lots of folks off the road. We resuscitated and drove an acute heart attack patient from a hotel to the hospital and then a middle-aged woman who stroked from an aneurysm rupture. I'm sure your dad would have performed surgery on her had he been on call," Casey said to Annabel.

"Has that ever happened?" Bob asked. "You bring a patient straight to the hospital and your brother-in-law does surgery on them?"

"A few times," he said with a smile. "We call it tag-teaming and our patients do quite well."

Bob nodded. "Can I pour you a coffee?"

"Sure. Since I'm going straight to bed, you can pour me my one and only cup. What time are you two leaving?"

"I'll leave the decision to Annabel," Bob said.

"What do you think?" she asked. "By 11 o'clock the latest?"

"Yes, if not sooner. Don't forget we're on Eastern Time up there, an hour later."

"I'm glad you reminded me. You'll have to keep me straight for a day or two. My mind may be on home and the loss of Dakota."

"You can count on me; longer if necessary."

The basement door opened and Danny, Sara, and Nancy came ambling over into the kitchen.

"Here you all are," Sara said. Her hair was still damp from a shower and she fidgeted to button up a pink sweater. "How about Danny and I whip up some eggs so everyone starts the day with protein?"

"Or in my case, ends the day," Casey said.

"Then it's a yes," Sara said.

They scrambled eggs, made toast and bacon, and sat down at the long table. Danny let out a big sigh. "Dakota loved eggs," he said. "Let's enjoy these for him."

Annabel brought her book and bag up from downstairs and placed them on the counter while Casey went to bed and Bob was quietly upstairs getting his things.

"We enjoyed meeting Bob," Mary said as she put away dishes. "Bring him back any time you'd like."

"Sure," Annabel said, "but we'll probably be going our separate ways after this rotation."

"Aren't you two good friends?"

"We have a fun time together and we're forced into similar, or the same, learning situations because of our patients." She opened the freezer and packed ice cubes into a large plastic bag for her cooler. "Do you mind if I bum some stuff out of your refrigerator? I took a few things from Mom and Dad's, but you have a better selection of cheese."

"Take anything you want."

Bob came down and the rest of the Tilson family gathered in the kitchen to say their good-byes.

"Here," Bob said and took Annabel's things. "I'll go take these outside and start the car." He turned to each of them. "Thank you so much for having me here and I'm sorry about Dakota."

"You're welcome," Sara said. "Have a safe drive."

"Come back any time," Danny said and shook his hand.

"I'll come up and visit my sister soon," Nancy said. "I'll pick your brain and we can all go out."

"See you then," Bob said. He nodded at all of them and kneeled down to say good-bye to Melissa and Tommy. He went down the hallway with their bags propped under his arm, the cooler in one hand, and disappeared out the door.

Annabel put on her jacket, gave all of them a hug, and Sara and Danny walked her to the door.

"He's a very nice young man," Sara said.

"Your mom is right about that," Danny said. "Call us when you get home."

Annabel nodded and embraced them again. "You two are the best-est," she said. "I am going to miss Dakota like crazy, especially every time I come home in the future. Walking into this house is never going to be the same again."

"I agree," Danny said. "But he will be in our hearts. And his spirit will live on with each of us."

Danny lightly massaged Sara's back. "Down the road when the dust settles, our tears stop, and we rejoice in Dakota's memories, let's discuss the possibility of bringing another Chesapeake into our lives."

CHAPTER 16

With discretion in the ICU's kitchen, Annabel grabbed a cup of coffee and went back down to the medical floor. She chose one of the cubby-hole desk areas away from the nurses' station and sat down with May Oliver's chart and results she scrounged up after arriving at 7 a.m. She needed to process it all before rounds, try to make sense of the information with the little clinical experience she had, and anticipate what her resident and chief resident would recommend for her patient.

The results were terrible. The thirty-two year old's lung cancer had metastasized before even being diagnosed. She thought of the pathophysiology going on in May's body and felt anger at a process that humans could still not halt. Adenocarcinoma cells had broken away from May's primary tumor – the one that the pulmonary doctor had viewed and sampled - and traveled to other parts of her body through her blood and/or lymphatic system.

Over the weekend, the results of her bone scan showed areas of bone where too much tracer, or radioactive substance, had been absorbed. Annabel took a sip of coffee. Radiology had then placed her flat, to lie motionless, and be high jacked as slow as a snail through the MRI machine.

Annabel thumbed through the results and found the radiologist's reading of the MRI. Later with the team, she knew they'd all look at the images themselves, but right now the report would arm her with the needed knowledge for rounds. She moved the paper cup into the corner and stared at the words. May Oliver had "two significant lesions in her brain." To her, this was a game changer. The invasive cells had targeted the rest of her body and the heart of her nervous system. She squeezed her eyes shut. And she thought that she had problems!

She wondered if surgery was an option for May's brain tumors and thought of her father – one of the best neurosurgeon anywhere. She frowned because she could not really refer someone outside of her teaching hospital or sphere of physicians. But if she could ...

She drank down the last bit of coffee and put the paperwork where it belonged. After taking a deep breath, it was time to see May before the team gathered together. As a student, she needed to avoid any specific questions from May regarding the findings of their work-up. Someday when she was a resident that would be part of her job … a skill that must be cultivated and carried out with compassion.

May's door was closed and, after Annabel knocked, she yelled for her to enter even though she was getting dressed. She hooked a bra up in the front and placed her pajama top on the bottom of the bed. "Hi," she said, going to the closet and slipping a plaid blouse off a hanger. "I understand you had some time off. I bet you went out partying."

"I wish," Annabel said. "Life sometimes has its own plan; one you can't foresee; one there is nothing you can do to change."

"I have my own thoughts about the topic," May said. "Social workers and psychologists are always advising people to plan ahead and sculpt their own destiny. That is only possible in limited circumstances."

Annabel ran her fingers through her hair. "So true," she said.

"Dr. Schott and Dr. Burg told me over the weekend that the bone scan was suspicious, so they sent me for an MRI. I can't figure out which was less fun – having the MRI or watching my boyfriend Jeff's reaction. I told him I was having a nuclear medicine test and they were going to inject a radioactive substance into my vein. He wobbled on his feet; I thought he'd pass out. These tests sound horrendously scary, like I'm being tested for cancer from my toes to the top of my head. I don't think he wants any part of it, so he's coming to see me less and less."

"Hospitals scare off a lot of people. He'll come around, May."

"I don't know. As it is, I weep over my dog every night I'm imprisoned here."

"I understand. My family and I lost our beloved family dog two days ago. I don't think I'll ever get over it."

May finished buttoning her blouse and sat on the edge of the bed. "I'm so sorry. That was God's plan for your weekend. I didn't know." She took Annabel's hand and squeezed.

Annabel forced a small smile. "Thank you. And yet we face each new day despite what happened the day before."

"I have more time available to grieve than you do," she said, letting go of Annabel. "You make sure you shed those tears when you're able to or they'll build up like water behind a damn."

Annabel nodded, yet wondered. Her patient might not have the time she thought she had to grieve. Not since her lung cancer was moving around her body like sand in a dust storm.

"I better start moving for morning rounds," Annabel said, checking the time. "Are you having any new symptoms this morning?"

May shook her head and Annabel listened to her heart and lungs before leaving.

Annabel grabbed a spot on the couch next to Jordan, whose fingers bounced around his iPhone keyboard in haste. He texted more by 9 in the morning than she did all day. Bob came in and sat on the desk next to her.

"You doing all right this morning?" Bob asked.

"I'm hanging in there. Thanks again for this weekend."

Jordan paused his fingers and tilted his head at both of them. Stuart put his index cards on his lap and glanced over.

"What?" Bob asked. "I drove Annabel to Nashville because she needed to go home at short notice."

"Unfortunately," Annabel said, "I took Bob away from studying. I hope his grade doesn't suffer because of me."

"Nah," Bob said. "Maybe Stuart can give us both a crash study session before our midterm test."

"If you want me to," Stuart said, "I will."

"A study evening could help all of us," Annabel said as Dr. Schott and Dr. Mejia peered into the room.

"Come on, let's round," Dr. Schott said.

The four of them and the two residents tumbled out the doorway and followed. Annabel dug out chocolate-covered blueberries from her pocket and shared with Bob. They walked in silence with smiles on their faces, but the enthusiasm for rounds lessened when Dr. Schott mentioned that one of Bob's patients had deteriorated and was transferred to the ICU.

Clenching her index cards, Annabel presented May Oliver last. "Mrs. Oliver's vital signs are normal, although I noticed that since she's been here, she dropped another pound. Her hemoptysis had an acute flare-up last night which worried staff and the doc on-call made several visits to her bedside. She stabilized overnight and this morning, she had no complaints. All of the results from the work up we ordered are in. The bone scan indicates cancer and the MRI shows lesions in her brain."

"You can stop there," Dr. Mejia said. "I'll clear up the semantics of metastatic disease to the students right now because sometimes this point is overlooked. Cancer may form a tumor in a new location in a patient's body, but it is still named after the part of the body where it started. In Mrs. Oliver's case, any lung cancer that spread to her brain or bones is called metastatic lung cancer … not brain or bone cancer." He placed his hands on his tie and made sure it was dead center on his shirt and continued.

"Also, another term you may hear is 'recurrent lung cancer.' That is not a metastatic disease. If Mrs. Oliver's cancer in her lung is removed and there are no more signs of it there, but later it reappears, that is recurrent lung cancer."

"This terminology," Dr. Schott said, "is important. Doctors need to be on the same wavelength. We must understand when one of us is talking about a container of blueberries and not a container of chocolate-covered blueberries."

"Annabel will share," Bob countered immediately with a smile.

Donn put his hand out and Annabel quickly dropped two into his hand.

"Let's hear from Dr. Burg," Dr. Mejia said, now straightening the top of his tie. "What are our principles of treatment for lung cancer and what are the options for the metastases?"

Melody shifted her weight from one high-heel shoe to the other. Dr. Mejia and Melody took pride in their fashion statements, Annabel thought, but it was far easier for Dr. Mejia as a specialized cardiologist with a bulging salary.

"There are several options for the primary lung cancer," she said. "Surgical resection, chemotherapy, and/or radiation therapy. They can be used in different combinations depending on several factors, but the intent must be clear – whether we're trying to cure the tumor or be palliative. And, along with what Dr. Mejia just said, we would treat the metastatic cancers based on the treatment we use on the original cancer. That makes sense because the cancer cells have not changed but simply are living in a new place."

"Perfect," Dr. Mejia said.

"New medical advancements may be used in her case," Dr. Schott said, "but the results are much more variable. Targeted therapy against mutations."

"Mutations?" Annabel asked.

"Due to the glory of modern medicine, because of laboratory scientists serving their eight-hour days with flasks and pipettes, some mutations are known to be prevalent in adenocarcinoma subtypes."

Annabel nodded.

"Time to explain the diagnosis and treatment to Mrs. Oliver," Dr. Mejia said. He carefully scrolled their faces. "I try, and am not always successful, to not overwhelm a patient with data. They have enough to process with the diagnosis itself."

"I figured you were going to tell me that," May said after Dr. Mejia broke the lung cancer news to her. "I kept telling myself it wasn't going to be me. Each person always thinks that something bad is going to happen to the other guy, not them."

"It's sad that we have to sometimes be the 'other guy,'" Dr. Mejia said.

May fidgeted with her hands and didn't look up.

"It appears that some of the cancer cells have already travelled to other areas of your body," Dr. Mejia added. "Let's consider your options right now for treating your lung, such as surgery, chemotherapy, or radiation, as well as more lab work to identify mutations in those cells. I would suggest surgery first. Then we can discuss where to go from there. Whatever treatment we use can then be used for two areas in your brain and your bones … other places your cancer has seeded to."

"Oh my god, you're kidding. My brain? No way am I going to see my boyfriend again when he hears that."

Everyone stayed silent. Annabel worried she was correct and May was going to need a support system.

May stared wide-eyed at Annabel. "What would you do?"

"It's difficult to say," Annabel answered, "but perhaps I would feel better knowing the primary tumor was rooted out. So I would have surgery and then discuss how to treat the other areas with my doctors."

May nodded slowly and leaned forward in the chair. "I think so too."

"Lung surgery is complicated," Dr. Schott said. "I always want my patients to know that. But if you agree, we will send a thoracic surgeon to come talk to you."

"It couldn't hurt," May said.

"We'll set up the consult," Dr. Schott said. "In the meantime, you have much to digest and questions to think about."

The team walked away and Annabel lingered. "I'm sorry we had bad news," she said.

"I know you are. These are dark days. I'll say a prayer for your dog and can you say a prayer for me?"

"Consider it done," Annabel said and left with a big sigh and a heavy heart.

Gloria folded laundry on the kitchen counter and separated her mother's day clothes from her night wear and stacked towels and wash cloths one on top of the other. From a second load, she shook out Darlene's mattress pad, which had needed washing and fitted it on the bed, making sure the rubbery area to collect body fluids was squarely in the middle. She then untangled the sheets and snagged the elastic corners of the bottom sheet around the edges of the mattress. By the time she made up the top sheet and pillow case, the lavender fragrance from the fabric softener made the area smell a lot better than before the wash loads.

Darlene was propped into her chair with the TV in front of her, which aimlessly streamed cartoons. SpongeBob ran across the screen, his skinny legs in hot pursuit of a starfish, and laughing with his mouth fully open. With mouth agape as much as the yellow character, the elderly woman stared with an empty expression and a busy tremor in her hand.

"I hope you don't mind, Mama," Gloria said, stepping away from the bed, "I'm going to stop buying those heavy-duty nutritional drinks. From now on, it'll be a tasty, sweetened shake for lunch. Enough calories for a meal too, so don't worry about that." She rolled her eyes why she bothered talking to her, but she knew it was the right thing to do. Her principles were steadfast.

She placed the towel pile into the linen closet and came back to the kitchen. From the refrigerator, she took out a twelve-ounce vanilla shake bottle and unscrewed the cap. She poured a third of it into a cup and gulped it down. Not bad, she thought. Before continuing, she practiced her germophobic habit and spilled hand sanitizer on her hand. She rubbed it in, leaned forward below the sink, and took out a container. After opening it, she used some of the liquid to top off the rest of the contents of the shake that she had sampled.

In front of Darlene, Gloria positioned the rolling table, secured a bib around the woman's neck, and patted it down on the front of her shirt. "Here you go," she said, putting the shake she'd formulated to her mother's lips. Every time she tried to give her mother a drink, she wondered if it would be in vain. Darlene could clamp down her mouth as efficiently as a snapping turtle and not open back up.

Gloria managed to get a few droplets past Darlene's lips and the woman darted her tongue as if figuring out the new flavor. Gloria tilted the bottle gently and her mother let the liquid slip in, slowly and over ten minutes, which seemed like ten hours.

"Hallelujah," Gloria said. "As sweet as the apple pie you used to bake, isn't it, Mama?"

At the end of the woman's liquid lunch, Gloria shoved down a quick sandwich for herself, the first thing she'd eaten all day. She began the preparation to tuck Darlene into bed for an afternoon nap.

"This time tomorrow will be my first day of work at your old hospital, Mama," Gloria said. "You'd be proud. Not to worry, though; someone will be here looking after you like always."

Darlene decided her mother's diaper could last longer and she supported the woman into bed. When she was finished, she redid her hands and turned off the TV. Her next task involved cooking homemade soup for dinner.

CHAPTER 17

While everyone emptied out of the office at the end of the day, Annabel's phone dinged with a text message. She hung her jacket back up and leaned against the desk.

Hi, sweetheart. Just checking on you. Are you doing okay?

Carrying on, Dad, she texted back, *because there's no other way. Sad weekend.* It amazed her that she heard from him now; most likely, he was still at the office or in the hospital. She typed again. *'You all must feel Dakota's loss there more than me. I'm thinking about that. Love and hugs.'*

I'll pass on your hugs. And say hi to your friend, Bob.

I will. Thanks, Dad.

She stayed where she was; a rare silence filled the room as patients in their rooms ate dinner and nurses did chart work. She wished she had made more trips home since starting medical school and spent more time with Dakota but, instead, the last two and a half years, she was too far away and too engrossed to make the journeys. It would be different if the relationships weren't close, but she was blessed with every one of her family members. With serious reflection, a pensive mood came over her.

Another consideration she needed to tackle, she realized, was Robby Burk. Why wait to contact him since she had broken their weekend plan? She decided to take the chance and text him.

Robby, sorry again about the other night. How about I take you out?

She smiled at her message and pressed 'send.' At least it would start a discussion going about when and where they could see each other. She checked her watch, not expecting a quick response, but a reply came back.

Gracious thought. I'm going home soon. What's your plan tonight...let's give it a shot. No formality!

She skipped a breath, and texted him back.

I'm leaving the hospital now. That would work.

I live over the bridge. Never mind....I'll call.

Her cell rang in a moment. "Hi," she said.

"Hello as well. How about we meet now? A simple bite to eat. Somewhere near your hospital or before the Ohio? I believe you said you live south of the hospital, too."

"I do. I'm on this side of the bridge. How about a dependable, relaxed place with fine coffee and a sandwich and salad menu in my neighborhood?"

"That may be too casual but, under the circumstances, we'll make it easier for you. And it will be my treat."

Annabel clutched her cell with a firm grip. Finally, she thought, and gave him the name of the place and directions.

"I'm leaving in five minutes," he said. "See you there."

"I'm headed out, too."

Annabel drove off the interstate exit and veered east towards her neighborhood. This was it. This was finally the time and the place. No mix up over what restaurant to show up at and no family crises. She breathed deeply with a see-saw of emotions. On one end, the anticipation dissipated over wondering when they would meet again but, on the other hand, her adrenaline kicked into gear and her heart raced. Soon she would be sitting across from those gorgeous eyes.

Her nervousness only ramped up as she circled the street looking for a spot anywhere between her apartment and the corner café. Had she known about their meeting, she would be dressed much more stylishly. Her white coat was thrown on the passenger seat; underneath her jacket, she wore nondescript brown pants; at least they were form-fitting, more attractive for her figure. On top, she wore a tan turtleneck sweater; not exactly first date material.

Darn, she thought, she couldn't make her debut more boring than this. She had been in such a hurry in the morning, she had not even slipped on a pair of earrings. She eyed a vehicle pulling out of a parking space.

"Come on," she mumbled. The car jockeyed back and forth several times and then squeaked out with little room to spare. She glanced at her watch. He must be here by now, she thought. It was taking her forever to show up. She rolled her eyes at the cautious driver and parallel parked with little adjustment. Her heart beat like a metronome on speed as she removed her keys and grabbed her pocketbook from the passenger floor. She slipped out her change purse and let go of the big bag. After wiggling the change purse into her pocket, she opened the door to face the cold air and wondered what he would look like after not seeing him for several months. She took a few steps away from the car and realized she needed to beep the door locked, but she heard the automatic sound of the door locking.

"Oh no," she mumbled and froze on the spot. Her car keys were not in her hand and, loudly, she blurted out an expletive. She had let the key ring slip into her pocket book without thinking. Like a child having a tantrum, she pounded her foot on the pavement and couldn't believe what she'd done. Her heart still raced, but now it was for a different reason other than seeing Dr. Burk. What a mess. And what would Robby think? Foremost, she needed to unlock her car so she could leave again tomorrow morning at the crack of dawn.

Annabel needed to focus and think and doing that would require her to stop daydreaming about her heartthrob. She stepped up to the door and tried to open it to no avail. Then she tried all three of the other handles to check if one of them defied the odds against her. But no such luck. Her hands were cold; her gloves were in her purse.

She walked with purpose across the street and into the coffee shop and café. The little bell announced her entry as Robby was ordering something across the counter from Pete.

"Hi, Annabel," Robby said. "I'm grabbing dinner because I thought maybe you were held up. Nice to see you."

"How are you tonight?" Pete asked, looking at her skeptically. "You two obviously know each other."

"Yes, from the hospital," Annabel said to Pete.

Annabel stood right next to Robby. He wore a blue knit cap and his complexion shined; he was a ski magazine's best bet for a male cover; she shook off his appearance the best she could.

"Hi, Robby. How's surgery?" she asked and immediately regretted it. What a mundane question, she thought. Couldn't she come up with something better than that?

He extended his hand over the counter to take a hot mug from Pete. "Surgery is fine as usual. Why don't you order and we'll talk at a table about surgery and medicine and whatever else."

"Except for a problem," she said nervously. She glanced between Robby and Pete. "I locked myself out of my car."

"I take it you are outside and your keys are inside?" Pete asked, finding it amusing yet serious.

"My car keys are in my purse ... which is inside my car."

"Good thing you're not a doctor rushing off to do an appendectomy on a patient," Robby said.

Annabel frowned. "But I need my keys to start my car in the morning," she said. "Do either of you know how to get into a locked car? I don't."

Robby pulled out the nearest chair and put his food on the table. "Easy," he said. "Call Triple A."

"Triple A? That's for senior citizens over sixty-five or something."

"You're thinking of AARP, the American Association of Retired Persons. You want the American Automobile Association."

She stared blankly at him while he took his jacket off and hung it on the chair. "As far as I know," she said, "I'm not a member."

"You would know," he said. "You get slammed with mail asking for more money for additional services."

Pete came from around the counter and moved shakers of salt and pepper to Robby's table. "Sorry to interrupt," he said. "Why don't you call your automobile insurance company? Many policies have roadside assist coverage."

"Smart idea," Robby said and stirred a spoon around in a cup of soup. "Don't mind if I eat, Annabel. I need to wrap up lecture material later at home, so I can't be here too long. I'm giving a talk in the department tomorrow at 8 a.m."

She shook her head, not caring about food right now for either one of them. "I don't know if I carry roadside assist and my insurance paperwork is in my car. I could call my folks. They carry all of our car policies." She frowned and slumped into the chair next to Robby. "I'm in bigger trouble than I thought. I don't even have my cell phone or apartment keys!"

"Here, Annabel," Pete said, pulling out his cell from under his apron.

"Thanks. I'll give them a call."

She walked over to the back corner of the room and paced. After calling the house number, Nancy picked up.

"Nancy, hey. Put Mom or Dad on or ask one of them a question for me."

"Dad's still in the office and Mom came home late and jumped straight in the shower. She'll be out soon and I can ask her. What's the matter?"

"I need to know if we carry roadside assist on our insurance policies." She lowered her voice as much as possible and continued. "You can't believe it. I'm finally with the chief resident I told you about. The date of all dates, although we arranged it at the last minute. Stupid me locked myself out of my car."

"You doofus. Isn't he acting like a hero and breaking into your car?"

"No," she whispered. "I don't think he'll even be staying here very long. He's got to go."

"O….kay," Nancy said. "Where are you?"

"Near my apartment, the corner coffee shop."

"I hope you get your date situation figured out. The car key problem will fix itself no matter what. A damsel in distress always gets what she needs."

"Really?" Annabel said with disbelief.

"Mom stopped running the water in there. I'll go ask her."

Annabel continued a slow pace. Robby was chowing down on some fantastic looking sandwich. Her stomach growled as Nancy got back on.

"She said yes. Call the insurance company or she said to call the Nissan dealer."

"The car dealer will be closed," Annabel said. "Give me the car insurance phone number, would you?"

Nancy went away again, came back, and began rattling off the number as Annabel walked over to Pete, waving her hand in a writing gesture. He handed her a pen and paper.

She wrote it down and said, "Thanks. I better call right now. My situation is gobbling up my whole night."

"Annabel," Nancy added, "Mom said to call or text her later to let her know the outcome."

"All right," she said. She hung up and gave Pete back his pen. "I have roadside assist," she said.

"If there is a problem with them coming," Pete said, "you can mind my store a few minutes and I can try breaking into your car with a coat hanger."

"Thanks so much. Let's leave that as my last resort."

"You can also call a locksmith," Robby said between bites. "They'll charge at least two hundred dollars, but they'll get the job done."

Annabel shrugged. "That's a good idea too. At least now there are choices. I'll stick with the safest method first, although I may still be waiting here in two hours."

"Don't worry, Annabel," Pete said. "You can chill here. Go make the call to your insurance company."

Sara came out of the bathroom and went straight over to Nancy at the kitchen table. "What was that all about?" she asked. "Annabel's not on the side of the road or anything, is she?"

"No, she's in her neighborhood at the coffee shop."

"At least she's not by herself. Besides the insurance company, someone there can probably help her out if she needs it."

"She's with the surgery chief resident she has a crush on. Another date that's blowing up in her face."

"At least she has a man with her."

"Mom! She can take care of whatever needs to be done without a man. Besides, it sounded like he's not being of much use anyway. Not like Bob, who dropped his entire weekend and whatever plans he had to drive her down here." She closed a text book while her mother still towel dried her hair.

"Hmm," Sara said. "Safe to say that Annabel's learning more about the doctor's character by having failed dates with him rather than having a steady, established relationship with him."

"But she doesn't see that," Nancy replied.

"That's why they say 'love is blind.'"

"Her stupidity will work for me."

"Your sister is far from stupid. I assume she is also blinded in this situation because of hormones."

"Like I said, this will work for me. I'd like to meet her friend, Bob, again. You don't mind if I make a trip to Cincinnati in the next month or two, do you?"

Sara shrugged. "No. However, be sure and coordinate it with your sister's workload.

"And my own."

Annabel called the insurance company and then carefully considered the menu on the blackboard.

"What'd they say?" Pete asked.

"They'll send someone. They were kind enough to inform me it would take no less than an hour or two."

"They'll probably just call a locksmith like you would have, except that now the fee will be covered under your policy."

"Unlike many situations," she said, "I only care about the end result."

"I see your point. Anyway, what'll you have?"

"The soup's delicious," Robby said, handing the empty bowl across the counter to Pete.

"How about a cheeseburger? They always smell great when I come in here." She leaned across the counter and handed him back his phone. "Thanks," she said.

"Don't mention it. One cheeseburger coming right up."

Robby asked for a coffee refill and they both sat down. "I'll stay a bit longer over this coffee," he said, "and then I'll let you focus on your situation. If the insurance company has your cell phone number, you could even go home after you eat and before your help arrives."

She would like that, she thought, but didn't want to remind him again that she was also locked out of her apartment. She watched him swallow; his eyes were on her and his mouth formed into a charismatic smile.

"Since you are giving a lecture in the morning," she said, "will you also have surgeries waiting on you tomorrow morning?"

"Yes. I'll go straight to my cases. There is never a slack in the day. You may have learned that already in your third year of medical school."

She nodded. "Are you still going to volunteer in Africa?"

"Yes. In a few short months. It will be an experience."

Her heart panged in her chest; she would feel a void when he leaves … even if this was their first and last date; although so far it was as removed as a date as getting the wrong entrée at a restaurant.

Pete came over with a glass of iced tea and her burger. "I threw some grilled mushrooms on the side in case you want to toss them on your burger. I also brought you an iced tea because you didn't mention what you wanted to drink."

"Thanks so much, Pete. I forgot the drink. I'm too preoccupied to think. Plus, our family dog died this weekend. That's upsetting all by itself."

"No problem about the drink and I'm sorry to hear about your dog. I bet he'll stay in your heart forever." He turned and left while the front door opened and another customer came in.

"Did your family put the dog to sleep?" Robby asked.

"Unfortunately. My father and all of us feel like rats for doing it."

"It happens," he said. "So what's your impression of medicine? Are you enjoying it enough that you're considering it for residency? Many students choose it or family practice when they're at a loss about specific specialties."

"You make internal medicine sound like a default area of medicine, like using a default internet browser because your primary one is offline due to technical issues."

He laughed. "Your analogy is not far from the truth. Think about it. You can google medical issues and treatments all you want, but when it comes to surgery, you need a practicing human being to wield the knife."

"Like you," she said, "I may want to use my hands. I'm too naïve this early on, however, to make a decision."

He continued smiling at her. She took a swig of tea, trying not to stare his way.

"I better head out," he said. "I need to read through my lecture once more and copy it to a usb thumb drive." He rose and put on his jacket.

Annabel was sure her face registered disappointment as he stepped next to her and put his hand on her shoulder. She felt his gentle squeeze.

"Good luck with getting into your car. I'm sure it's going to work out fine."

"Thanks," she said.

He took a step but stopped, looking back at her. "I'll call you next time," he said.

CHAPTER 18

Totally vexed at herself, Annabel dropped her keys, purse, and backpack on the kitchen counter. At least now she knew what to do if she ever sabotaged herself again by leaving her keys inside the car; she also learned that the insurance company delivered what they promised in two hours.

She sank into her big chair after she called home and assured her mother her problem was solved and that she was home, but she lacked the motivation to open a book. The night would be gone by the time she took a shower and went to bed.

What did Robby think of her now? She contemplated the hours he works and that he only squeezed in seeing her on his way home. He was also more dedicated than most residents at his level to plan a year abroad volunteering his services. She frowned. Had he seemed the least bit interested in the passing of her dog?

Annabel stopped tallying up Robby's negative attributes. From the surgical rotation, she had come away with the clearest picture of him as a sharp, concerned surgeon, a super teacher, a likeable guy, and one heck of a looker. That was the real Dr. Burk. She stopped frowning. She hoped he called her again, especially since bad things happen in threes and they had hit their quota as far as dates were concerned.

Annabel rushed into the office after seeing her patients. She had done the unthinkable, rare thing and overslept because she failed to set her alarm. At least she managed to see her patients in a hurry so she would not be blindsided on rounds with some unexpected overnight occurrence. She heard from one of the nurses that the thoracic surgeon would be by this morning to see May Oliver and, if she could, she wanted to listen in on what he had to say.

She assumed Dr. Schott was the individual sitting on the couch with the newspaper covering his face.

Donn peered over the paper. "She's here!"

"Sorry I'm a few minutes late," she said. "It's been one thing after another."

"Your situation can't be worse than what I'm reading in the state-by-state news section," Dr. Schott said. "Some maniac in Maine pressed the accelerator instead of the brake and drove off a cliff."

"An accidental Thelma and Louise," Bob said.

"What does that mean?" Stuart asked.

Donn shook his head. "You need to take an occasional breather from studying, Stuart, and watch old movies."

"I would have been unable to drive here this morning," Annabel said, "if I had not gotten back into my locked car last night. Keys were on the wrong side of the door."

"Ouch," Bob said. "Not like you."

"It is now," Jordan said.

"Still," Donn said, waving the top corner of the paper. "Two rednecks in Alabama also have you beat, Annabel. They robbed a bank in Mobile and were quickly caught thanks to their bragging about it - with photos on social media."

"Good thing you didn't say Tennessee," Bob said.

"Or Louisiana," Melody said.

"All right, y'all," Annabel said. "There are more than enough examples of stupid fodder from every state in the nation as well as from this bunch."

"What, like Jordan?" Donn asked. "Tapping on social media over there like I don't see what he's doing? The light it emits shines through his fingers like the sun rising and beaming between the trees."

Jordan slipped the iPhone straight into his lab jacket, raised his eyebrows, and gave a little shrug.

Dr. Schott folded over his paper. "I better not read one more state-by-state news item, or we'll never start rounds. But I'll let you all in on one of my own," he said, smoothing his fingers over his beard and mustache. "When I was selling real estate before going to medical school, I was ready to close on a property that had been sold the day before. Talk about not knowing what's going on!"

"How can that even happen?" Bob asked.

"Precisely," Donn said and began walking out the door.

"Sounds like your evening got messed up last night," Bob said to Annabel as they walked behind the residents and Dr. Schott.

"And my car key issue was the prelude to a date with Robby Burk," she said, "a spur of the moment arrangement which blew up in my face."

"Ouch. Are you going to see him again?"

"He said he'd call. Who knows?"

"Karla was locked out of her apartment one night two weeks ago because she left her keys in her lab coat. We had to drive all the way back to the hospital to fetch them."

"Still seeing her once in a while for a sleep over?" A hint of jealousy shrouded the question.

"You're direct today. I'm not even seeing her this week. But usually we meet for more than a sleepover, you know."

"Sorry. I didn't mean for it to sound snippy. I need to get my head aligned this morning. I didn't even have time for coffee." She took out espresso beans and shared. "By the way, my dad texted before I left the hospital yesterday. He mentioned to say hello to you."

"Give him my regards. The rest of your family, too. I really enjoyed meeting them. Too bad about Dakota. I could tell he was a special dog."

Annabel nodded as the group stopped.

"Dr. Palmer," Donn said, "you can start us off by reporting on your congestive heart patient from your last admission."

"Mr. Hogan's vital signs are normal today," Bob said, "but his weight has not budged since yesterday with our attempted diuresis of his fluid overload and he still has pedal edema on physical exam. His posterior-anterior and lateral chest films show a minor pleural effusion."

Donn nodded with his hand rubbing one side of his mustache. "How do we classify heart failure, Dr. Palmer, and what did you and Dr. Watts decide about his classification?"

"Since CHF or congestive heart failure is a chronic and progressive disease, the New York Heart Association designed criteria to assess it." He made eye contact with everyone on the team. "The method used is to determine the patient's exercise tolerance. Dr. Watts and I believe he is now a Class III because he has marked limitation of physical activity. He is symptomatic with light activity. However, with this pleural effusion, his symptoms this morning are at rest, which makes me wonder if he is now a Class IV."

"Nice job," Dr. Schott said. "What are more symptoms of CHF, Dr. Tilson?"

"His low cardiac output produces fatigue and lethargy as well as the dyspnea, peripheral edema on physical exam like what Bob mentioned, and ascites."

"The dyspnea or difficulty breathing makes it hard for him to even tie his shoelaces," Bob said.

"Dr. Watts, tell us about Mr. Hogan's ascites. Inform the students again what that is and what are we going to do about it?"

Chineka smiled. Dr. Schott made sure the students learned on their feet. "Ascites is the abnormal accumulation of serous fluid," she said, "in the spaces between the tissues and organs in the cavity of the abdomen. It accounts for the increasing abdominal girth as well as much of the increased weight you see in patients like Mr. Hogan. We have treated him with diuretics and slashed his dietary salt, but the time has come for a paracentesis."

"A para what?" their chief resident asked, goading them on and turning back to Bob.

"A surgical procedure that internal medicine doctors get to do!"

Dr. Schott lightly smiled. "Yes, we do play surgeon once in a while."

"Anyway," Bob added, "it is a procedure to draw off the abnormal fluid or effusion from the abdominal cavity."

"What for?" Donn prompted him.

"To make him less symptomatic. He'll breathe much better when his abdominal girth is gone."

"Dr. Watts," Donn said, "fine tune what student Palmer just said."

"I will perform it for both diagnostic and therapeutic purposes," she said.

"That's correct. This will be the first paracentesis for this group. Dr. Palmer, be sure you're there when Dr. Watts performs it."

Dr. Schott and Dr. Watts disappeared into Manuel Hogan's room first. Annabel gleamed at Bob. "You're sharp today," she said softly.

"Only today?"

Inside, Mr. Hogan's thick white head of hair matched his furry eyebrows which practically fell down obscuring his eyes. His legs rested on the foot rest of the recliner and the swelling and redness in them made Annabel squirm. Mr. Hogan adjusted two prongs in his nose which delivered supplemental oxygen, making it slightly easier for him to breathe and help reduce the workload of his heart.

"Mr. Hogan," Dr. Schott said, "good morning. Dr. Watts will be back to talk to you about draining some of that fluid off of your belly. How does that sound?"

"I bet it can't hurt any more than how I'm suffering with it." He patted his belly over the hospital gown like a pregnant woman in her ninth month.

"I'll go out on a limb and assure you … you'll be glad we do it."

"How about a new heart while you're at it?"

"You'd never survive a heart transplant, Mr. Hogan. Your age is a big factor. We'll keep treating you with the proper standard of care."

"My wife took off for heaven without me; she beat me to the pearly gates. Saint Peter is tapping his feet waiting on me to join her, so all's I want is another six months here, doc, to clean up my affairs. Just give me that, will you?" He pleaded with his eyes and Donn furrowed his brow with sympathy.

"We'll try our best."

After rounds, Annabel wrote her morning progress note on May Oliver at the nurses' station and jumped up when she saw a man in a white coat enter her room. It must be the thoracic surgeon, she thought, who they were waiting for.

Annabel followed him in as he introduced himself as Dr. Barrett. "I'm here at the request of the Internal Medicine doctors," he said, "to evaluate you for lung surgery."

Annabel was surprised to see May's boyfriend, Jeff, by the window as Dr. Barrett glanced at her.

"I'm the medical student taking care of Mrs. Oliver," Annabel said. "May I listen in?"

"Certainly," Dr. Barrett said. He wore a studious look but a carefree pair of sneakers.

"I was just leaving," Jeff said.

"You don't have to," May said.

"No, I came for a quick visit. You have important matters to discuss with the doctors." He passed May and slid between Dr. Barrett and Annabel and rushed to the door. A look of abandonment crossed May's face, but she managed to peel her eyes away from the back end of her boyfriend in flight and settle on the surgeon.

"Mrs. Oliver," Dr. Barrett said, "you are aware of the adenocarcinoma that has been discovered in your lung. I am here to offer you one solution - to operate on your lung to remove it as best as we can. Hopefully, the entire mass." A comfortable silence ensued as he let her think about it. "Lung surgery is risky because we must deflate the lung we're working on so it won't be breathing for you at that time. Fortunately, with some organs, we have an extra one - like your lungs and your kidneys - so your other lung will do all the work while we work on the first one. Skilled anesthesiologists do this, allowing surgeons like me to root out the tumor in question."

May glanced at Annabel and she nodded.

"Like with many surgeries, there is a risk of infection, bleeding, stroke, or death; also technical problems whereby I can't deliver what I promised. An anesthesiologist will also talk to you if you decide to proceed."

Dr. Barrett stood over six-feet-tall and finally sat on the bed and leaned forward. "Having a thoracotomy is a reasonable and expected procedure in this situation especially since some of the objectionable cells are seeding themselves elsewhere. But, the decision rests entirely with you."

"My mind was made up before you arrived," May said. "Please don't think I wasted your time because I needed to hear what you had to say. I would like to proceed."

"Never would I consider my explanation to you pointless or unnecessary. We shall go ahead, then. Expect to be on tomorrow's schedule."

"Thank you. Dr. Tilson, will you be there?"

"I am on a medicine rotation, not surgery, but I'll ask Dr. Schott if I can."

"He's a reasonable chief resident," Dr. Barrett said. "If it serves educational purposes and you can help with the care of your patient, I'm sure he won't mind."

Dr. Barrett stood and focused again on May. "Someone in the anesthesia department will be by today to talk to you and both services will be writing orders … such as nothing to eat or drink after midnight."

Annabel lingered after he left.

"He stayed but five or ten minutes," May said, her eyes clearly glued on Annabel. "My boyfriend, that is. When I told him I might be having lung surgery and then the surgeon walked in, he fled out of here like he was on fire. That's the last I'm going to see of him." She bit her lip and her face crumbled with despair.

"May," Annabel said, "please don't lament over him. If I may say so, the relationship wasn't meant to be."

May's head gave a little bob. "Perhaps it was an imaginary relationship that I had with him all along. It was one-sided and I kept trying to make it work but, luckily, it wouldn't cooperate that way. Sometimes circumstances make it easy on you because they are telling you something. It's about time I listen." She rubbed her hands back and forth like she was brushing off crumbs.

Annabel ate lunch by herself figuring she had missed everyone in her group. When she got back to the office, only Stuart was quietly hunched over the desk, reading. With relief, she realized she was caught up with medical "errands" and had time to study like Stuart. She wanted to know more about Mr. Hogan's procedure that afternoon and opened a text from the shelf to "thoracentesis."

A text message made a ding on a cell phone; maybe her own because Jordan wasn't in the room. She weeded it out of her pocket and found an update from her sister.

I'm on campus but Mary and Casey just brought Dakota's ashes home.

Annabel slipped out the door and leaned against the wall. She dialed Nancy instead of texting back. "Hey, thanks for the message. I wanted to talk."

"That's fine," Nancy said. "I'm in a lounge where students are goofing off. Mom and Dad are working but Casey came off a midnight shift and wouldn't have it any other way but to go with Mary to the vet's and pick him up."

"It figures," she said. "I'm so glad Dad did that. You know, he also said he wants Dakota's ashes to be buried with him."

"I hate to think of that day."

"But would you ask him something? I would like a small urn with some of Dakota's ashes with me up here."

"I can ask. If he says yes, I'll bring them up. I'm coming to visit. Would next weekend or the following weekend work for you?"

"I don't know if I can stand you that long but I'll let you know."

"I have something else you may like."

"What's that?" Annabel asked.

"I brushed Dakota regularly. Two or three times before he passed, I saved samples of his hair in baggies. I can bring one to you."

"I'd appreciate that. I carry a plethora of stupendous memories but that would be one more thing to cherish."

"Consider it done. And I bet Dad won't mind sharing a bit of ashes. If you don't hear from me, he has granted your request."

When they ended the call, Annabel closed her eyes, thankful for mutual family support.

CHAPTER 19

"Annabel, Dr. Watts and I are going to do Mr. Hogan's paracentesis," Bob said as he passed her in the hallway going the opposite direction.

Annabel stopped short. "Can I come along?"

"Sure," Dr. Watts said. She kept moving and, inside the supply room, she barked orders at them. They stacked the necessary supplies in Mr. Hogan's room.

"Mr. Hogan signed his consent form already," Chineka said. "For procedures like this one, you would never do it on a patient with a bleeding disorder or thrombocytopenia."

"Thrombo what?" Mr. Hogan asked.

"A low platelet count," Chineka said. "Mr. Hogan, you may lie on your back and we'll adjust the bed so your head is raised a little."

Bob rolled over the blood pressure machine and wrapped the cuff on Mr. Hogan's arm while his patient wiggled on the bed to get comfortable.

"I'll get a baseline blood pressure and pulse," Bob said. He cycled the machine and listened with his stethoscope.

Chineka began cleaning Mr. Hogan's abdomen, gowned and gloved, and draped sterile towels around the site. "I'm going to make a little bee sting on your skin while I inject some numbing medicine," she said, drawing up lidocaine.

"I always use the lower left quadrant," she said to the students and gave the local anesthetic a minute to take effect. "An ultrasound can also be used for guidance, especially if there isn't too much fluid." She slowly put the larger paracentesis needle into Mr. Hogan's belly.

"Ouch," Mr. Hogan said.

Chineka tilted her head. "You should feel pressure, not really pain."

"Pressure," he said. "You shoulda knocked me out for this."

"This is much safer for you," Bob said. "The needle in the abdomen is similar to what awake pregnant women go through for an amniocentesis."

"That's why men don't have babies."

Annabel suppressed a chuckle as Bob glanced at her.

Carefully, Dr. Watts began to aspirate fluid into a large syringe. "Be sure to lie completely still," she said.

"What else am I going to do? Do you know what I'm gonna do when I am sprung out of here?"

"You are going to get your affairs in order," Bob said while Chineka continued focusing on the procedure.

"Right," Mr. Hogan said. "I told you young folks that. Specifically, I'm going to go pick out a headstone. Of course, I want to be buried, but why shouldn't I be the one to select what will be resting above me for God knows how long? Maybe just a century because the world's population is burgeoning and my plot will someday be needed for land area under a high-rise apartment building. And I want to write a creative inscription ahead of time, something which will make people stand there and ponder over the nut case underneath. Something like 'Stayed still for a Paracentesis.'

"I see you students half-grinning," he said. "You two have such baby faces, you're young enough to be my great-grandchildren." He glanced down and, for the first time, studied what Chineka was doing as the heat from the baseboard kicked on and made a steady drone.

"More than a liter drained already," Dr. Watts said.

"I don't feel so great," Mr. Hogan said. "I mean, I haven't felt fantabulous since getting CHF, but now I'm going to droop."

Annabel and Bob exchanged glances and nodded. Bob cycled the blood pressure cuff while Annabel positioned her stethoscope on his forearm. "110/76," she said when it finished. "I'll run and fetch fluids."

She hurried out to the supply area again knowing that, for Mr. Hogan, he was hypotensive. His pressure had been a lot higher when they first started, so it was not unusual for him to be lightheaded, especially after spying on the needle and the procedure. She grabbed only an IV bag and tubing.

Annabel came back into the room and Bob wheeled over a pole from the corner. Between the two of them, they hooked the fluids into Mr. Hogan's hep-lock, took his pulse, and recycled his blood pressure. He rested with his head back and his eyes closed. Bob patted his forearm, which was speckled with previous bruises from attempts at starting IVs and bumping into things.

"I'll be okay," Mr. Hogan said softly.

"This will do," Chineka said. "Over two liters. We'll let Mr. Hogan readjust to the loss of volume and not drain anymore." She took the needle out of his abdomen and applied a bandage over the site. "I'm sending some of the fluid for testing, but we don't expect any surprises. The white cell count and culture will probably not show signs of an infection.

"How are you doing, Mr. Hogan?" Dr. Watts asked.

"Hanging on. I haven't had this much attention since my wife rubbed horse liniment into my aching muscles."

"Glad we can be of service," she said and turned to the students. "Mr. Hogan needs his blood pressure, pulse, and temperature monitored over the next hour. I'll write the orders. Staff should call me if his vital signs deteriorate from what they are now."

"If we stay free to do so," Annabel said, "Bob or I will pop back in too."

With Mr. Hogan looking peaceful and feeling better, they stepped out.

"You two worked like a team in there," she said, "without my even telling you what to do. I'm impressed."

"Thanks," Bob said. "Those words would shine if they were written on our clinical evaluations," he added with a pleading smile.

"Dr. Palmer," she said, "sometimes you're priceless."

The next morning, Mr. Hogan appeared more comfortable as the team congregated around him. Every light was on in the room with the gray sky a contrast through the window. His fork dabbled with the scrambled eggs on his breakfast tray.

"These would taste like a filet mignon if I could sprinkle salt on them," he said.

"No salt," Dr. Schott said. "Not under my care."

"I figured you'd say that."

"You look no worse for wear after your paracentesis yesterday."

"That motley crew of yours drained my belly yesterday like they tapped open a beer keg."

"It's a heck of a way to lose weight," Dr. Schott said. "How did you fare with the procedure?"

"Besides getting all dizzy and your medical students rescuing me, I hung in there."

"They come in handy once in a while," Donn said.

"Mr. Hogan's weight is down two pounds today," Bob said to Dr. Schott, "and the lab values from his ascitic fluid so far show no sign of infection."

"A little more tuning up, Mr. Hogan," Donn said, "and we'll try and discharge you to home."

Dr. Schott led the team outside. "I am not optimistic about Mr. Hogan. I believe his ejection fraction is much worse than the last time he was evaluated. Dr. Watts, please order an echocardiogram on him and give the students a small primer on the topic."

"This is a subject I have pored over in my own life," Chineka said, "since my mom has CHF. When an illness or disease is personal in nature, then I use it to my advantage to learn every last morsel about it."

"You students have heard this before," Donn interrupted, "and you'll hear it a thousand times. Standing on your feet on rounds, hearing a subject over and over, is what makes it sink in so that it is second nature. Go ahead, Dr. Watts."

"The heart's ejection fraction," she said, "is a number that is a percentage. It is the percentage of oxygenated blood that is pumped out of the left ventricle, the main pumping chamber of your heart, with each heartbeat. Fifty-five or higher is considered normal, but below forty may be evidence of heart failure or cardiomyopathy. The last percentage assessed for Mr. Hogan was below 40 percent.

"Since Dr. Schott wants us to reevaluate Mr. Hogan, the best, most common method to assess ejection fraction is by doing an echocardiogram. That test uses sound waves to produce images of the heart and the blood pumping through the heart. The result can guide us with our patient's treatment plan and tell us if he is going down a slippery path."

Donn nodded with approval, took off his thick glasses, and rubbed a cleaning cloth on the lenses. "Mid-term test is coming up soon. I don't expect one bad grade from this bunch."

"I'll be ready," Jordan said.

Donn peered over at Stuart.

"No problem, I hope."

"I'm not comfortable yet," Annabel said.

"Annabel always feels that way," Bob said tentatively, "but she comes through every time."

"What about you?" Donn asked.

"I squeak by. I can't compete with Stuart or Jordan."

"Stuart, maybe," Donn said. He slid his glasses back on. "Dr. Tilson, any pertinents about May Oliver before we step in?"

"She'll be transported over to the preop area any minute for her lung surgery."

"You can break from rounds to watch once she goes into the OR." He pointed to the room.

Inside, May Oliver twisted her hands together like she was sweating it out at a poker table with high stakes. A man and a woman in their early sixties sat on the bed facing her. They were dressed smartly and stood immediately to greet the group.

"We're May's parents," the man said. "I'm Ken and this is Louise. We came as soon as we could; we're thankful we'll be here during her surgery."

"We only have one child," Louise said, "so May means the world to us."

Louise's cheekbones were prominent and high like her daughter's; she was an attractive woman with an air of humility. After sitting down, she reached for May's hand and held it in her own.

Annabel was glad to meet them; she hoped their appearance made up for May's boyfriend and his cowardly avoidance of her situation.

In a series of efforts, May coughed, trying to clear the irritation coming from her respiratory tract. Stuart handed her the emesis basin from the nightstand. She clenched it close to her mouth and expectorated slimy blood. More came with repeated coughing as Louise and Ken Oliver's faces registered fear and uncertainty.

Even though Annabel finished her medical school surgery rotation, it had not included thoracic cases. She realized she would be watching a much more dangerous surgery on a grander technical scale and wished it wasn't going to be on May Oliver.

In the OR, the anesthesiologist and senior resident busily prepared May for her case as the surgical team waited. She had a soft spot for the importance of the anesthesia care team and watched with diligence as they hooked her up to all the monitors, inserted an arterial line in May's wrist for constant blood pressure monitoring, and then a central line for better IV access.

"Sweet dreams," the resident said, as the attending doctor injected a narcotic and sedative-hypnotic to put her to sleep. With a face mask, the resident breathed oxygen into her after she fell asleep and he opened her mouth with a laryngoscope to intubate her. From hearing Dr. Barrett's previous explanation to Mrs. Oliver, and having talked with the anesthesia resident, she knew this endotracheal tube was different. She stayed out of their way as they inserted a one-sided lung tube, which had to be placed perfectly to ventilate May's non-operative lung. They checked the placement by sliding down a flexible bronchoscope and taking a look.

With anesthesia satisfied, the OR team, anesthesia, and the surgeons placed May in a lateral position with the operative lung facing up. Dr. Barrett and his resident scrubbed outside at the sink, anesthesia checked placement of the tube one more time since May had been moved, and when the surgical team came back in, they began surgery on May's lung.

No one asked to turn on music; May's age and her case were disconcerting to everyone present. Annabel was allowed to stand near the anesthesia team and peer into her chest cavity where she saw the rubbery deflated lung. After Dr. Barrett expressed concern about the whereabouts of the tumor, he isolated it, his scalpel went to work, and blood began seeping into the hollow of her chest cavity.

"Hold onto me, Mama," Gloria said to deaf ears as her left arm encircled her mother and her right one jimmied up a clean pair of trousers. The elastic waistband settled on her mother's waist and Gloria straightened the ends of the adult diaper underneath. She gently lowered Darlene and decided her blue print top was fine for her clinic appointment. She reached for a nylon hairbrush and detangled the back of her mother's short hair. "Look at you," Gloria said. "Now you're the belle of the ball."

Darlene's face was set in a scowl, like it had been baked in clay. "Mama, on the other hand, I need to crack your face with a hammer to bring back the beautiful expressions you used to wear."

"Damn," Darlene scowled; or at least that's what Gloria thought she said.

Gloria moved the tray table close. She scooped up a teaspoon of left-over yogurt and her mother cooperated by letting it slide down her throat. A portion of the liquid lunch Gloria had prepared was still left so she tipped the bottle up twice to her mother's lips until the liquid was drained.

Gloria lined up their jackets and hats on the bed and readied her purse. Her mother's clinic appointment was in an hour and a half. She squeezed sanitizer on her hands, moved the bottle back to the counter, and left a moist trail on every item she subsequently touched. Glancing at the clock, she knew moving her mother out of the house and situating her in the car took longer than the actual drive to the clinic.

Annabel fretted because May's thoracotomy extended over the time allotted for it on the schedule. She noted the proficiency of the experts above and below the surgical drapes hanging across May's neck area to both sides of the arm boards. The senior anesthesia resident swept his eyes over the monitors as a constant ritual, kept his record updated, and adjusted his anesthesia dosages when the need arose. He peered into the lung, watching carefully the amount of blood loss and transfused the second bag of red blood cells. Every thirty minutes, he ducked under the table and noted May's urine trickling into the Foley catheter. So far, her renal function was fine.

At the end of the surgery, anesthesia had yet more to do. Besides inflating the surgical lung back up, the team then removed the double-sided endotracheal tube and immediately replaced it with a single lumen tube.

"May needs to go to the ICU and patients don't tolerate the larger tubes well when they're waking up," the anesthesiologist said to her, noting her curious expression.

Before they transported May to the unit, Annabel left the OR dazed at the complexity of what she'd seen. Her patient would now be an ICU patient, hooked to a ventilator until the medical specialties deemed she would be able to breathe on her own.

Out in the waiting area, May's parents approached her with questions.

"What took so long?" Ken asked.

"Is our daughter's cancer gone forever?" Louise asked.

Annabel wished she was more than a third year medical student but, nevertheless, she tried to appease them.

"The other doctors will be out to talk to you and answer your questions. May, however, is stable and will be going to the ICU. There she will be sleeping off her anesthesia and feeling no pain."

CHAPTER 20

Gloria pulled her car up below the awning and jumped out. The beauty of bringing her mother into the hospital or clinic was that she didn't need to bring along Darlene's wheelchair for the trip. All she had to do was pop into the front door of the facility and grab one of theirs. She wasn't getting any younger to be hoisting medical equipment into her car, she thought, and realized her birthday was the next day – a whooping thirty-nine years old. She should stage a celebration with her mother. Birthdays deserved a special cake; all the years that Gloria was growing up, her mother saw to it.

Snow flurries swirled around in the unloading zone like they didn't know where to go and peppered her thick black shoes. She stomped on the mat after she entered the building and grabbed a wheelchair. A considerate elderly volunteer rushed over to help her and followed her back out.

"You'll catch pneumonia out here," she yelled at him as she opened her car door.

He ignored the remark and heaved Darlene out of the front seat and lowered her into the wheelchair.

"Thank you so much," Gloria said inside. "I don't have a shred of help 24/7 when I'm caring for my mom. You don't know it, but your kind act is like a ray of sunshine on this dreary winter day."

The man's eyes smiled with deep wrinkle lines as he pushed Darlene inside and Gloria parked the car. In a little while, both women were riding the elevator upstairs to the outpatient medicine clinic.

All four students ate lunch together and grabbed refills on their coffee; or in Stuart's case, a hot chocolate. A buzz of conversation sounded from the waiting room as well as an overhead local news station as the students walked through to the outpatient clinic. "You may need an umbrella later today if it warms up any more," the newscaster said, "and if this light precipitation hangs around."

"Warms up?" Bob said when they entered the exam area. "That'll be a miracle."

Stuart peeked at a chart outside the first door. "This is a new patient, not a follow up. I'll take her."

Dr. Burg heard him and stopped filing her nails behind the desk. "Come on, then," she said. "He should be ready for the A-team."

"What does that make us?" Jordan asked as they disappeared into Room 1.

"We're the BTA-team," Bob said, "better than average. Which can mean A+."

Annabel shook her head at him and picked up the next chart. "This one's mine; my Parkinson's patient for a follow-up."

"I'll see another patient in the interim," Chineka said, plucking out a different chart in the next bin. "You go in there and examine Mrs. Pratt. Evaluate if her Parkinson's symptoms are stable and not worse than when she left the hospital."

Annabel turned the knob, grateful for the opportunity. She loved seeing patients by herself. It not only made her feel useful and important, but then she could compare her assessment with her resident's and realize the things she missed.

"Mrs. Pratt and Mrs. Pratt," she said when she entered. Darlene sat in the wheelchair and the women's jackets and hats were lumped on the exam table. Gloria stood, a canvas tote bag brimming with a diaper and toiletries next to her on the floor.

"How is your mom doing?" Annabel asked.

"She's in her own world but no worse for it. Her motor control hasn't gotten any worse, thanks to that levodopa and carbidopa."

"And is the clozapine that the psychiatrist recommended helping with her psychosis?"

Gloria shrugged. "She may be calmer, come to think about it."

Annabel noted Darlene's blood pressure was acceptable and then leaned into her patient. She lacked any facial expression, the trunk of her body stayed catatonic, and one hand fidgeted with a tremor. How awful, Annabel thought more seriously than before. Her patient had no pleasant moments as far as she could tell. And unlike some of the psychiatric patients she had taken care of who had thought processes they could not escape but their bodies were fine, this woman's mind and body were like she was locked up inside plaster without any escape.

Annabel hovered over her with her stethoscope. She appreciated

Darlene's clean clothes as well as the light lavender fragrant smell coming from the woman. Gloria was amazing, she thought, like a Mother Teresa in the Pratt home. She wrapped her stethoscope back around her neck after listening to near normal breath and heart sounds. Her patient's heart rate and respiratory rate were a tad elevated, but nothing concerning.

"How are you holding up?" Annabel asked Gloria.

"I landed the job that I interviewed for."

"Congratulations," Annabel said. "I don't know how you juggle a job and taking care of your mom."

"The way I always have. Someone's at the house when I'm gone. Yesterday was my first day. The personnel office gave me two choices of where I wanted to work and I chose the medical floor. Basically, I had to follow around nurses and other medical assistants, but next time, I'll be on my own."

"You'll be an asset with all your care-giving experience."

The door opened and Chineka entered. She gave them a greeting and Annabel told her a short update on Mrs. Pratt.

"I'm going to order some labs," Dr. Watts said, "to make sure your mom doesn't have a recurrent UTI. After an assistant draws her blood, you may be more comfortable outside in the waiting area."

"We'll be fine here," Gloria said. "Mom will most likely shut her eyes. She's missing her nap."

Annabel and Chineka left and Gloria helped herself to an ethyl alcohol wipe next to the sink to kill any new germs on her hands. As her mother soon rattled off some snoring, Gloria also closed her eyes.

"Only one more hour to go," Annabel said as she combed the side of her hair with her fingers.

"But then we have rounds on the wards," Bob said, holding a chart next to her.

"The day is going too slow and I'm anxious to study tonight."

"Here," he said. "I have a new box of espresso beans." He took them out and quickly found Jordan and Stuart hovering behind his shoulder.

"All right. They're small boxes." He spilled some into each of their hands as well as his own, crumpled the box, and tossed it underneath in the garbage.

"Bob, this is perfect," Annabel said letting the chocolate bean melt on her tongue.

A woman from the lab peered at the students' charts in front of them. "Here," she said, "this is for Pratt."

"Thanks," Annabel said, and looked at Darlene's results. "I'll be back," she said and updated Chineka. The two women compared new lab results with old ones.

"Let's go back in," Chineka said.

Inside, Darlene's eyes stayed closed. "I hope my mama hasn't had too much rest," Gloria said opening her eyelids. "Otherwise, she'll be up half the night."

"We'll let you get out of here," Chineka said. "Results are fine except that your mother's renal function seems to have slipped in the wrong direction, but there's no UTI. I'm sure it's not easy for you, but try and make sure she stays hydrated. The creatinine is creeping up and we'll have to watch for further renal insufficiency. Instead of bringing her back in a month, we'll schedule you back in two weeks."

"Okay, doc," Gloria said. "You know you can count on me."

Gloria began softly rocking her mother's shoulder to stimulate her. "Mama, it's time to wiggle you into your coat so we can go home."

Outside, Annabel wrote a clinic note on Mrs. Pratt for Chineka to counter-sign. Gloria soon passed, pushing Darlene in the clunky wheelchair, and waved good-bye with the appointment slip in her hand.

However, Gloria thought, there was a scant chance she'd be back in with her mother for that visit ... which was sooner than she anticipated.

Back on the medicine ward, the students and residents hurried to gather any new patient data for rounds. They ached to go home. Tomorrow was a call day.

Dr. Schott pitched in too. "All right, did they expedite Mr. Hogan's echocardiogram this afternoon?" he asked no one in particular.

Mr. Hogan's nurse, a young woman named Susan, handed him several sheets, paper-clipped together. "Here are incoming results from today for his chart," she said.

"Thanks." He glanced at Bob. "Which means even the eager medical student here hasn't seen them."

Bob frowned. "Don't hold it against me."

"I would never," he said and took off his glasses. Instead of wiping his lenses, he rubbed his eyes as if he didn't want to see Mr. Hogan's echocardiogram assessment.

Donn read the results with his glasses back on and with Susan still standing by. He shook his head and leaned back. "His ejection fraction is estimated to be 34 percent. Very bad heart failure. That means the pumping ability of his heart is severely below normal. Among other fatal complications, he is capable at any time of having a life-threatening arrhythmia or having the left and right ventricle pump in an unsynchronized manner."

Annabel placed her head in her hands on the counter. She liked Mr. Hogan. She could tell that Bob did too; he not only didn't have a humorous thing to say, he didn't say anything at all.

"Thanks for letting me listen," Susan said, "because now I can keep a closer eye on him."

Donn nodded and she left. "I feel it's our duty to tell him now," he said. "Unlike many patients with their illnesses, I think he absorbs and understands what we tell him about his heart failure. And when he doesn't, he asks more questions."

"Somewhat like our other patient, Mr. Harty," Bob said. "He was a really smart old man that I admired. I still feel bad about him"

"I tell you," Donn said. "Sad cases multiply like leaf piles in the fall."

Annabel had never seen Dr. Schott with a crestfallen face before, but for a flash, his beard and mustache and demeanor made him appear ten years older. He was not even an attending yet, she thought. Clinical medicine, as well as many other specialties, was not for the faint of heart.

When the team shuffled into Mr. Hogan's room, he was absorbed with watching the history channel. Old footage of World War II had him on the verge of tears: antiquated-looking airplanes dropping bombs, boys in uniforms wielding rifles, and disheveled families seeking refuge from homelessness.

Dr. Schott cleared his throat and Mr. Hogan flinched.

"Didn't notice my cavalry came in," he said. He muted the television and grinned. "What are you going to tell me this time?"

"Your heart function worsened since your last echo." Donn pursed his lips. Mr. Hogan deserved getting his medical news like whiskey. Straight up.

"Bad, huh?"

"That bad."

"Thanks for telling me. Of course, you already told me you aren't going to stick a new heart in me. You better send me home then ... ASAP."

"Not so fast. I'm still responsible for monitoring you after that paracentesis."

"I'll grant you that. Only because I like you and the rowdy group behind you. I don't want to get any of you in trouble with a medical review board or something like that."

"Thank you," Donn said, "but do me another favor. After the war story, tune into an old *I Love Lucy* or *Carol Burnett* show. A little humor is the best prescription."

"Most of you were in diapers when I watched those shows," he said softly.

Driving home, Annabel wore a smile, happy to be finished for the day. She wanted pampering; something she was scarce on these days. Stepping out of the car, she didn't dare leave her keys in there, something she had stupidly reserved for her Robby Burk night. She decided to forego rummaging through her sparse refrigerator contents or dreaming up what to make herself for dinner and went on up to Pete's café.

The pleasant jingle sounded when she stepped in. Customers occupied several tables. She dumped her things on the bench against the wall and strolled to the counter.

"I was wondering when I'd see you in here again," Pete said, rearranging sweets inside the see-through case. He looked towards the door and leaned over. "No date tonight?"

"No man with me. I can't tell any more when they're considered a date or not. I messed up the last one."

"Having a crisis on a date is a good test if they're possible marriage material."

"Yikes, I wouldn't go that far," she said. "I'll order your house salad and if you could throw on some grilled chicken ..."

"Coming right up. Especially since I've got help today." He nodded towards a stout woman preparing a sandwich plate.

"And just some water," Annabel added and went back to the bench. She needed to catch up on her cell phone; unlike Jordan, she had not scrolled though emails or texts for hours.

Nancy had texted her earlier in the day. *Dad said it would be fine – for you to have some of Dakota's ashes. Can I come up this weekend?*

You don't have to come up just to give them to me, she wrote back and sorted through her backpack for her medicine paperback. She began studying the classification criteria for CHF when Pete put her water and salad on the side of the placemat.

"Thanks," she said as Nancy's next message showed up.

I want to visit my sister, that's all.

All right, but bring books and an air mattress. I DO need study time.

Can we go out Saturday night? (Invite your friend Bob).

All right.

She pressed "send" and chewed a slice of chicken. A guy and girl laughed loudly at a nearby table and then swapped their plates but Annabel wondered about her upcoming plan with Robby Burk. She had enough dignity to refrain from calling him because he had been clear ... he would call her.

Another thing, she thought, she had enrolled in medical school but that didn't mean she was a nun. It was time to search for a fling via the different app she had selected since having too much trouble with the social app, Findar. She vowed to be more careful and listen more to her intuition. After all, she had had some fantastic experiences. Like the guy on the boat on the Ohio. That was a memorable one-night stand. What was his name anyway?

By the time she finished her meal and scrolled through the profiles of men who had left messages for her, she decided to contact a man five years older than her who had sun-kissed surfer's hair. He hinted about some kind of secret police work under "occupation." His name was Ben Rogers.

CHAPTER 21

Gloria first tended to Darlene. The home aide would be at the house soon and would change her mother's clothes and make her bed, so she only did what was important. She reached under the sink and then into the closet and mixed liquid from two containers … the one ingredient she'd been using to poison her mother and the other to make it easier to drink. As far as her calculations went, she made enough for what she wanted accomplished during her absence. She brought over the glass.

"Good morning, Mama. You slept like a champ last night. No one knows like me since I sleep with one eye and ear awake for you." She sat on the edge of the bed and held Darlene forward enough to let the drink slide down slowly. "I'm going to bring home a cake today after work and we're going to celebrate my birthday. Your little girl is getting old too."

Gloria stroked her mother's grey hair and looked into her icy eyes. "You have no idea how I'm going to miss you, Mama," she said as she put the used cup on the nightstand.

She hated that her mother would have to wait a few minutes to be cleaned up, but she needed to get ready for work. She stared into her closet and pulled out a camel blouse, which was becoming with her golden honey hair. Lastly, she pulled on her solid shoes - a blessing for a long shift on a hard floor.

The doorbell rang when it was supposed to, allowing Gloria to sigh with relief. She opened the front door and greeted the caretaker, Marabeth, an olive-skinned woman with a shining smile and a helpful attitude.

"Mom is ready for you," Gloria said. "I know deep down inside, she's happy to see you."

"She's a fine woman," Marabeth said, "except for when she mumbles out a cuss word." She put a big black bag on the chair. "Don't worry about a thing, dearie. You go off to work."

Gloria bundled up in her jacket, grabbed her belongings, and headed out. When she started the engine, she praised her efforts. She had left under no different circumstances or changed behavior than normal. Nothing that would raise a red flag.

Annabel read May Oliver's new chart notes since late rounds the day before. For being on call, her day was starting on a promising note for her patients. May's breathing tube had been pulled last night by the on-call team and the pulmonologist and specialized cancer doctor had come up with a plan for her chemotherapy. She walked into May's ICU room, where her patient gave her the faintest of smiles.

"I made it through having more than a slice of my lung cut out," May said with a hoarse voice. "Unlike some colleagues over in Afghanistan who had different body parts operated on, I escaped that because I wasn't in the thick of battle. But back in the states, I fall prey to the knife anyway." She grimaced with a twinge of pain along her ribs.

"It was an important surgery," Annabel said. "The surgeon performed a lobectomy and by doing that, he removed the entire tumor."

"That's what they told me."

Annabel readjusted the pulse oximeter probe on May's finger and listened to her shallow breaths with her stethoscope. Her vital signs were acceptable, but Annabel recognized the weary, strained look on her patient's face.

"The doctors don't want to waste any time," Annabel said. "Dr. Schott will probably brief you on rounds, but if he's satisfied, we may be transferring you out of here today back to the medical floor. Chemotherapy is next."

"As long as they remove the rest of these IV tubes."

"The one in your non-operative upper chest may be needed for some time."

May wiggled her finger at Annabel; the one with the bulky probe. "Thanks for filling me in with my care," May said. "You've been an asset ever since I landed in the hospital."

Annabel smiled. "You would do the same if our roles were reversed."

Annabel passed the east nurse's station on the medical ward when Bob joined her.

"My sister's coming up this weekend," she said. "How about we grab a bite to eat on Saturday?"

"Go out before our test next week?"

She laughed. "Maybe it'll do us some good. We can spare a night."

"I'm game. Should we ask Stuart and Jordan?"

"Sure. Ask Karla too, if you'd like."

Bob shook his head. "She won't come. She's gone crazy as far as studying. Some kind of new thing, like she wants to score the highest on her rotation. She's thinking of applying to the country's most prestigious residency programs in her senior year and wants her grades to shine. That's put a wedge between us and, like I've mentioned, we don't see each other much. The relationship has dwindled away."

"I'm sorry, Bob. In the fall, it seemed like you two were hitting it off."

"I don't blame her for her changed attitude. I hear residency spots can be pretty damn competitive."

"I can't think that far ahead."

He looked at her, considering what to say. "And I can't think about being on a rotation without you, let alone residency."

Her forehead wrinkled as she slowed to look at him, trying to catch his meaning.

"Who would I have this much comradery with, share snacks with, or acquire these memorable patients with besides you?" he quickly asked. "Besides, the two of us end up in medical dramas about new drugs or eccentric patients."

She didn't have time to respond as they rounded the corner into the office and Jordan and Stuart also appeared.

"Amazing," Dr. Schott said from behind his newspaper. "It's rare for twin calves to be born, but in Kansas recently, there were three calves born twice on either side of the state."

"Fodder for the world record book," Bob said.

"Fodder for farmers who want to replicate such a thing." Donn pushed the paper aside and pointed towards the bulletin board. "Who's taking the first admission today?"

"I'm up first," Dr. Berg said.

"I'm the student up first," Stuart said.

"Enthusiastic group," he said. "Let's go do rounds and you students have to attend a grand rounds lecture later at the medical campus."

Annabel grabbed a rolling cart from behind the central desk and Dr. Burg and Dr. Watts pulled patients' charts from the rack and stacked them on top. Stuart rolled the noisy antique out of the nurses' way.

"Dr. Palmer," Donn said, "give us Mr. Hogan's update."

"He had a low grade temperature overnight and he's almost put a pound back on," Bob said. "On physical exam, he has a trace more pedal edema as well. He is still on doses of IV Lasix."

Their chief resident fidgeted with his mustache. "What are we going to do with Mr. Hogan?" he asked and took off through the doorway.

Inside, Mr. Hogan ambled over to the sink in brown, clunky slippers. "I thought I heard you all coming," he said. "I'm going to brush my teeth - the highlight of my morning besides breakfast. Plus, old people can't sit around all day in a chair or they may be caught dead."

Donn rolled his eyes. "There's truth to that. Move around when you can and don't let blood clots form in your legs. And put your legs up when you're resting. We're trying to get that edema to subside."

Mr. Hogan turned and sat back in his chair. Donn crouched and pressed on his ankles, noting Bob's assessment to be correct.

"We're going to increase your Lasix today," Donn said.

Before they left, it was clear no one mentioned any plans for his discharge.

Gloria reported to the west wing of the medicine floor eager for the change of pace in a new facility. Ten-hour shifts could be grueling but she was ready for the challenge. In essence, previous work days at other jobs were often less tiring than being at home with Darlene. She hoped she would stay focused during the day; it would be difficult to not let her mind drift to her mother, who would be getting more obviously sick for the caretaker as the day wore on. But she would say good-bye to her at the end of the day with all the love and affection they had shared for each other over the almost-four decades they had been together.

She saw her boss get off the elevator and she whispered silently to herself, "Mama, it won't be long. I made a promise to you and I intend to keep it."

Her new boss approached her with a clipboard and a colorful headband around her hair.

"Gloria, welcome." She ushered her new employee to the counter, explained her tasks for the day, and handed her a list from her paperwork. "Some days, I may break this routine, depending on what needs to be done," the woman said, "but this is a nice manageable introduction to the floor. I have you slotted for two twenty-minute breaks and a half hour for lunch," she added, pointing to Gloria's schedule. She wore a blue hospital coat and gave her instructions in a friendly tone. So far, Gloria was more than happy to be in the government hospital.

The woman left after introducing her to the east and west wing staff at the nurses' stations. Gloria went back to where they had started. She readied her designated cart of machinery, making sure the rack on the side of it housed a bottle of hand sanitizer.

She didn't have to do it, but she committed the first woman's name to memory from her list of patients. After all, she also had a name and a face and was more than just a medical assistant taking vital signs; caretakers and patients in the hospital environment were co-dependent on each other. She put a spring into the step of her black shoes, and went in the corner room.

"Morning, Ms. Baker," she immediately said to a woman brushing her hair. "I'm Gloria and I'm here to take your vital signs. Let's put a heartbeat number to that lovely heart of yours ticking away in your chest."

After morning rounds, all four students piled into Bob's Chrysler sedan and headed downtown to the medical campus for grand rounds. Dr. Schott gave them leeway to eat lunch while they were gone and they decided on a familiar independent restaurant on the medical campus. As they walked from the parking lot, Annabel spun around once, taking in the deep blue sky with a splattering of billowy clouds moving fast above the tall buildings. They filed through the revolving door and joined medical folks escaping the hospital and offices.

The students formed a line, put in their orders, and paid. Soon a man was calling their names and they were busing their food to a table.

Annabel placed her tray down and took a sip of cappuccino. "This tastes like a million bucks. Cinnamon on top of the frothy hot milk like it should be."

The students opened utensils and acknowledged other people they knew. Not wanting to check messages during the lecture, Annabel scrolled through her phone to find that Ben Rogers had suggested a definitive plan for them – to meet Saturday night.

She frowned and thought about it while she speared an avocado slice from her salad. There was already a plan in place with Nancy and Bob and she didn't want to start changing things around. She took a look again at his profile on the dating app. He had a pleasant smile. He also mentioned in the same text that if they agreed to meet, he would alleviate any concerns she had about his identity. Since he had listed some kind of police work, he would show a picture of his credentials if she confirmed the date.

How about meeting at 7 p.m.? his message said. *At Stone's west of the interstate ... it's a great new bar with craft pizza. A young crowd. And later...that'll be up to you.* ☺

Jordan was bragging about making a correct diagnosis on a previous rotation as Annabel contemplated her response. Bob sat across from her and, although he chowed down on a warm pastrami sandwich, his eyes stayed on her. She could always link up with Rogers after going out with Nancy and Bob and it wouldn't preclude her from sleeping with him if she wanted.

Her last thought before messaging him was that she'd waited for Robby Burk long enough. Even if he happened to call, Saturday night plans would already be a done deal.

She scrolled her fingertips with a message. *Sounds fine. Mind if we meet at 8 p.m. instead?*

"Did you hear us, Annabel?" Stuart said.

"Uh, I guess not," she said.

"You better catch up to us and quit being so Jordan-like with your cell phone."

"Sorry," she said. "I'll eat faster, but you all go ahead if I'm going to make you late."

"We're fine for a few minutes," Bob said, wiping his hands.

Annabel finished what she could and looked at her cell one more time as her colleagues rose. She couldn't believe what popped through. Ben Rogers delivered the picture ID he promised and it was better than she imagined. There was a picture of his badge as a Secret Service agent. *For your eyes only,* he said.

She rose with a smile and put on her jacket. If she was going to have a one-nighter, Ben Rogers gave her little to worry about. Now she had something fun to think about; something to help her get through any depressing aspect of the rest of her week. Every relationship she had right now was platonic – she craved for something physically intimate.

Gloria worked her way down to the east wing. She gathered vital signs, recorded them on bedside charts and her own log, and made friends with patients. As she rubbed her hands, the cold sanitizer clinging to her palms, she glanced at the next name, knocked on the door, and entered.

"Mr. Hogan," she said, "I've come to take new vital signs on you. Looks like the docs want you weighed too." She stared a moment at his face. "You're my first Santa Claus look-alike for the day."

"I'm missing the beard and mustache," he said, "but you're right. My hair and eyebrows more than make up for that." He laughed and patted his belly. "And this too."

She motioned for his arm and wrapped around the blood pressure cuff.

"But my belly isn't just fat, you know. I've got bad congestive heart failure. I swell up. They even siphoned fluid out of here a few days ago." He pointed toward his left lower quadrant. "Like an elephant sucking water out from a watering hole."

"That sounds miserable," Gloria said and quieted to get his pressure. She unwrapped the cuff and asked him to stand on the scale.

"They did that earlier," he said. "They only do it once a day before the doctors come in for rounds."

"Okay," she said. "I can understand." She put the pulse oximeter on his finger for a reading.

"There is only so much monitoring I'm going to take," he said. "My heart is shot and I'm just trying to go home for end-of-life stuff. Clearing my plate, so to speak." He grinned at that, happy with his choice of words.

Gloria took a step back. "Will that be soon, Mr. Hogan?"

His face soured. "I'm taking one step forward and two steps back." He pushed forward like he was going to tell her a secret. "The only reason I want to live right now is to take care of my will and go through small assets at home. If I can't go home, I don't want to waste oxygen. I want to meet my maker because my ticker is pumping inadequately … way below normal. It's so bad, I'm not even a candidate for a heart transplant."

"You sound pretty sure of yourself."

"I've lived a good life and was fortunate to make the right decisions most of the time. Like the woman I married. There's nothing wrong with me wanting to join her."

CHAPTER 22

The students sat as far back in the lecture hall as possible. Grand rounds brought students, residents, and attendings from their hospital as well as the one downtown. She sat between Bob, Jordan, and Stuart while the resident on stage readied his power point presentation of "An Overview of Antibiotics."

Annabel looked to her right while putting a few index cards on the pull-down desk top in front of her to jot down notes.

"Either of you want to go out for an early dinner on Saturday?" she asked Jordan and Stuart. "My sister's coming to town. Bob's joining us."

"Why not?" Jordan said.

"I'm game," Stuart said.

"Super. Let's meet at five thirty."

A stout chief resident began his presentation. Annabel knew Donn was holding down the fort for their team on call. She hoped admissions hadn't started this early as she began selectively adding antibiotic information to her cards. They would be handy study material for their test.

Next to her, Jordan put his elbow on the desk top, half covered his face in his hand, and then all at once became interested in what she was doing. "Smart," he whispered and proceeded to do the same thing with his own index cards. Bob slouched and put his head back but payed strict attention. Annabel's thoughts drifted to Robby Burk, but she quickly replaced him with curiosity about the Secret Service agent she was yet to meet.

Gloria owned nothing more than an antiquated cell phone. For a long time, when she would try to install some new app, her phone would warn her that she had an old operating system that could not download the software. Yet she couldn't update her operating system because the phone was too old. The phone, however, had the basics, which was all she needed. She could retrieve email, text, take pictures, and surf the web to a limited extent if she had lots of time. The phone came along with her to work and was snug in one of her blue pockets. She realized she couldn't brazenly use it while working, but she could and would take any short call from her home aide.

Sure enough, the phone buzzed early in the afternoon and the caller ID registered the call made from home.

"You know I wouldn't be bothering you at work," Marabeth said, "but I don't want ya having any surprises when you get back."

Gloria stood behind her cart and against the wall in the hallway. "What is it?"

"Your mother," she said with concern, "she threw up twice and is quite droopy, with no energy to spare."

"Poor Mama. Do you think she has a fever?"

"No, dearie. She hasn't picked up a fever."

"Do you think a hot cup of tea or two antacids will help settle her stomach?"

"I'll try that. If she'll keep them down."

"Okay, then. Thank you, Marabeth, for letting me know. Tell Mama I'll be home in a couple of hours."

Gloria ended the call and slid the phone back into her pocket. Before she started rolling her cart again, she took a deep breath and said a little prayer that the nausea and vomiting were not much of an issue. She had picked her plan with thoughtfulness and understanding and wanted her mother to pass like Dr. Kevorkian had helped out himself. She wanted her mother to die by her hands ... not with the ideas about death that they practiced in the Dark Ages.

On the drive back to the hospital, Stuart announced that Dr. Berg and Dr. Schott already had an admission and he needed to show up in the ER as soon as he arrived. The students peeled out of Bob's car in the parking lot and hurried for their afternoon patient care. Annabel checked on May Oliver, hoping her patient had made it out of the ICU. She found May's chart on the west wing of the medical floor and flipped open each section.

She was encouraged to find the pathologist's report from her patient's lobectomy already on the chart. She read through every word. The area of the lobe which had the adenocarcinoma was larger than they previously thought. Reading the description of the cancerous alveoli and its invasion into the terminal bronchioles made her shudder. After all, it was the only organ and tissue responsible for taking oxygen out of the air necessary to sustain life. The only good thing about May Oliver's case, she had heard Dr. Schott say, was that she was young and not an old smoker, which meant she had no underlying cardiopulmonary disease.

That was all well and good. However, the evil cells had invaded other organ systems and that was what May Oliver had going against her. Annabel walked into her room, trying hard to bring along a sunny attitude. Louise and Ken clung to either side of May's bed, fussing at her while May slumped like a rag doll against the pillow as if the transfer had drained her of every last ounce of purpose.

Annabel greeted the couple and stood at the foot of the bed. "May, having read your chart, it's official. Your chemotherapy starts tomorrow morning."

May's eyes wandered down to Annabel and she took her mother's hand. "All right," she said and tried to clear her throat. "I'll give it a shot and see where it takes me."

Louise grasped her daughter's hand in the air. "Of course you'll give it a shot. We won't have it any other way."

Annabel took a step to leave and Ken locked his eyes on her. He frowned and tossed his head back and forth to the side in a small gesture to keep from his wife and daughter. She frowned back at him as well, worried that chemotherapy might be nothing more than a butterfly Band-Aid.

Gloria rattled her cart around the corner and wheeled it into the supply room, where she figured the next shift worker would retrieve it. She massaged her hands and left the hospital with a new sense of vigor and purpose. Now she had quite a repertoire of sick patients besides her mother to oversee and, unlike her mother, she could engage in meaningful discussions with them. At least for the allotted amount of time she spent in their rooms.

The bakery downtown would be closed, she realized as she climbed into her car and started the engine. She drove to a supermarket near the house, went in, and stared at the case in the bakery section. There was no shortage of a selection for layer cakes or sheet cakes. She chose a small square vanilla cake with buttercream frosting and asked the aproned woman behind the counter to write "Happy Birthday Gloria" on it.

She left carrying the confection in a box, a delicious symbol of all that was presently festive in her life. Her birthday, her new job, and granting her mother her wish to die under the present circumstances. She would continue to miss their old times together after she was gone, but she didn't mind because what was about to transpire made more sense than her mother hanging on to a meaningless and terminal life. It was like a mountain climber at ten thousand feet holding onto a crevice with his fingertips while an avalanche approached from above, his necessary backpack descended to the earth below, and he dangled with two broken legs, unable to mount further.

Gloria parked behind Marabeth's car and scurried to the front step carrying her things. She unlocked the door and walked into the main room. The heat was up too high and she smelled an odor of sickness as she went straight to the counter to put down the cake.

Marabeth sat flush up against Darlene's bed. "She's looking worse than I've seen her," she said. "But she hasn't vomited again, thank the Lord."

Gloria slithered out of her jacket as she went to the other side of the bed. "Mama, I'm home. Let's hope you feel better and can taste the birthday cake I brought home."

"Is it your birthday?" Marabeth asked as she got up.

"It is. Whenever Mama and I were able, we celebrated each other's special day with a cake. I bought her favorite flavors."

"I'll leave you, then. She's cleaned up for now and I'll be back in two days."

"Thanks for taking excellent care of her today. Maybe she just had a stomach bug that is already out of her system."

"No problem. I hope you enjoyed your first day at a new place." She left expeditiously without looking back.

Darlene was in a different floral pajama set than when Gloria had left and her eyes stayed focused on the bed sheet tossed lightly up to her abdomen. Gloria scanned around. An emesis basin was on the nightstand as well as the cup she'd used in the morning.

Gloria couldn't waste much more time. She stepped across to the kitchen and squirted sanitizer into her hands, rubbed a little, and went under the sink to her container and unscrewed the cap. Then she opened the cabinet and pulled out a vanilla meal substitute. She mixed them both in a cup but used less of the real drink this time and put the first bottle back.

She cut a sample piece of cake and went over to the bed with the plate and fork and Darlene's drink. "Mama, your baby girl's birthday is today and I got us a cake to celebrate. We'll pretend about blowing out the candles, but my wish is that you rest in the hereafter with pure serenity. I'm sorry you got Parkinson's disease, but we won't let it cause you any more pain. For my birthday, I'm granting you your wish and not one for me."

Gloria sat on the edge of the bed and worried that her mother wouldn't drink. But the drink was so tasty and tempting that Darlene slowly took the necessary swallows. Gloria stopped for a half minute and ate a forkful of cake.

"This is scrumptious, Mama." She put a small forkful to Darlene's lips and her mother only managed to lick the icing. Her hand slowed down in the middle of a tremor and she seemed to want more vanilla shake. Gloria obliged and sighed with ease that the liquid had reached its target.

Gloria bused the cup to the counter and, having sampled the cake, she cut a normal size piece and went back over. "Mama, I have to tell you thanks for being so strict with me about doing homework when I was little. And thanks a lot for helping to teach me to drive."

Gloria laid down a towel on the top of Darlene's pajamas. In an hour, her mother upchucked very little stomach contents and it broke Gloria's heart to see her wrench forward with such weakness. She replaced the dirty towel and threw the soiled one into a bucket in the laundry room, went back, and cleaned off her mother's mouth and chin. She took breaks between sitting alongside her to disinfect her hands and once use the bathroom. But the vomiting stopped.

After another two hours, Gloria turned up the lamp switch to increase the brightness in the room. She searched her mind for more things to tell her mother. There were so many things and, yet, nothing more really needed to be said, except for those four timeless words which she'd uttered a hundred times in the previous weeks. Having her mother leave this world while hearing those special words, she imagined, was better than the icing Gloria had given her from the cake.

"I love you, Mama," Gloria said again before midnight.

Darlene's eyes barely stayed open now as her face registered peace and contentment. Her last breath was but a puff, a morsel of air with oxygen, and the last one of her seventy years.

Stuart and Jordan had both acquired new patients in the afternoon. Annabel and Bob were up next and, within minutes of each other, they received pages from their residents in the ER.

"Students are the only people ever in this stairwell," Bob said as the two of them descended the stairs on their way to the ground floor.

"It's quicker than the elevator and better for our waistlines."

"You have a gorgeous waistline without ever using the stairs."

"Thanks. I think that's the first direct remark you've ever made about my figure."

"I practice restraint every day. It's not easy, you know, side-by-side with you every day. Plus, you're smart."

They reached the first floor and Annabel put her hand on the doorknob as Bob went to do the same. She chuckled at their attempt at the same time, but she knew he was being his usual gentlemanly self and trying to open the door for her.

As she stopped giggling, she glanced up at his face - his tapered blonde hair and round face with the cheerful expression he almost always wore. His eyes searched hers. She absorbed his countenance with clarity; his admiration for her, his fondness for her, and his loyal friendship. In the dim light, she realized for the first time how blue and rich his eyes were. Like beacons of a lighthouse on a rough shore.

Bob retracted his hand away from the doorknob and, for another second, their eyes held. Astonished at the moment, Annabel deliberately blinked to shake the sense of attraction she felt and she quickly jerked the door open. She felt so uneasy, she couldn't bear to glance at him again as they walked to the ER.

"Hurry up and get over there," Dr. Schott said upon seeing Annabel and Bob walk into the ER. They both looked a bit dazed.

"Bob," said Dr. Schott, "go see Dr. Watts. She's working up a COPD patient who needs admitting. And Annabel, you're with Dr. Burg. Go try your first intubation with your new patient, a twenty-nine-year-old who tried to do himself in with a tricyclic-antidepressant overdose. Put that breathing tube in like you've done it a hundred times and decide with your resident what proper settings to use for him on the ventilator."

Annabel inhaled deeply. Was Dr. Schott ramping up her responsibility like she was a seasoned resident? She wanted so much to intubate someone, especially after the extra attention she'd paid the anesthesiologists during her surgery rotation. They were the ultimate airway experts and she wanted to learn that skill as best she could ... no matter what field she went into. But for Dr. Schott to allow her, a medical student, to do it was a thrill.

Thoughts of her encounter with Bob in the stairwell drifted to the back of her mind as she leaned over her new obtunded patient, Mick Rhoden. With the ER doctor and Dr. Burg on either side of her, she opened his mouth with a laryngoscope and slid in a #8 endotracheal tube between his vocal cords.

CHAPTER 23

Gloria leaned against the bed and kissed her mother's forehead.

"Rest in peace, Mama," she said softly. She sat in silence for several minutes and then stumbled to the kitchen, wiped her eyes with a tissue, and absent-mindedly sanitized her hands. Back at the nightstand, she picked up the phone and dialed 911.

"Hello," Gloria said. "My elderly, sick mother just passed away at our house. Her death was expected, but I'll need help with what I'm supposed to do."

"What is your address, Ma'am?"

After the exchange of more information, Gloria hung up and waited. Her sole goal was to remain calm, focused, and sad because of her mother's departure. Remaining calm was easy. The execution of her plan had worked like magic; her mother would be proud of her. She managed to suppress the elated joy she felt because Darlene was finally sprung from a life of imprisonment with Parkinson's disease. Her mother was in a better place and she was the one responsible for the brave and kindhearted gesture to move her along on her path to freedom.

It happened without much fanfare. A police car and EMS parked out front almost simultaneously. No blaring sirens from either one of them. It was after midnight and Gloria didn't think one household in the neighborhood could tell that emergency vehicles were on their block.

The two officers, Dustin Lowe and Edgar Banks, were partners through thick and thin and were working the graveyard shift for the week. Of the two, Dustin was younger and sported a dimple in his chin, which bemused most women. He beat his partner and the paramedics to the front porch and Gloria opened the door.

"You all were fast getting here," Gloria said and pointed. "My mother is over here in her bed."

The male paramedic went over and began checking vital signs while the woman asked what happened.

Gloria shook her head with despair and wiped away moisture in her eyes. "She's had Parkinson's disease for years and I take care of her here at home. Her stomach turned a bit sour today. I work outside the home very little compared to how much I take care of her, but the homecare lady who helped out today said my mother had some vomiting. It seemed to have mostly passed by tonight because she only upchucked once. Like I said, her Parkinson's was really bad and her mind didn't understand what transpired around her."

The paramedics kept Gloria engaged with questions and they kept looking over Darlene while the two officers strutted around eyeballing the hospital-like environment Gloria had provided. Dustin Lowe wasn't fond of corpses, so he only listened to the conversation taking place and began poking at things like he sometimes did. Encountering dead people in his profession, he always pretended he could make a case out of a situation that appeared as innocent as a baby sleeping.

Officer Lowe took a bird's eye view of the kitchen island. The lid of a small sheet cake was open and one used plate sat next to it as well as one red plastic cup. His eye caught a shimmering to part of its surface and he looked closer at a thin substance which looked gooey, but had dried. Inside the cup, he detected a trace amount of a whitish drink. He hunched over and sniffed it. Distinctly sweet. His eyes roamed the rest of the counter and around the room and he saw another cup like it on the nightstand. He walked over in no hurry, picked it up, and wondered if it had the same glaze on the outside; he was sure it had the same sweet odor as the first one but not as strong.

"Do you mind if I poke around, Mrs. Pratt?" Dustin asked nonchalantly.

Gloria frowned, but it was not aimed at Dustin. Sadness welled up in her throat that her mother was finally gone and would be taken away by the paramedics.

"No," she said, "and if you officers want a bite to eat, help yourself to some birthday cake."

"Thanks for the offer," Edgar said. "Whose birthday is it?"

"Mine," Gloria said, "but celebrating makes no difference now."

Edgar nodded as Dustin continued to pry around. An emesis basin was also on the nightstand, a diaper bag on the counter, and a jacket on a chair. In the kitchen, he opened some cabinets to find dishes, paper products, and the shelves with food items. On a low shelf, he spotted what he liked to think of as old people's drinks. He opened one up and sniffed. Just a light fragrance of vanilla.

Over in the big room, the paramedics still had Gloria engaged with questions, which Dustin listened to as well. His partner was doing his own police work and making mental notes of the corpse.

Dustin stepped into the laundry room, the first door off the hallway. The dirty cloth that permeated his senses verified the fact that Darlene Pratt had been sick. Vomit usually smells pretty bad, he thought, but the cloth smelled ten times more potent. Nothing that a good police lab couldn't figure out, he thought. It's probably nothing, but it wouldn't hurt to check.

He sauntered back into the big room and watched as Gloria helped the paramedics take the pillow out from behind her mother's head and tied a string at the neckline of her pajamas. As the male and female medic moved her to the edge of the bed, Gloria clunked into the kitchen, dabbed her eyes with a tissue, and then squirted sanitizer on her hands.

Officer Lowe's instincts were nagging at him as he watched Gloria and contemplated questions for her. His hunch at the moment was that there was something potent smelling in those cups besides vanilla drink.

"Mrs. Pratt," he said, "did you say there was a caretaker here all day?"

"Yes. I usually work a long shift two or three times a week and someone else stays with mother. Otherwise, I take care of her 24/7."

"That must have been taxing for you day after day."

Gloria waved her hand at him. "People say things like that to me. I take a break by working a little bit but, no, I never complained about minding and doing for my mother. It was my duty. She would have done the same for me." She worked at massaging her hands and scowled at him like he should know better than to make such a remark.

"I'm sorry. What I do want to ask you is about the woman who was here today."

"She has been here before. Today, she worked a good twelve hours."

"Before we go, please write down her name and where we can reach her."

Gloria nodded and stepped over to be closer to her mother. She put an extra bed linen on her as the paramedics readied to place her on the stretcher.

Dustin contemplated the sweet smell again and went back to investigate

166

further. He opened more cabinets below the counter. Mostly pots and pans and towels and plastic containers. He checked under the sink. Strange items like a toilet bowl cleaner and brush, disinfectants, and bug and rodent traps. Antifreeze too.

Antifreeze?

He grabbed the silver liter container, put it on the counter, and unscrewed the cap. After sniffing it, he jerked his head back and frowned.

"Officers," the male paramedic said, "we're leaving unless you need something from us." They had hoisted the stretcher up and were ready to approach the door.

"No," Edgar Banks said. "We'll track down what we need or make the necessary calls."

Gloria scribbled down Marabeth's name and number, hustled into her jacket, and picked up her purse and car keys. "I know this sounds crazy, but I'm following you boys to be near my mom. Wherever you're bringing her, I can provide more information about her if someone needs it. Honestly, I'm not ready to leave her side until someone tells me to."

The paramedics shrugged; it didn't matter to them. They all left after Gloria told the officers to lock the door behind them.

Dustin Lowe rubbed his chin as he scanned the room one more time and stood next to his partner. "Along with legal permission, let's have one of the lab specialists come over quick and take a few things I'm curious about."

"Don't see the need," Edgar said, "but if a morsel of interest exists in that thick skull of yours, I don't mind."

"And," Dustin said, "let's pay the aide a visit. The deceased was sick today. I wonder how concerned she was or how tired she may have been nursing the deceased."

"Whatever you say," Edgar said, knowing that the two of them worked well together and fed off of each other's hunches. "I'll make the lab call."

With a strong sense of self-esteem, Annabel used her stethoscope to listen to Mick Rhoden's breath sounds. His lungs went up and down with the respiratory therapist squeezing on the Ambu bag and she smiled at Dr. Burg.

"My first intubation," she said, "and I nailed it."

"Nice job," Melody said.

"I spent extra time with anesthesia on the surgery rotation and it panned out." She rarely took delight in her own accomplishments, but she was all too aware of the necessity of airway skills and what it meant to save someone's life by establishing a patent method to breathe. She felt like she had taken a huge step.

"Let's go sit down and talk about the ventilator settings in more detail," Melody said. "The ER doctor is also going to pump Mr. Rhoden's stomach."

For the interim, Melody gave the therapist the orders she wanted and then considered their patient. "We also have the dilemma of a patient without a medical history. That's a problem and leaves us with writing a lot of 'unknowns' on our H&Ps."

The nurse in the closed-draped area listened while she removed the used airway equipment from the patient's bed. "Someone called Mr. Rhoden's mother," she said. "She's in the waiting room."

Before leaving the ER, Melody sat down with Annabel and gave her a mini course on ventilators in addition to what she had already learned. "There are always questions on the internal medicine exams about respiration, ventilators, and settings." She crossed her legs and Annabel was all too aware that she was in her teaching and on-call mode. She had substituted her heels for sneakers.

"Tell me about PEEP," Melody said.

Annabel bit the inside of her lip. "I hope I explain it correctly. It's the alveolar pressure in the lungs above atmospheric pressure which is present at the end of expiration."

Melody nodded. "And how does it come into play in a mechanically ventilated patient like Mr. Rhoden?"

"You residents order it as a setting almost all the time," Annabel said. "But I honestly don't understand why."

"We order a small amount of PEEP to mitigate end-expiratory alveolar collapse. Usually five centimeters of water."

"Makes sense," Annabel said. "Thanks."

"You're welcome. Let's go find Mr. Rhoden's mother."

Middle-aged with hunched shoulders, Mrs. Rhoden paced the waiting room like an expectant father during his wife's delivery. She stood still when Dr. Burg introduced herself and Annabel.

"Is my son going to be okay?" Mrs. Rhoden asked.

"His most immediate problem has been addressed," Melody said. "The need to breathe."

"If he hadn't been found by his roommate, he could be dead." Her eyes grew bigger. "Which is what he wanted anyway."

"It appears he'll be fine, but we're not out of the woods yet," Melody said. "Once we have him stabilized and over this hump, he'll need to be under the psychiatry department's care."

"I can't imagine. A shrink. For my own son."

"In the interim, we'll be taking care of his medical care. Can you help us out with his history? Illnesses? Medicines? Surgeries?"

"Easy enough. No surgeries. No medical problems except seasonal allergies and recent depression. And only allergic to sulfa drugs."

"And family history?"

"Negative except for a history of depression."

"Anybody ever try to take their own life?"

She looked away. "Me," she said.

After leaving Mrs. Rhoden, Annabel and Melody thought about the same thing – a cup of coffee - before tackling their paperwork. ER staff did their best to keep fresh coffee available through the night shift, so they ducked into the small kitchen. The aroma of a rich Columbian roast wafted through the room. Annabel picked up the pot and poured some into two clean ceramic cups.

"Thanks," Melody said, taking a sip. "What do you think about Mick Rhoden?"

"My last attending on psychiatry told us that the National Institute of Mental Health says that a family history of suicide is a prevalent risk factor for suicide." She leaned against the counter. "So there we go."

Melody warmed her hands with the toasty mug. "You make us upper residents proud."

"What do you mean?"

"You quoted what one of your previous teachers told you, which means that you were paying attention and you remembered what he had to say.

You have developed excellent listening skills early on in your training."

"Thanks," Annabel said. "It's easy to be stashing all of this information away when Bob and I are learning from excellent clinicians."

They took their coffee with them and sat at the ER desk where the activity after midnight slowed down. Since there was little in her new patient's history, it took Annabel no time at all to write up his history and physical. In a few hours, she hoped he would be in the ICU.

Mick Rhoden's case was too ironic for Annabel to make sense of and she wished she could follow his care when he made it to the psychiatry department. Mick took prescribed tricyclic antidepressants for depression and yet he almost succeeded in committing suicide on the very drug used to lessen his depression. She looked back at Melody's orders and it was clearly stated that he would be on suicide precautions, particularly when he came off the ventilator. However, she sighed, she knew from her limited clinical experience that suicide precautions didn't always work.

Too tired to think about patients wanting to hurt themselves with such finality, she placed her head in her hands and rubbed her eyes, her forehead, and the rest of her face to rejuvenate herself. It was time to head to the call room for some sleep. She straightened out her white jacket, which could use a washing and an ironing, while being glad about wearing scrubs. So much more comfortable than the street clothes she wore earlier in the day.

After rinsing off the two mugs they'd used, Annabel sauntered away to the call room. With her beeper within a few inches of her pillow, she fell asleep without further thoughts about patients and new admissions. There were only a handful of hours to sleep, but when she startled awake in the morning before her alarm, she realized Robby Burk had been in her dreams. She pictured him doing surgery in a remote hospital in Africa and she was by his side, handing him his instruments and wiping his brow from the heat.

As she leaned over to find her clogs from under the bed, she wondered why, in her dream, she had followed him overseas instead of pursuing her own course of medicine and why she was his helper instead of functioning as an independent doctor. Interesting, she thought ... what a strange scenario had surfaced from her subconscious. It made her uncomfortable, but was that truly any different from their last encounter or messaging?

CHAPTER 24

Annabel freshened up in the bathroom, gathered her overnight bag from the call room, and stashed it in the office. She needed her first cup of coffee. Mick Rhoden was now in the ICU, which was the second best place in the hospital to grab some. The morning shift was coming alive with staff going in and out of patients' rooms, but she found the coffeepot empty. After setting up a batch of a Hawaiian brew, a nutty odor began filling up the room, luring Mick's nurse in for a cup herself.

"I'm the student taking care of your patient with the effective overdose," Annabel said. "How's he doing this morning?"

The nurse reached over and grabbed two disposable cups. "In report, they told me his stomach was suctioned out in the ER. He's starting to wake up and, without other medical problems, I bet you all get him out of here fast."

"He has that in his favor." Coffee stopped dripping from the coffeemaker and Annabel poured for the two of them.

"I never thought this would be a big part of my job," the nurse said.

"What?"

"So many young people trying to kill themselves. I'm only twenty-five and my whole first year here, I nurse one to two patients like this every week. So I looked it up. Did you know that suicide is the second most common reason why adolescents die, after traffic accidents?"

"I believe it. You and I are young. I would never think about that for a second. How can people our age get to that point? I took psychiatry, but I still can't wrap my head around the idea."

"I had a classmate who did it," she said. "Compared to other students, I always thought she magnified her problems. Things I perceived as minor inconveniences, she considered to be major problems. She told another student one day that life was painful."

Annabel swallowed and shook her head. "My psychiatry attending said that some depressed patients see no alternative other than death. The sad part is that, most of the time, no one else is attuned to that and helping them. Part of giving these patients help is to be asking them the right questions. And if that isn't happening, they're not getting the right answers."

The nurse sighed. "You and I may not be helping them beforehand, but at least we're helping in their after-care."

"But then it's as important that they get the psychiatric help they need and never attempt it again. That they realize life doesn't have to be so cold and so dark."

With a magic marker, the nurse marked her Styrofoam cup and snapped on a lid. "I'll finish it in a little while. Thanks for being our barista." She took a step. "Nice talking to you."

"Likewise," Annabel said.

Instead of expeditious rounds, Dr. Schott announced to the team that their attending was joining them. Annabel sunk into the desk chair, subtly took out espresso beans, and shared them with all the students.

"Thanks for these," Jordan said, "but bummer that Dr. Mejia is coming along."

"I would think his cardiology input is always useful to you," Stuart said.

"Less so than getting a letter of recommendation from him when I apply to residencies."

Bob squinted his eyes. "How can you be thinking of that already?"

Sebastian Mejia showed up at the doorway. His eyes settled on Dr. Schott and he made a small "follow me" gesture. Donn pushed himself off the couch and they all followed in single file. The senior doctors talked among themselves as they swept through the medicine hallways. Dr. Mejia was calling the shots of who he wanted to see and in what order. He summoned over the main desk for May Oliver's chart, thumbed through it, and paraded into her room.

A cot was set up on the other side of May's bed and the white hospital blanket stirred from someone underneath. May's mother, Louise, peered over the bunched-up sheets by her neck.

"Oh, so sorry," Louise said. She threw off the covers and sat on the side of her make-shift sleeping arrangements. "Even though my husband and I are staying at May's place, I decided to stay with my daughter last night."

"That's fine with us," Dr. Mejia said. "Don't consider it an imposition on staff either. We want our patients to have as much support as possible from loved ones."

"Thank you," she said, staying put where she was.

"May," Dr. Schott said, "let's check your thoracotomy incision and make sure your lungs sound fine. Annabel, in the meantime, update us with any new information this morning."

"Mrs. Oliver remains afebrile and her other vital signs are stable. The thoracic surgeon saw her last night and is satisfied with her incision and progress." Annabel stepped closer to the bed and held May's hospital gown to the side while Dr. Schott untaped her bandage. "He tapered down on her narcotics as well because her pain is subsiding. And today is May's first day for chemotherapy over in the cancer center."

"How is her hemoglobin?" Dr. Mejia asked.

"It's twelve," Annabel said.

"That level will suffice," Dr. Mejia said. "I don't want you to be anemic for your treatment. We'll leave you now as both Dr. Schott and I are satisfied with your wound healing."

"Think of any questions you might want to ask the cancer doctor," Donn said to her. "Especially side effects of treatment."

Annabel lingered, wanting to be the last person to leave May's side. Mrs. Oliver was at her heels by the time she slipped through the doorway.

"Dr. Tilson," Louise said, "thanks for all you're doing for my daughter. She trusts you a lot. I'm worried, though. I understand her moods like no one else. It didn't help that her Misty died, but now the cancer problem and treatments are tying up her life, leaving room for nothing else. She's so much more despondent and even talked about not being a 'guinea pig' for chemotherapy."

"The most important role for you," Annabel said, "is to be a really good listener and to ask her lots of questions about what she's thinking. I'll do the same as much as I can. If you don't mind, I'll also ask the other doctors about prescribing her an antidepressant which may help her mood."

"Thank you," Louise said and took Annabel's hand and gave it a squeeze.

Annabel smiled at Louise and hurried to her group. The encounter warmed her heart; it was as important as all her book knowledge and clinical rounds.

After seeing every patient under the auspices of the team, Dr. Mejia dismissed the students. They took care of their chores, peeled out into the cold but windless day, went home, and caught up on sleep.

That night, Offer Banks and Lowe knocked on the homecare aide's front door. Dustin shuffled his feet on the wooden porch when the door cracked open.

Alarmed at the men in blue standing before her, Marabeth said, "Is there some sort of bad news?"

"Yes, ma'am," Edgar said, "unless you are already aware of Darlene Pratt's demise."

Her mouth turned down as she opened the door wider. "No, I didn't know that. How sad. I'm so sorry."

"Would you mind if we ask you a few questions?"

"Only if you come in. This air is making my bones cold."

The two men walked into a neat, modest room with pictures of children and adults on the two table tops. Two lamps were on with little other light. Marabeth wiped her hands on a dishtowel and then laid it on the back of a chair. "Sit down," she said.

Edgar looked at Dustin, giving him the opportunity to ask her questions first.

"Ma'am," Dustin said, "we won't take up too much of your time. This is just routine for us. We were called to Mrs. Pratt's home last night after she died. We understand you cared for her yesterday." He left the remark open-ended.

"I did. Lately, I've taken care of her routinely but not as much as her daughter. Darlene had real bad Parkinson's disease, the worst I've ever seen. But yesterday, she had some kinda stomach bug."

"That's what we understand. Were you able to feed her anything at all? Any food or drinks?"

"You're not thinking that I took rotten care of her?" she gasped.

"No, ma'am. Not at all. Besides the coroner's input, we're only trying to be clearer about her cause of death."

"But isn't it from her Parkinson's disease?" she asked alarmed.

"Marabeth," Dustin said in a soft voice, "don't worry. As far as we're concerned, you are a sympathetic caregiver otherwise you wouldn't be a home health care worker."

She eyed him cautiously. "I am a fine worker, for sure. I made her a soft boiled egg in the morning but, not long after that, she threw it up. After I cleaned her up, I tried to give her a little bit of apple juice, but she wouldn't take it. Then later, she vomited again. I was worried about her getting dehydrated, so twice during the day, I made her tea and she did sip some. I tried giving her yogurt late in the afternoon, but she refused to budge her lips."

"Those drinks you prepared for her … what did you serve them in?"

"You sure are being fussy. I used a small glass for the apple juice and a mug for the tea. But I always wash the dishes after whatever I give her. I didn't leave a mess, did I?"

"Not that we're aware of. You seem like a neat and orderly person. So you never used a plastic cup all day when you were there?"

"No, sir. Never. I don't believe in throw away cups which clutter up the waste bins. Now her daughter uses them, but that's her prerogative. She uses red plastic cups. I always see them around the house."

Dustin's eyes narrowed. "Did you give Mrs. Pratt any liquid meal substitute yesterday? There are vanilla ones in the pantry."

"I used them for Darlene regularly, but not yesterday. With an upset stomach, I thought they'd be too rich for her. Should I have?"

"Not necessarily. It sounds like you did the best you could."

"Thank you. You had me scared. Mrs. Pratt had wonderful care. Her daughter was totally devoted to her. As far as I could tell, taking care of her mother always came first."

Edgar slid to the edge of the couch. "Thank you for your time," he said. "We appreciate it."

Both officers stood and Dustin said, "I understand the daughter had a birthday yesterday."

"She brought home a cake in the evening," Marabeth said. "What a shame. She certainly didn't get a birthday celebration if her mother passed away."

Dustin and Edgar slipped out the door with a tip of their hats and Marabeth latched the door behind them. They stepped off the front step and walked towards the car.

"Interesting," Edgar said. "Looks like your intuition was correct, but you may have been barking up the wrong tree."

"If there was something amiss with this woman's death," Dustin said, "the daughter's innocent until proven guilty. But maybe her wish was for her mother to be on the other side of the ground. If there is foul play, I wouldn't have suspected it from her."

"Yes, if there is any."

"I'll be curious to know what and when the lab comes up with anything."

"And with what we've seen and heard, let's alert Ohio's BCI."

From a distance, Annabel saw Bob pull into the side entrance of the hospital lot and park. The top of her jacket was unzipped and she left it open as she hustled towards him. It was comfortably above freezing for a change and without a threat of precipitation. She stepped in front of the door he was heading for and waved at him with her free hand.

"A welcoming committee," he said when he reached her, wearing a smile.

"It'll cost ya."

"Coming from you, it's worth a few bucks or favors. I'll pay you triple if you do it every day."

She rolled her eyes and hit him on the sleeve while he opened the door. "Did you study last night?"

"Yeah, how about you?"

"I did. And my pesky sister called. She can't wait to hang out with us this weekend. Where should we all eat dinner?" she asked and shot him a glance. "In essence, I don't care because I'm probably going to grab a bite somewhere else afterwards."

"Wasn't it your idea to eat out?"

She shrugged her shoulders as they winded their way to the staircase. "Something else came up. Want to go to Pete's in my neighborhood? That would be great for my sister for when I leave. She only has to walk back down the block."

"Fine with me," he said, perplexed. "I'll tell Jordan and Stuart. And I'll tell them we've been half stood-up by our female colleague."

"Bob, I'm sorry. Everything always wants to happen at the same time, doesn't it? We both know that already," she added.

Dr. Schott was embedded in the couch when they turned into the office. He didn't move the newspaper. "Did you both hear that today is some kind of movie blitz day? *Star Wars* or *Star Trek*, but I can never get them straight because I don't follow movie stories that jettison to twenty sequels and then end up flipping back to prequels."

Annabel grinned. "Don't ask me. Movie time is a short commodity for medical students. You sure are early, Dr. Schott. I'm hurrying to see May Oliver. I can't wait to see how she did with her chemotherapy." With that, she sped away while pulling on her short student's coat.

Their chief curled an end of the paper. "I wonder if she'll be this enthused in a few years."

"I've met her father," Bob said. "I think she's a chip off the old block."

"I detect a compliment there," Donn said, covering up with the paper again.

"Just don't tell her I said so."

Annabel rounded the corner of the hallway and almost bumped into Ken Oliver.

"It's you," he said, "the medical student. My wife is still in our daughter's room, but I'm going to the cafeteria. I can't take being in there at the moment."

"How come?"

"Because of what she did to herself. You'll see." He walked away with a slow gait and slumped shoulders.

Louise Oliver's hand was kneaded up in a fist as she rubbed it into the other one like a baseball in a mitt. She paced back and forth right inside the door and locked eyes with Annabel for a moment and nodded towards the window.

May stood against the wall next to the window with a blank, sad expression. She wore a smart, soft pink robe and all her hair had been shaved off except for a short buzz all over her head. It was a stark and shocking look, yet despite it, May had stunning features and was a beautiful woman even though she'd grown so thin.

Seeing her, Annabel almost gasped out loud, especially when noticing the despair written all over her face. She cautiously stepped over.

"May, what's going on?" Annabel asked softly. "What happened to your hair?"

"I shaved it all off. Only a little while ago."

"Why?"

"They told me yesterday I'd lose my hair with treatments. Why wait to watch it drop off like a sick cow with brittle hair because of low quality nutrition?"

"There was no need to do that," her mother said.

"Why, Mom? Just because you don't want to see me this way?"

"I give up!" Louise said and stormed out of the room.

"May, she's just upset and worried about you. Maybe you'll feel more comfortable with your hair shaved off or maybe you could buy a wig. There's a fine selection of them in catalogs, but you are pretty enough without one."

"No thanks about covering up with some stupid wig. You mean well and I appreciate that."

"As usual, if there's anything I can do for you, holler. In the meantime, I do need to know how the chemotherapy went and how you're feeling this morning."

"I'm still nauseous since yesterday. The nurse said Dr. Burg could order me more anti-nausea medicine."

"No problem. Is there anything else you'd like to talk about?"

May shook her head and proceeded to stare out the window.

CHAPTER 25

Gloria Pratt weaved her way through the back stretch of the parking lot where hospital employees parked. Her mind was busy thinking of everything she needed to do at home. She wanted to get rid of the huge hospital bed sitting in the living room as well as other ancillary equipment that had been needed for Darlene. There was a void at the house not constantly cleaning and feeding her, turning her in the bed to prevent bed sores, getting her up and down in the chair, and giving her all her meds. She missed her mother as well as doing all those things for her. However, now poor Darlene was out of her misery and rested pain free either in heaven or some other restful state of mind that Gloria believed could exist. If her mother could communicate from the afterlife, she would be squeezing Gloria in a loving, thankful embrace.

She pulled off her knit hat and stuffed it into her pocket as she neared the front door of the hospital. The weather smacked with a hint of spring and the sunshine warmed her face. Besides the fact that her own life was on its way to becoming so much easier, she felt renewed and powerful for what she had accomplished. Even the visit by the paramedics and police had been a snap; all she did was tell them the truth about how sick her mother was with Parkinson's disease and how she had been ill that day. Which, apparently, they were going to corroborate with her aide, Marabeth. Routine police work.

She floated on cloud nine, elated and intoxicated with her own importance because of pulling off a feat as humongous as terminating her mother's life. A life which needed taking because it was inhumane for her to live like that. And she had had the guts to do what was necessary!

Her mind continued to race as she left her jacket and pocketbook in the woman's room locker. The cart she needed sat behind the medical charts on the ward, but she personalized the side basket with her hand sanitizer and tissues and kept her cell phone in her pocket. She was fortunate to be only working part time; it would allow her all the time she needed for her mother's arrangements, she thought, as she nodded good morning to the staff at the desk.

Gloria's direct boss, Anna, came out of the supply room and called her over. "You can leave that one," she said. "Come in here to the pharmacy cart. You'll be giving out patients' medications for the foreseeable future."

The red cart had drawers with prescription drugs, a black binder with a list of patients, their diagnoses and medications, and an uncluttered top counter where medications and dosages could be prepared.

"This requires utmost attention," Anna said. "You'll be going through the whole medical floor three times today giving out prescription and non-prescription drugs except for IV drugs. You'll be doing this job in the future, or taking vital signs, or both. Just check in about your assignment each day."

Anna spent thirty minutes showing Gloria the details of her new assignment and when both women were sure about the day's details, Gloria set out rolling her new shiny cart. It even had a fresh bottle of hand sanitizer on the top shelf by the railing. She smiled about the new task because it seemed to carry more responsibility.

The hallway smelled like a freshly mopped floor as she walked along with her heavy, comfortable shoes, came to the window at the end, and turned. While with Anna, she had already assembled the first patient's pills to take, so she went straight into the first room.

The first patient wasn't happy with Gloria disturbing her. The geriatric woman rubbed her eyes; her only overnight sleep had been in the last few hours. After Gloria dished out her medications, she closed the door behind her.

Outside Mr. Hogan's room, Gloria went through, one-by-one, the doctor's orders for his medications. She searched through the drawers where the drugs were stored alphabetically and put the needed ones into a miniature paper cup. She frowned at the long list: heart medications to make the heart pump better and to help maintain a normal rhythm; blood pressure drugs; diuretics; antacids and drugs for reflux; narcotic and non-narcotic pain medications; and drugs for benign prostatic hypertrophy. It took her several minutes to select each pill and plop them into two cups. The color and variety looked like a stash of candy to pop into a child's mouth and suck on.

She rapped her knuckles on the slightly ajar door and peeked into Manuel Hogan's room.

"Come in," he said. "I'm not getting up for you." He pointed to his swollen ankles resting on the foot rest.

"I don't think you've budged, Mr. Hogan, from two days ago." She glanced again at his awful diagnosis and recalled her conversation with him. The poor man had verbalized his despondency and how fed up he was with his congestive heart failure and astutely said that the pumping ability of his heart was all downhill from now on. The doctors informed him of some concrete number from a heart test he'd taken, like thirty-five, which proved it.

"I haven't," he said as Gloria parked her cart in front of his chair. "This is no way to live. Sitting in a hospital room in a chair. They tried taking the fluid off of my belly, but it's come back. Death is not going to be pretty. I heard that with CHF, a patient can choke on his own bodily fluids building up in his lungs and I told them never to put me on the ventilator."

She poured apple juice into a paper cup, filling it halfway. "That sounds awful."

"They want to try what they call inotropic support. Put in more IVs and infuse heavy duty drugs that will make my heart squeeze tighter. I'm only itching to get out of here to take care of things." He leaned forward and put out his hand to accept the first pills she tapped out. "After I do that, I would prefer to die at home."

She watched him put the pills on his tongue and handed him the drink as the importance of what he told her registered more clearly. Who wouldn't feel the same way with such a pitiful heart? A ticker that doesn't even let a man climb a few steps or carry in groceries? He deserved his despondency and he was clear in the head, not like her mother had been.

Mr. Hogan continued talking, but she only pretended to listen. The feeling of power, control, and authority she possessed over influencing her mother's death ramped up further. What if … what if she could help Mr. Hogan just like she'd helped Darlene? He was justified with his wishes even more than her mother and verbally declared his desire not to live the last stage of his life in hospital bondage. The heartless medical care system wanted to strap him to a chair and wrap chains around him.

She wanted to ask him a dozen questions but stopped herself because the questions and the answers were secondary to the main issue at hand, which was his desire to not live under the present circumstances. What difference did it make if he had family, who weren't by his side anyway, or if he still needed to clean out his house? Let the absent family take care of that.

Gloria's bold sense of empowerment sprouted after the roots had been established by assisting her mother. How practical and easy it had been to take care of Darlene. If she could continue to make a difference, a real impact on patient's end-of-life care, then she needs to step up to the task at hand and help Mr. Hogan. Like her mother, he needed assistance, and she was the perfect guardian angel to come to his rescue.

Something akin to a thunderclap exploded above her when she left his room and a plan, as simple as a child's magic trick, seeded in her brain.

May silently liked that she woke up without her mother having slept in her room. Her parents would be in to see her later but at least she could get a breather to be by herself to wallow in her own self-pity. If she wants to feel sorry for herself, then who was to stop her? She was entitled to her own feelings. After all, it was not every day such a critical diagnosis and treatment was handed down to a relatively young person and she definitely pulled out the short straw when it came to looking forward to a future.

At least so far since she opened her eyes, her nausea had lifted with the anti-emetic the medical team had started her on. Maybe she would enjoy a small bowl of oatmeal when breakfast came around. However, the antidepressant the team prescribed for her hadn't done a thing yet, but she really didn't care.

She pushed away the bedcovers, slipped her feet into her slippers, and stood. For some reason, she wondered, her muscle tone was not up to par and she slumped forward as she grabbed her robe from the chair. She put it on awkwardly and instead of tying the ends, she began wringing her hands excessively at the fluffy cotton belt. As she took a step to head for the bathroom, a strong smell of oatmeal came to her nostrils … the food she had concentrated on but a few moments ago.

May managed the first step with decreased muscle tone, but the second step completed the new turn of events. Confused, with her vision turning blurry, she fell back against the mattress and onto the floor. Her body became tense, and fast jerking movements took over her arms and legs. Her tremors lasted briefly, but she lay clumped up on the floor with a memory lapse of the fine details of what happened.

The next thing May knew, her young medical student was above her, talking to her. But what was she doing on the floor?

Annabel had a restful post-call day and she studied two whole internal medicine chapters. She was glad, however, that it was Friday and she was scheduled back in the hospital. Her sister would be in for the weekend late in the day and then she looked forward to Saturday night. Besides going out with her colleagues and Nancy, she had the date or tryst set up with Ben Rogers, the Secret Service Agent. It was a toss-up which part of the evening would be more fun.

Dr. Schott was not yet in the office with the newspaper clouding his face, nor were any other students. Their jackets were all hanging on hooks. She went to the nurses' station and read all the new posts and lab work in May Oliver's chart, and then knocked on her door. She waited a few moments, wondering if Louise Oliver slept inside on a cot from the night before. The only sounds she heard were the occasional paging to physicians or staff members over the hospital PA system and not a peep came from inside May's room.

Annabel eased the door open and quietly stepped in. May must be out strolling a hallway, she thought … a good sign. The bathroom was empty, the door open, and May was not in bed. She stepped in further to check if the cot was occupied against the window. It was empty but, beside the bed, May was sprawled on the floor and stirring like she had slept.

Annabel crouched down beside her. "May, what are you doing on the floor?"

May's right arm appeared bruised and she was not able to respond right away; she seemed confused and weak.

"Did you fall?" Annabel asked.

May stared back at Annabel with sleepiness and memory loss over what had happened. After attempting to support herself, she took Annabel's arm and leaned into her.

Annabel helped May get up; her patient had some weakness, at least in her left leg. She shifted her straight into the chair, called the desk, and asked someone to call in Dr. Burg or Dr. Schott. At least one of them should be in the hospital by now, she thought.

Annabel focused back on May. "I'm the medical student. Do you remember me and what happened? Are you having any chest pain?" Annabel took her vital signs and listened to her chest as May thought about her questions. She evaluated her pupils and did a short neurological assessment.

Dr. Schott hotfooted into the room and narrowed his eyes, standing beside her.

"I wonder if she had some kind of stroke," Annabel said. "I found her sprawled on the floor."

Donn physically assessed May in a few short minutes. "Do you know where you are?" he asked.

May blinked multiple times like she was uncluttering her brain of unneeded information and then her vision fell on Annabel. "I remember you now. The medical student."

She looked at her chief resident. "I think I'm in the hospital."

"You fell," he said. "There is a bruise on your arm, but otherwise, I don't see any other injuries. Is anything hurting you?"

"Not so much. My thoughts are fuzzy and my leg is weak."

Donn stood straight. "We're sending someone in with you while I order some tests. Have you ever had a seizure before?"

The question caused a look of fear on May's face. "No. Not ever."

"I suspect that's what happened, but we'll figure it out."

"Why?" she mumbled but lost her train of thought.

Donn decided not to explain things to her that she might forget. He ordered a stat EEG and a neurology consult.

After they made sure she had extra supervision, Donn and Annabel headed to the office.

"A seizure was on my differential after I found her," Annabel said.

"Good thinking," Dr. Schott said.

"If it was a seizure, it was caused by her brain tumor, wasn't it?"

Donn frowned. "A sure bet. From her metastatic lung cancer."

CHAPTER 26

Annabel and Bob stood in the back of the group as Stuart gave a flawless update of one of his patients with unmanageable diabetes. After he rattled off the plan for the man's dietary and lifestyle modifications and change in medical therapy, they cluttered the hallway to go see the next patient.

Bob and Annabel faced each other as they weeded out espresso chocolates from the palm of her hand. Donn watched and cleared his throat.

She read the room number by the side of the door and realized where they were. Her overdose patient from the ICU had been transferred. "Sorry," she said. "Mick Rhoden is status-post day two after a tricyclic antidepressant overdose. Yesterday, he was successfully extubated and sent to the floor. He complains of a sore throat this morning which he says is due to 'the stupid breathing tube.' He also mentioned there will be no more anti-depressant overdoses in his future because he never wants to go through that again.

"His vital signs are stable and all his lab work this morning is normal. Psychiatry will be by this morning to do a consult on him. Although his affect is dull, he actually smiled this morning while we talked."

"You students and residents," Donn said, "are performing miracles with your patients and your presentations."

"We can't take credit," Melody said. "The on-call team yesterday supervised Mr. Rhoden's extubation after we left."

"But the patient smiled at Annabel," Bob said. "Her presence with a patient counts for lifting their spirits."

Annabel rolled her eyes, but then she decided to go along with the compliment and bowed her head.

"There's some truth to that," their chief said. "Now let's go in."

Mick Rhoden's eyes widened when he counted all seven of them parade into his room. "This is more attention than I deserve."

"We're just thankful you're still here to shower attention on," Donn said. "Dr. Tilson briefed us on how well you're doing."

"Better than the last two days," he said.

"Psychiatry is coming by today. Are you amenable to that? They can help treat your despair. We all like you, but we don't want to ever see you admitted under the present circumstances again."

"I don't mind talking to them."

"Any chance that you're still contemplating hurting yourself?"

He shook his head. "No. And especially not after what I've been through."

"What do you do? Are you employed?"

"I own a small computer store. I sell computers, but mostly I'm a tech geek and repair them."

"Excellent," Donn said. "That's a modern career for a young person and you should be proud."

"I suppose," he said.

"Don't suppose. It's the truth. We'll wait to see what psychiatry recommends. Most likely, we'll transfer you to their service or we'll be discharging you soon. In the meantime, would you like to share with us why you took the overdose, before talking to them?"

Mr. Roden fidgeted with his hands. "My girlfriend dumped me. Cold and hard. We were going out together for five years. Now I realize what I don't have."

"I'm not an expert in the relationship department, but maybe there's a reason and there's someone more special out there for you."

The team left in the reverse order that they arrived and Donn announced, "There's no man or woman worth killing yourself for. Let's go see Bob's patient, Manuel Hogan."

Dr. Schott stood under an old photograph of the hospital hanging on the wall and asked for Bob's update.

"Mr. Hogan was the last patient of mine that I saw right before we started rounds. He complained of his usual concerns: wanting a better heart, wanting the puffiness around his ankles to go away, and wanting to breathe better. Above all, he wants to go home.

"Interestingly enough, his beside vital signs were as good as after we did his paracentesis and drained off the fluid from his belly. His blood pressure was 150/86 and there is a documented one to two pound weight loss. I weighed him myself to make sure and found that to be accurate. On physical exam, his lungs sounded clearer than yesterday and his pedal edema was also better."

Donn shot a look at Mr. Hogan's resident, Dr. Watts.

"Mr. Hogan's diuretics in the last two days caught up with him," she said, "and there has been an improvement. He certainly can't take a stroll around a block, but he is better than he was on admission."

"How are his labs?"

"His BUN and creatinine are stable," Bob said, "and his electrolytes are slightly improved. Of course, he doesn't know any of this yet, and in his head, he believes that he's going to die any day."

"Can't blame him," Donn said, "because that has been the reality of his situation. However … I clasp on to some hope that this may be the window of opportunity we've been bargaining for."

"You mean discharge him home before his next acute flare up of congestive heart failure?" Bob asked.

"What do you think?" Dr. Watts chimed in.

Donn stroked his mustache, continuing to give it meaningful thought. "Although Mr. Hogan has been desperate to die to escape his CHF, he's more desperate to go home one more time before that happens. I say we discharge him home tomorrow morning if his condition stays stable where it is and we can schedule him back in clinic within a week."

Everyone nodded in agreement.

"He'll be so happy," Bob said.

They neared the doorway and heard Mr. Hogan's voice. "Don't be talking about me out there. Let me hear what terrible things you're planning for me today."

Donn walked slowly as he wiped the thick lenses on his glasses. He sat on the end of the bed and smiled.

"If your CHF behaves in the next twenty-four hours, how would you like to go home?"

Manuel Hogan tilted his head and adjusted the nasal cannula oxygen in his nostrils. "I must be hearing things. Saints alive! You betcha. I'll push my own wheelchair if I need to." He lit up with a smile.

Dr. Schott was about to read May Oliver's chart for an update when his pager went off and he called the number from the nurses' station. His tone became serious and he talked at length while the residents and students waited.

"It must be the neurologist," Annabel said to Bob. "He's talking about May Oliver. I didn't get to tell you yet, but I walked in on her earlier and it looked like she had just had a seizure."

Bob leaned his elbows on the counter. "What did you do?"

"She was safely over it. The boyfriend I had in Nashville while in college ended up having seizures after a sports-related head trauma, so I have a little bit of experience with the matter. No fun."

"You've mentioned him. Do you two still talk?"

"Every once in a while," she said turning around from Dr. Schott on the phone. "We're good friends. Unfortunately, the whole experience railroaded his studies, but my dad invented a new device for certain seizure patients."

"You're so fortunate to have broadened your medical education because of your father."

"But your mom was a nurse, wasn't she?"

"Yeah, but she never felt confident enough to work in a hospital. She stayed in doctors' offices her whole career. And Dad, he tinkered with wires since he was an electrician, but he was so good at it, he should have been a vascular surgeon working on people's leg veins."

Annabel laughed. "Or a neuroscientist working on synapses."

Dr. Schott put down the phone and stopped leaning on the desk. "That was one heck of a fast consult," he said. "The neurologist was in the vicinity, saw May right away, and hustled her off for an EEG. It showed abnormal brain electrical activity. She had slowing, or for you students, her brain waves were slower than we'd expect for her age. He said the problem electrical activity traces came from the region of her brain where her metastasis is." He frowned. "We're chasing something which is three steps ahead of us."

They stepped into May's room, dreading to tell her the bad news. Her parents had arrived for their daily visit and Louise stood immediately.

"The neurologist confers that May had a seizure this morning," Dr. Schott told them. "He is going to select the best anticonvulsant for her and her situation and hopefully we can prevent another one from ever occurring."

"What's next after that?" May asked. "A wheelchair because my leg bones become too breakable because of my bone cancer? Or as you doctors would call it, the metastatic lung cancer in my bones?"

Gloria only had thirty minutes for lunch, so she wolfed down a sandwich in the cafeteria as fast as she could. She bused her tray to the stack of dishes, massaged in hand sanitizer, and hurriedly walked to the outpatient pharmacy off the front lobby of the hospital.

Attractive displays at the beginning of the aisles advertised happy people popping antacids for their indigestion and smiling couples satisfied with male erectile dysfunction drugs. Small bottles and flat and square miniature boxes lined the shelves in the three aisles. She considered carefully what she wanted to buy; over-the-counter drugs as neutral as possible. It would be best to also have pain relief pills because she would be substituting what she bought for real narcotics or strong sedatives in her drug cart. She wanted to make two purchases so she would have a variety.

In the section for aspirin and acetaminophen and nonsteroidal anti-inflammatories, she lingered while thinking about them. She picked out a generic bottle of an anti-inflammatory. Hopefully, the pills inside won't have any markings on them, she thought, just in case a patient is wise to scrutinize every pill she dished out to them. She stepped over to the next aisle.

A middle-aged man in a security uniform left with his purchase and a gray-haired woman behind the counter focused on Gloria. "Can I help you find anything?" she asked.

"No, I'm fine," Gloria said. In front of her were vitamins and minerals. Vitamins never killed anybody, she thought, and selected a bottle of fifty small pills. She didn't want to use some chunky pill that someone would have difficulty swallowing. Next, she pranced up the end aisle looking for hand sanitizer to restock at the house. With her ethyl alcohol cleaner, vitamins, and nonsteroidal anti-inflammatories, she went to the register.

The woman at the counter rang up her items. "Taking care of your pain, your health, and the germs around here." She grinned. "That'll be $16.32."

Gloria paid and hustled back to the medicine floor. In the locker room, she threw away the pharmacy bag and opened up each bottle, dispensing with the child-proof covers underneath the screw caps. She tapped the contents of the two bottles into the two front pockets of her work jacket and slipped the empty bottles and sanitizer into her purse. The pills from her pockets needed to be inconspicuously dispensed.

Gloria had a mid-day medication round to dispense right away. There were now less medications to hand out than in the morning or later in the day, but she could nevertheless begin implementing her plan. By the last round later in the day, before her shift ended, she figured her visit to Mr. Hogan would be the last time he would have to bother with swallowing a handful of drugs. She was such a guardian angel and thoughtful person - she had just spent most of the $16.32 because of him.

As she wheeled her red cart out, she noticed a note from Anna sitting on top:

Go by May Oliver's room first. The docs want her to take her first dose of anti-seizure medication.

She parked herself outside May's door with her back against the wall and faced her cart with only enough room to open each drawer. The poor woman's list of diagnoses was bad enough, but now they added seizures to the list. She shook her head, thanking the Lord that she was years older than May. The young woman would be struck dead well before reaching Gloria's age. She was sure of it.

First, she needed to make sure May received her newly prescribed medication, so she went to the drawer with the appropriate first drug letters, took out one Phenytoin, and put it in the cup on top. Next, she scrutinized May's other early afternoon meds and suppressed a smile. The narcotics to be dispensed from her cart were so easy, she thought, because the hospital doctors didn't bother with trade names because of the increased cost of them to the hospital. They were all generic and May was taking hydrocodone with acetaminophen. She was disappointed over the acetaminophen part of it because she only wanted to steal the narcotic for Mr. Hogan. However, it didn't really matter that he would later be getting extra acetaminophen or what she knew as Tylenol.

She took May's dose of hydrocodone and acetaminophen and slipped it into the front pocket of her pants. Her hand then dug into her right jacket pocket and pulled out a vitamin, which she plopped into May's cup as the substitute. She noted May's prescriptions for late in the afternoon and sighed with relief that there was another narcotic dose and even a sedative/hypnotic for the evening, which she could also steal and give to Mr. Hogan instead.

"I hope you enjoyed lunch," Gloria said to May as her patient sat near the window inside. "Although you didn't eat much, did you?"

"What's the point?" May almost cried.

"Think of it as comfort food. Especially that coffee that's getting cold.

I would be happy to ask them to warm it for you."

"No, thank you."

"Besides your regular meds, I have the new medicine for you that the neurologist and medical doctors prescribed."

May held out her hand and popped one pill into her mouth. "I'll chase these down with some water." She grabbed the large plastic cup with a straw on her tray table and took a sip after each of the three pills Gloria handed her.

Gloria monitored the situation and, satisfied, rolled her cart to the side. "Have a nice afternoon. I'll be back later, but I hope they discharge you one of these days."

"Ha," May said. "I'm getting chemotherapy; I'm sick enough from that, but now I developed seizures from the metastatic lung cancer which invaded my brain. It's in my bones too, and although they already chopped away at my lung, I still cough up blood once in a while. And besides that, I lost my dog and my boyfriend since I've been in here." She wiped one side of her face because of the tear that had built up and rolled down her cheek.

Gloria was frozen where she stood. "I'm so sorry. I know the toll serious medical problems inflict on people's lives. My mom had Parkinson's disease and I took care of her until the end. Just hang in there and do the best you can. Can I bring you a book from the library?"

May wiped the other side of her face and looked up. "I'll try not to be so morbid when you come back later. But a book is not a bad idea. I'll stroll the hallway in a little while when my parents come back from lunch and visit the hospital's library. Then they are sending me over for my second chemo treatment."

"Good luck," Gloria said and left. Next, she went down the east and west wing to dispense the rest of the scheduled patients' drugs. She acquired two more narcotic pills and one anti-anxiety medication with sedative properties in the pocket of her pants and put vitamins and a nonsteroidal anti-inflammatory in their place. She gloated at how easy it was and how the patients all seemed clueless.

CHAPTER 27

Poised to go home, the students gathered and waited for their chief to come back from a medical consult. He strutted in waving his newspaper and Annabel spoke up first.

"Dr. Schott, thanks for letting us do rounds earlier this afternoon."

"I did it as a favor so the four of you can leave earlier than usual and use the extra time to study this weekend. I'm giving you Saturday morning off too. Dr. Burg, Dr. Watts, and I will do rounds tomorrow morning. The first medicine test is Tuesday, so be prepared."

Annabel sneaked a peek at the other students, hoping no one would mention their get-together tomorrow night. They had agreed that the one night going out would be beneficial. Each of them could do solid studying and cramming on Sunday.

"Now get out of here before I start reading from this out loud." He waved his paper at them with a hard frown. "I haven't read one line of this yet."

Annabel gulped, reached over into the corner, and pulled out her backpack. She grabbed her jacket from the hook and slid it on while Bob, Stuart, and Jordan did the same.

"Then we'll see you on Sunday morning for rounds," Annabel said.

Donn's head was already buried behind the paper when he mumbled something they didn't understand.

Annabel's phone dinged as the students piled into the staircase and headed downstairs. Nancy's message came through as she noted the time - 4:00 p.m.

An hour or two left for my drive. Stopped for gas and a milkshake.

"My sister's almost here," Annabel announced. "She's going to grill you all about medical school tomorrow night. My opinion doesn't usually count."

"We can help with that," Bob said. "Stuart can tell her that studying is required every breathing minute when you're not on the wards."

"Time put into studying depends on how smart you are to begin with," Stuart said.

"You can tell her that too," Annabel chuckled.

They weaved through the first floor lobby and split up for the revolving door at the exit.

"Even when it's not beautiful outside," Bob said, stepping off the curb, "I find it refreshing to leave the hospital. The air seems invigorating like we've been inside breathing stale air, disinfectant, and germs all day."

"That's why I like to take a walk in my neighborhood whenever I can," Annabel said. "So I'll meet the three of you at Pete's tomorrow, up on my corner?"

"I'm in," Bob said.

Stuart gave a thumbs up. "Me too."

"I'll be there," Jordan said.

When Annabel arrived at her car, she texted her sister.

See you soon!

As she turned on the ignition, another text message came through, but it wasn't Nancy.

Looking forward to tomorrow night at Stone's. I'll be wearing a brown leather jacket.

She looked at Ben Rogers profile picture and could picture him in a leather jacket. But she better not set her expectations too high, she thought, and texted him back.

Yes, I'll meet you there and enjoy the day.

I hope I stay 'free.' Because of the delicate nature of my job, I could always be called in.

As long as he doesn't get called tomorrow night, she thought. If they both found each other attractive, she would love to have a fun time in the sack with the Secret Service Agent.

She responded with two emojis in lieu of continuing the discussion and started for home.

Kitchen staff pushed the bulky dinner cart along the medical hallway and a woman with a disposable bonnet read and checked off her master dietary patient list. She plucked trays from the shelves and delivered them into patients' rooms.

Gloria was aware of the routine for the delivery of meals and she banked on the progression of the familiar schedule. It was her last, late visit of the day to dispense patients' medications and she would make Mr. Hogan her last stop.

Against the wall and below old photographs of the hospital, she substituted the fictitious pills she'd bought from the pharmacy for every patient who was taking a narcotic, sedative, or hypnotic. Gloria went into each patient's room either right before or after their dinner tray was placed before them. She made sure that patients accepted and gulped down the pills she provided.

When she only had Mr. Hogan's room left to go into, the front of her pant pockets bulged with the drugs she had confiscated and hoarded for him. On the other hand, the two front pockets of her work smock were now almost half devoid of their over-the-counter pill stash.

Gloria keenly watched earlier as the woman with the bonnet scurried into Mr. Hogan's room with his dinner selection. When the kitchen crew finished their job on the east and west wings, they checked back into everyone's rooms and, luckily, took the empty or partially finished dinners from the first wing, which included Mr. Hogan's.

Now Gloria leaned against the wall outside his doorway and flipped the pages in the black binder to his name and went to his medication list. She assumed no one paid her much mind in the hallway; she was not paying him a visit in sequence with the other patients. She had finished everyone else and had backtracked to him.

There was nothing to worry about, however, Gloria thought. Although people nowadays should be more alert and cognizant of other folks and events transpiring around them, it seemed like people just didn't actively think these days. However, she concluded that giving out medications didn't matter to anyone; no one gave her a second look.

She needed to pay attention with utmost focus on her pill switching. First, she went to the drawer and weeded out all the nine medications on Mr. Hogan's medication list. She put the heart medicines, antihypertensives, and all the rest of them one by one on the top counter off in the left corner by a box of tissues and the plastic drinking cups. A couple holding their winter jackets and wearing long, sad faces passed her and gave her a nod. She waited until they turned into a room two doors down.

Gloria reached into her right pants pocket under her work smock. Her fingers circled all the pills, she brought them out, and put them discreetly in front of her. Most of the oxycodone and acetaminophen looked the same, so she put three into each of the two small pills cups she needed to use for him. She selected four other pills other than the narcotics. Each one a hypnotic, sleep aide, or sedative. In essence, it didn't matter because everything she now had from her pockets had been carefully selected.

She contemplated the two baby pill cups in front of her with five pills each. Mr. Hogan wouldn't know the difference between nine or ten pills, but ten would make her feel more assured. This is overkill, she thought, because even six of these drugs would likely be a lethal dose for Mr. Hogan, particularly because of his severely compromised heart, as well as his lungs and circulation. Not much would be needed to put him to sleep and thereafter to make him stop breathing.

With the important preliminary task done, she slid Mr. Hogan's real prescribed drugs from the counter corner into her hand and dropped them into the pocket of her trousers. She took a deep breath and committed herself to the last part of her task. Her patient, Mr. Hogan, had been desperate in his discussion with her that morning and the other day; she felt relieved that his congestive heart failure would not snuff out his last days like a snake making a slow kill. In the next hour or two, he would only become sleepy and then fade away to meet his maker. No pain, no suffering, no more needle sticks, no more heart tests, or false hopes from anyone about getting better.

Gloria gave a push against her cart and turned it into his room. Mr. Hogan's dinner tray was gone. The reclining chair was positioned halfway back with the old man's legs on the foot rest. He rested in a post-prandial slump and smacked his lips absent-mindedly as she positioned her cart.

"Mr. Hogan, time for your medicines and then no one will disturb you until they take your vital signs around ten o'clock. You can slumber off into a better sleep than the nap you're taking right now."

He wiggled a little in the chair and nodded.

"Would you like to wash these down with water or apple juice?"

"Water," he said.

She poured water from a bottle into a plastic cup and he reached for it. Then she proceeded to hand him the first little pill cup. He barely glanced at her as he put one after the other of them into his mouth and chased them with the drink. As he took a break for a second, Gloria pulled the window drapes closed.

"Thanks," he said and put another pill on his tongue.

She put the pill cup into the waste basket hanging off the side of her cart and picked up the second cup.

"Ugh," he said. "Too many pills."

But despite his small complaint, he continued downing the medications.

"This one is colorful," he said. "They must have changed things around because I don't remember seeing a blue one."

"Nice to see some color in the mix," Gloria said with a smile.

"Hey, I didn't mean to complain so much this morning."

"That's all right. You're entitled." She put the second empty pill cup into her trash and, after his last sip of water, she took back the paper cup.

Gloria sighed with great consolation that her task was over. As she made it to the door, she wished she could witness the final serenity on Mr. Hogan's face as her mercy killing propelled him to his last breath.

"Since I may not see you tomorrow," Mr. Hogan added from his chair, "keep up the good work."

She threw her arm up and gave him an acknowledging wave as she pushed her wares out the door. That was a strange thing for him to say, she thought. She wondered if he had a premonition that he would die overnight. She pulled the door to a closed position but didn't snap it shut. Unless Mr. Hogan used his call button, there should be no reason why anyone would enter his room for a few hours.

A smile crept over Manuel Hogan's lips as he jostled his rear end tighter in the chair and let the post-prandial sinking spell overtake him again. The doctors had given him such hope that morning. He would go home one last time; that was all he wanted and all he could ask for. He eyed his ankles and he agreed with their assessment. The swelling was still there, but it had definitely subsided. Plus, he was sure about that because his ankles didn't feel as tight as before with fluid.

By tomorrow night, he could be sitting by his front window with his favorite home brewed coffee, a newspaper, and the nightly news on in the background. He'd make sure the front porch light is on and perhaps if it is cold enough, there will be an icicle or two hanging down from the roof line.

After that, and before going to bed, he could pen the two letters he had wanted to write for some time. Notes to an old flame and a relative because he wanted to patch up previous differences. Or at least try. And the day after? He wanted to talk with his lawyer to make sure his will and last requests were in order and, before the end of that day, he would be sure to go to the movies to sit in the new stadium seating and marvel at the hugeness of the screen. Even if the flick was halfway enjoyable, he'd be happy. It's the simple things in life, he thought, as he sleepily leaned forward and scratched at his ankle.

He readjusted the nasal cannula on his nose and sank his head back against the soft chair. He yawned and as each minute ticked by, Mr. Hogan's conscious thoughts drifted away. His drowsiness succumbed to sleeping, which then acquiesced to a hard, deep sleep, and then culminated in his last breath.

Gloria hung around for another hour, just wasting time. She dawdled behind the nurses' station rearranging her cart like it was dirty and needed reorganizing. No call buzzed through to the nurses from Mr. Hogan's room and no one flew down the hallway as if a patient was in trouble.

"Some people like their jobs," Anna said, exiting from the storage room, "but what are you still doing here?"

Gloria startled. "After being slow as molasses, I'm leaving now."

"Good night." Anna gave her a look like she was crazy.

Gloria went to the locker room and slid Mr. Hogan's real meds into the bottles she had for the multivitamins and nonsteroidal anti-inflammatories in her purse. She thought to keep the substitute pills she bought in her lab smock. Maybe another patient would surface in the coming days who needed her help.

As she left the hospital, she drew in a big gasp of fresh, cold air. The adrenaline soared through her veins with the sheer ecstasy of what she did for Manuel Hogan. By now, he might have crossed over into the afterlife. She thought about watching the newspaper in the next few days for his obituary. With a broad smile and a clunking of her shoes along the asphalt, she decided to attend his funeral or visit his gravesite later. She hit her car remote button. Instead of one beep, she sounded it three times, like an uplifting trumpet signaling Mr. Hogan's death.

Upon arriving home, Gloria removed the multivitamin and nonsteroidal anti-inflammatory bottles from her purse, which had all of

Mr. Hogan's real hospital medicines in them, and placed them on her kitchen counter.

On the late evening medical assistant rounds, a tech just like Gloria entered Mr. Hogan's room. She found him in a restful pose in the recliner with his hands folded on his lap and the nasal cannula in his nose. But he was way too still; not even a hint of his chest rising with inspiration. She shook his arm but realized the gravity of his condition. She called the desk.

"I think Mr. Hogan is dead," she said with alarm.

One nurse came running in with a med student she signaled from the desk as he was writing a note. The student felt Mr. Hogan's carotid artery in his neck and shook his head.

"Get the crash cart," he said, "let's start a code and call for help."

"I don't think so," the nurse said. "He's a DNR, a do not resuscitate, by his own wishes." She closed his eyelids with her finger. "Too bad. Dr. Schott had decided to discharge him in the morning."

CHAPTER 28

With an internal medicine paperback in her hands, Annabel lounged in sweatpants and a hoodie against a pillow and a sham on her bed. She blocked out all other thoughts except for what she was studying; her sister would be showing up soon, and with a busy Saturday night, she needed to use all available time to study and review. Learning to focus immediately and intently on certain subject matter, she realized, would be a skill she could use for years to come.

A rap came at her door. She padded over in slipper socks and her sister knocked with the familiar seven raps they used at home. When she opened the door, Nancy stood there with her paraphernalia: a rolling suitcase with a wrapped-up sleeping bag perched on top and a small cooler and bag on the other side. Nancy's hazel eyes latched onto her and she broke out in a smile. Her light brown hair was clipped on one side with a herringbone clip.

"How'd you manage carrying all of that?" Annabel asked.

"Two trips from the car. Easy enough since I parked practically out front."

"I should be so lucky. Looks like you're moving in."

"You told me to bring a sleeping bag."

"That I did." Annabel grabbed the cooler and purse and let Nancy pull the suitcase.

"This okay?" Nancy asked while spreading the sleeping bag down on the bedroom floor.

Annabel nodded and her sister proceeded to position the suitcase next to it and unzip. From the right side, packed tightly between clothes, Nancy withdrew a white container four inches high and handed it to her.

Annabel took it in both hands. A white strip was taped horizontally across the front with only one word. *Dakota*. She held it to her heart for a few moments and then patted the top. "Thank Dad for me."

"I will. He said to tell you that he and Mom are getting another dog in a few months. Any of us are welcome to go to the breeders with them and pick out a Chesapeake puppy."

"You and I will be home less and less. I think the dog they select should be entirely their decision."

"It may come down to that anyway, Annabel. You can't race down there anytime you want."

"So true. I wish I could see them more often. Even Aunt Mary and Uncle Casey. You should enjoy all that time you spend with them right now."

"I've probably overstayed living there while going to college and I'm still not sure what I'm going to do in the spring when I graduate."

"You know we can never overstay being there. The whole purpose of Grandma and Grandpa's house was to be available for any and all of us. I know that's how Mom and Dad see it and we should feel the same way."

"I'll see how it goes."

Annabel carried Dakota's ashes over to the only shelves in her bedroom and placed them at eye-level. "I should place a tennis ball here," she chuckled. "This will be my memorial spot for him. He was so special."

She turned around and fetched a pillow from the closet and threw it over to Nancy. "This is for your sleeping bag."

"Thanks. So, can you tell me more about your friend Bob? Since you're not interested in him, I'd like to get to know him better at dinner tomorrow night. Perhaps I can influence him to pay more attention to me than just being his friend's sister. What do you think?"

Annabel shrugged. "He's been my dearest friend since we started clinical rotations. I can't prevent you from being attracted to him, but don't put me in the middle of something I don't feel comfortable with."

"Like what?"

"I don't know. I'm just saying. But, by the way, there's somewhere I need to be tomorrow night after we all eat dinner together, but I'm not broadcasting it."

Nancy tilted her head. "A date?"

"Yes … or something like that. I'm meeting someone for a light dinner that I couldn't really change. Just don't make a big deal about it with my med student friends because we give each other grief about stuff like extracurricular social events and I don't want to be the brunt of this week's jokes. Plus, the coming days are important since we're all taking our first internal medicine test."

"Okay," Nancy said. "I'm game if you let me sit next to Bob."

Annabel rolled her eyes. "Done. And I don't have to jump up in the morning to leave for Saturday rounds, but I do need to go on Sunday morning for a little while."

"I'll leave on Sunday after you come back and maybe we can eat lunch together before I leave."

"All right. I better buckle down again with my books."

Dustin Lowe and Edgar Banks started their 3 p.m. shift on Saturday by being called into the chief's office. Chief Erickson was a 27-year-veteran of the Cincinnati police department who held the esteem of all his men and women officers. He was all business except for when he topped off his coffee in the department's small kitchen and would ask fellow law enforcement how they spent their day off, or how their kid's soccer game went, or how they were tolerating their high protein diet.

The strikingly tall chief swung to the side in his chair, crossed his legs, and told them to take a seat. He updated Banks and Lowe on several matters and then shuffled folders on his desk, found what he was looking for, and put a thin one in front of him.

"Yesterday," he said, "our guys on internet detail tracked down a man with a previous police record masterminding a doozy of a scheme. Raking in serious cash from a scheme which put him on our radar for selling fake IDs online. We nabbed him yesterday along with a handful of his customers not much better than him. They all pick up fake IDs for all sorts of reasons."

The chief opened the file, pulled out a photograph, and handed it to Dustin. "Here's another customer of his that I want you both to pick up today."

Dustin studied the picture of a twenty-seven year old with a narrow face, blue eyes, and a chin dimple indented enough to fit a pebble. He handed it to Edgar as the chief waited.

"That one," Erickson said, "bought a fake Secret Service ID. Our guys searched social media, and this Ben Rogers shows up on dating sites flashing his false identity to impress women."

"Damn," Dustin said. "Why doesn't that surprise me?"

"Because if young people are going to meet people by using those methods, they never know what they're going to get."

"But," Edgar chimed in, "it's not just young people and sometimes the situation works out fine. I'm aware of someone in his fifties who married his spouse after meeting her on social media."

"Heaven forbid," the chief said and frowned. He leaned forward and handed over the rest of the slim file.

Dustin opened it and read the top sheet. His eyes grew wide as he started to laugh.

"What's so funny?" his partner asked.

"You won't believe what this guy really does for a living. He better legitimately train and become a Secret Service Agent instead."

"That won't be possible," the chief said. "For starters, he's earned a few years of probation and a big, fat fine. He'll no longer be attractive to women except for those with a record like him."

Dustin passed the information to Edgar. His partner suppressed a chuckle and rolled his eyes. "You can't make this up."

"We'll pick Ben Rogers up later," Dustin said and tapped on the open file. "Is this his current address?"

"Far as we can tell." He uncrossed his legs and rotated them back under his desk. "Next, I'll fill you in on the Bureau of Criminal Investigation's matter on that Darlene Pratt case."

"I was wondering about that Parkinson's patient," Dustin said, "especially after we talked to the caretaker. She ended up a surprise … a mellow woman without a mean bone in her body."

"Good thing enough suspicion popped up in this case because the medical examiner went ahead and did an autopsy." He paused, making eye contact with each one of them. "He found poisoning with ethylene glycol."

"Antifreeze," Dustin said. "Damn. I saw a bottle underneath the sink. Who's responsible? The caretaker, the daughter, a boyfriend of the daughter, or who else comes and goes in that house?"

"They're investigating and we're lending a hand if the need arises. Turns out the daughter, Gloria, is a model for sainthood. The mother was recently hospitalized at the government hospital and then seen as an outpatient. A nurse at the clinic said the daughter and mother came in recently and was seen by a medical school student and resident. No new medical problems with the patient and the staff there sang praises of the daughter's home care.

"They're looking at the home situation more carefully the way they found it and what you reported. They found antifreeze residue inside the paper cups and the outsides had traces of ethyl alcohol."

"Ethyl alcohol?" Edgar asked as he stood with the file.

"Hand sanitizer."

Edgar nodded and Dustin rose. As they made it to the door, the chief said one more thing.

"The BCI will probably be pulling more people in the next two days to question." The chief picked up the phone as they both slipped out the door.

"I've got a stash of paperwork on my desk," Edgar said.

"Me too," Dustin said. "At least the BCI is handling the Pratt case. Otherwise, we'd be wrapped up with it."

"Yeah," Edgar said and veered away from sitting at his desk. He needed an afternoon cup of coffee to start the shift off right.

Late Saturday morning, Annabel took a study break, the two sisters dressed warmly, and headed out for a jog. Annabel led the way down the street to the neighborhood park benches and dormant garden and then led the way over the highway on a walkway overpass. They both hustled down one hundred plus steps to the path between the road and Ohio River. The cold air plus sunshine invigorated both girls but Annabel found herself huffing and puffing more than usual.

Annabel stopped. "You're in better shape than I am," she said after leaning over to take a deep breath. "Medical school is taking a toll on my body. Maybe that will keep you from considering it as an option in the future."

Nancy kept jogging in place. "Lots of jobs can do that to you."

"Valid point. Let's walk some. What are you wearing later?"

"A rust blouse with a matching casual vest and faded jeans. Plus, date shoes."

"Date shoes? What are those?"

"Anything other than tennis shoes and with some height."

"I hope you like my group. You already met Bob; Stuart is extremely smart, quiet, and a little bit nerdy; and Jordan's okay but a bit of a know-it-all. They are all decent-looking, but Bob's probably the best all around. He's thoughtful and has a sense of humor."

"I gathered that. But who are you going out with after that?"

"I'll tell you about it later tonight if you're still up, or in the morning."

"You mean you don't really know him?"

Annabel shrugged. "Not too much but, like I said, don't say a word to my friends or I'll take grief about it forever."

"It's a deal, especially if the other two leave and I can spend more time with Bob."

Annabel exhaled into her hands. "I guess we better start running again to keep warm. Let's head back."

The girls turned. The muddy Ohio's current was swift and several birds flew above the middle of the channel. The traffic on the bridge between the two states was lighter than during the work week and Annabel wished it was already springtime when everything would appear more cheery. She wondered about her sister's preoccupation with Bob. Would she like him as much if he wasn't a medical student?

She also thought about the man she was meeting later that night. Pictures in profiles sometimes were better representations than the actual person. She was prepared for that, but he still looked decent. Being a Secret Service Agent, however, meant he could be trusted, and he must have a respectable background. With those three things in his favor, she hoped more than anything that they ended up in the sack. She was overdue for salacious sex and imagined strong biceps wrapping around her in a passionate embrace.

However, she thought, whatever happened to Robby Burk? He never called after their three failed attempts at dating and for that she was disheartened. Her gut instinct told her to not call him at all. She had to give him the benefit of the doubt that something else might have materialized in the hectic life of a chief resident, or he was holding off on dating for the time being, or he had changed his mind about her and was no longer interested. He was the one most responsible for ramping up her hormones and he was the one who she would sleep with in a flash. The sad lesson, however, was that she could not control other people's feelings or actions. If he didn't want to call her, there was nothing she could do about it.

"Annabel, did you hear a word I said?"

Annabel shook her head. "Sorry, I wandered off into thoughts about men."

"At least being in medical school hasn't stripped you of being a normal female who wants to date and have a good time."

"More than that."

Nancy's mouth flew open. "I can't believe you said that to me if it means what I think it means."

Annabel didn't respond as her heart rate quickened mounting the steep steps back up to her neighborhood.

Back in Annabel's apartment, Nancy showered and dressed first while Annabel read the highlights about acute lung infections and sepsis. Her sister put her vest on over her blouse and moved sideways and frontal in the full length mirror. She rubbed a gel into her hair, which added a shine and she made sure it covered her ears which, for her whole life, she considered too prominent. She always wished her parents had taken her to a plastic surgeon specialist when she was young to have them altered. Ear jobs were as important as nose jobs!

"You look fine," Annabel said, getting up from her bed and heading to the bathroom. She showered and put on a denim skirt, a white turtleneck sleeveless top, and a dark pink overhead sweater. She topped it all off with a pair of boots from Nashville.

With a little bit of makeup, and the long waves in her hair taking on a shine from the same hair gel as Nancy, she grabbed a purse and her phone. "Ready?" she asked.

Nancy nodded, they grabbed their jackets, and strolled up the block to Pete's Café.

CHAPTER 29

The overhead bells jingled as Annabel and Nancy entered Pete's. Half the tables were occupied and on the right side against the wall, Jordan and Stuart sat at a bench and dipped pita chips into hummus.

"Hey, guys," Annabel said. "This is my sister, Nancy."

Jordan rose and shook Nancy's hand. "I'm Jordan. Have a seat and welcome to our only party for four months." He pointed next to him and Nancy sat down. "And that guy across from you is Stuart."

"Pleased to meet you, Nancy. Any friend or relative of Annabel's is a friend of ours too. We share long days and bizarre situations; our cases are more dramatic than those in medical shows."

"You must be the smart one," Nancy said.

"Hey, I take offense to that," Jordan said. "Which one am I?"

"Hmm. Let me think about that over this appetizer, which I'm sure you're going to share." She gave him a second glance.

Bob strolled in, flung his coat on the jacket pile-up, and filled their ears with a gregarious laugh. "I guess I'm the late one. It won't be the last time either. Hi, Nancy, did you have a nice drive? We're glad you could make it." He pulled out a chair across from her and sat next to Annabel. Stuart was planted at the end of the table.

Nancy grinned, annoyed already that the seating had not worked out the way she wanted. "Thanks, Bob. The drive was boring, which is a good thing. I caught up with NPR shows and country music."

"A college girl listening to NPR?" Jordan asked. "Aren't you supposed to listen to the top ten count down?"

"Please, I can do without six hours of monotonous electronic music."

"Wow, you are a Nashville girl."

Pete appeared at the empty end of the table. "Just wanted to come over and say hi. Glad you brought a group tonight, Annabel."

"Thanks, Pete. Meet my classmates, my sister, and you know Bob already."

"Welcome to the neighborhood hangout. Feel free to order a killer specialty coffee to start off your night. I don't mind making them any time of the day. And when you come up to place your orders, the special today is a grilled pastrami with cheese and a side."

"He makes huge sandwiches," Annabel said. "How about splitting one with me, Nancy?"

"Okay, and if I need more, I'll order afterwards. I understand your reasoning for half."

Bob scrunched his eyes. "Annabel, I've never seen you diet."

"I don't, but I'm leaving in an hour to be somewhere else."

"You're inviting us back to your place to study, right?"

Annabel shook her head. "We were going to all study together before the test, but this is much better."

"But then you break our spirits by limiting us to one hour of your time?"

"All right, already, Bob," Jordan said. "She doesn't want to spend more time with us than she has to."

Annabel put her hand on Bob's shoulder. "Come on, let's go order."

The five of them lined up along the counter and ordered, and as they waited for their food, they dived back into Stuart and Jordan's appetizer.

"So what's it like living in Nashville?" Jordan asked Nancy.

"We're on the outskirts, but downtown is amazing. It throbs with country music," she began, "and tourists spill out of the bars at night. It's so much fun."

Meanwhile, Annabel, Bob, and Stuart began discussing medicine. "In a way, I missed rounds this morning," Bob said.

Stuart gave him a double take. "You must like internal medicine a lot."

"I develop attachments to certain patients and I wanted to see the happiness all over Mr. Hogan's face this morning when we discharged him. Dr. Schott believed his last twenty-four hours would be stable and his going home was a done deal."

"Funny you say that," Annabel said, "because I liked Mr. Hogan a lot too, and also sincerely wished for his departure. At least he lived at home and still took care of himself as much as possible, not like your poor Mr. Harty who did the final act of suicide."

"I hope I live to be as old and as sweet as Mr. Hogan. Mr. Harty, well, he left a dent in my soul. I already had one patient commit suicide on the psychiatry rotation, so his overdose made me feel downright sad."

Annabel leaned back to put distance between her and the chips. "We must derive pleasure from our successfully discharged patients."

"And acing exams," Stuart said. "After all, we won't go anywhere if we each don't get through each step of the way."

"We can drink to that," Bob said, and saluted with a cup of water.

Pete came over and put down a mocha cappuccino in front of Annabel. She picked it up and toasted with Bob and Stuart.

Across the table, Jordan had his right elbow on the table with his head resting in his hand as he focused on Nancy. "Surgery is one thing," he said, "but cardiothoracic surgery is on a different wavelength. My future is already determined."

"Sounds like too much responsibility to me," Nancy said, "but what is your opinion about med school? The pros and cons?"

Jordan launched into his opinions while Nancy stole a glance at her sister. Bob had one hand resting on the back crosspiece of Annabel's chair and, with the other, he scooped hummus on a chip and handed it to her. For a moment, her heart pattered. Bob's smile and charm were as refreshing as a waft of honeysuckle on a breeze.

But, she realized, the reason for her trip was in vain. Clearly, Bob adored her sister. If she had sensed it before when he had accompanied Annabel home for Dakota's death, she'd been too stupid to admit it to herself.

Checking her watch, Annabel quickly startled and sprang up from her chair. "That was delicious," she said. "I will see the three of you tomorrow morning and I'll see you later, Nancy."

"What's your hurry?" Jordan asked.

"I have another engagement." She grabbed her jacket and purse. "Thanks y'all, and, Nancy, thanks for splitting a sandwich with me." She waved at Pete as she crossed the wooden floor and disappeared out the door.

"What was that all about?" Jordan asked.

"She's got a date," Nancy said and then realized she shouldn't have said it. "Please don't tell her I told you." She frowned and tapped a clean knife on the tablecloth.

"We'll keep quiet, won't we?" Stuart said.

"I'll try," Bob said with disappointment hanging on his words. "Did she give you any details?"

"No," Nancy said. "She didn't divulge any information to me, but it did sound like she was meeting some guy for the first time."

"So it wasn't her surgery chief resident?"

"She's talked about Robby Burk, but she would have been jumping all over if she was seeing him."

Bob's face sulked more and Nancy regretted the whole conversation came up.

On the west side of I-75, in a row of two-story apartments, Dustin and Edgar rang Ben Rogers' doorbell to no avail. Dustin peeked at the address again to confirm their location and began rapping at the door. The sun had gone down; he figured most people were home from work and he was bound to disturb someone. Edgar butted in and gave two louder bangs on the gray door.

A door cracked open from the adjacent apartment. A skinny young male in sweat clothes wore a surprised face upon seeing the two men in blue.

"Wait," Edgar said. "Know the whereabouts of your neighbor?"

"Is he in trouble?"

"He'll be in more trouble if we don't find him."

"It's Saturday night, when he meets new women at Stones a few blocks away. Friday nights he goes to the one east of the highway."

"Why Stones?" Dustin asked.

"Lots of chick food; their menu is jammed with salads. Plus, good wine and intimate, dimly lit booths."

"He's got his social life down to a science," Edgar commented.

"Hey, don't tell him I told you where to find him."

Edgar nodded and the man withdrew back into his apartment.

"Let's go pick up the sleaze-bag womanizer," Dustin said.

They hopped back into the patrol car and rode over in silence until Edgar said, "We'll probably find this Rogers guy with some gorgeous woman who you or I could never attract."

"Don't forget brains. She'll also be the CEO of a major company or a college professor who thinks she's hooking up with a Secret Service Agent."

Restaurants lined the city street with every ethnic choice Annabel could think of as she pulled into the back of Stones and found a parking spot. She freshened her lip gloss in the rearview mirror, left her purse on the floor in the back seat, and only put a card holder with a credit card into her pocket. She weaved her way through the lot and entered the front entrance.

A mixed assortment of art dotted the walls, from wood sculpted animals to photographs of major cities. She smiled at the Nashville print over the cash register as the maître d asked her if anyone was joining her.

Her fingers smoothed her hair along the side of her face as she looked deeper into the restaurant. "I'm meeting someone. Ben Rogers."

"Take her back to Ben," the man said to the waitress grabbing a menu. "Enjoy your meal."

Annabel wondered about the maître d's comment as she passed the busy bar. Sounded like Ben was a regular commodity at Stones. She spotted him before the waitress put her menu down.

Ben slinked out of the booth, put his hand on Annabel's upper arm, and gave her a warm smile. "Your picture is only half as flattering as you are."

"Thank you, I think," Annabel said.

They both slid in from either side and the waitress asked Annabel for her drink order. "A glass of water as well as a chardonnay."

Annabel stole a glance at Ben. His deep set eyes were blue as an ocean on a sunny day. As he smiled, his right cheek flashed a dimple, which made him look like a school boy. He was trim like a runner and didn't look like the type investing in rigorous gym time and protein powder drinks.

"Have you been here before?" Ben asked.

"No. When I get out, I mostly stick around a few favorite spots."

"Check out the menu. I'm going to try what's on today's blackboard."

Annabel looked it over. "I had a small bite with my sister, who's visiting, so I'm glad there are some salad choices."

"Is she older or younger?"

"She's almost three years younger. So tell me, because of your job, do you travel a lot?"

"I go back and forth to Washington at least once a month. I'm primarily on the criminal investigation side of the Agency, so that does involve being out of town quite often. But enough of that, I shouldn't be talking about this subject anyway."

The waitress put down Annabel's drinks. "You two ready to order? You ordering the special, Ben?"

"Sure," he said.

"And I'll have a small house salad with grilled chicken," Annabel said.

"Coming right up."

"However," Annabel said when the waitress stepped away, "I'm dying to hear. Have you ever been assigned to presidential security?"

He tilted his head and narrowed his eyes. "That's for me to know and for you to find out. Later tonight, maybe?"

"Maybe so." She smiled and raised her glass.

Ben tapped his beer bottle against her wine glass and they both took a swig. Annabel's cheeks warmed; tonight might turn juicy by the time they finished their date.

Dustin and Edgar parked in the back lot of Stones and hopped out of their patrol car.

"Let's keep it low key," Edgar said as they sauntered to the entrance. They opened the door and the maître d raised his eyebrows.

"Just routine," Dustin said. "We're looking for someone."

The two officers peered inside from both sides of the helpdesk. The lighting was dim and they didn't spot their mark, so they both walked down the aisles.

Dustin looked over at Edgar and nodded his head towards the back right wall. Ben was facing their way and, as both officers gathered attention from other diners, they approached him and stopped at the end of the table.

Both officers failed to spot her beforehand, so they both took a double take when they saw Ben's date. The officers and Annabel knew each other from when Annabel rotated on psychiatry. Their interactions had stemmed from both a police matter with a patient and a robbery, as well as a personal situation when Edgar dated Annabel's attending doctor and Dustin dated Annabel.

"Annabel Tilson," Dustin said. "We meet again."

Annabel smiled. "What a coincidence. How are you?"

"Can't complain."

Edgar leaned his knees against the seat cushion on Ben's side. "Are you Ben Rogers?"

Ben's hand nervously tapped the table. "What's it to you?" he groaned.

"I understand you bought a fake ID. Come on down to the station and we can talk about it."

Ben froze. A saying his mother used to say to him popped into his head. *Caught in the act.* He finally took a breath, didn't know what rights he had since he knew he was guilty as hell, and slithered to the end of the bench. Edgar stepped back and Ben rose.

"I'll take him to the car," Edgar said. He nodded at Annabel and Ben didn't look at her.

"I'll fill her in," Dustin said. "I'll be a few minutes."

Ben and Edgar walked out of the restaurant to many arched eyebrows and Edgar put him in the back seat.

Annabel cringed. She couldn't believe what Edgar said about a fake ID. He must be referring to Ben's Secret Service Agent identity card. Now her heart palpated as Dustin sat down across from her and frowned. He pushed Ben's beer to the side and leaned forward.

"Didn't you learn your lesson yet about meeting strange men from social apps? That guy possesses a fake government ID, which he uses to lure women via dating apps."

Annabel put her hand over her eyes and her forehead. Of all people to show up, it had to be Dustin Lowe. She was a freaking magnet for dreadful situations.

"I guess I should thank you, but I only met him for dinner. I had no plans to marry him."

Dustin raised his eyebrows. "You're smarter than most women and you're cut out to be among the next generation of doctors, however, you need to practice more discretion. You're getting mixed up with shady characters."

"However, I did date you," she said with a soft voice.

"All right. I give up. It's none of my business. But did he show you his ID?"

"Yes, he posted it online. Goes to show, you can't trust anyone."

"Bingo!" Dustin cackled. "And dare I tell you what he really does for a living?"

Annabel shook her head but then nodded.

"He owns a small business that takes care of scooping up pet poop in shopping mall lots and business areas."

Annabel coughed and then took a gulp of wine. To heck with sipping on it.

"Anyway," Dustin said after letting that news sink in, "how's your training coming along?"

She sighed. He was a gentleman for changing the subject. "As you know, I finished psychiatry. Now I'm almost in the middle of internal medicine. My team and I manage vets and service people in Cincinnati's military hospital."

Dustin sat tall. "We're involved with a case right now ... a patient who was recently hospitalized there and seen in their clinic. A Parkinson's patient. Turns out she was murdered by poisoning."

"How awful," she said and wrung her hands. "I took care of a Parkinson's patient, but she's alive. What kind of poison?"

"Ethylene glycol. Anti-freeze."

Annabel turned her hand over like she didn't understand. "How does that work?"

"Dangerous stuff. People and pets are poisoned every year because it is odorless and colorless and it can be easily mixed into food or drinks. The major danger is because of its sweet taste, so kids and animals are attracted to it."

Annabel stayed glued on his explanation.

"I'm no medical examiner, but I've been told that once it's ingested, it degrades to a toxic product which affects the central nervous system, the heart, and then it accumulates in the kidneys. The only way the degraded compound, ethylene glycol, can be discovered is on autopsy. It's almost a fool-proof method to kill somebody!"

"People are so horrid."

If anti-freeze is toxic to the kidneys, Annabel thought, then renal failure would be one of the pathways to death. Based on what Dustin just said, Darlene Pratt's circumstance nagged at her. They'd seen her in clinic after her hospitalization; Dr. Watts had mentioned they should see her again soon because her renal function lab work had crept up; they needed to monitor that more closely. Annabel stroked the waves of her hair. She believed Mrs. Pratt would be back in clinic in another week or less. Luckily, her daughter took excellent care of her and accommodated all her appointments.

Annabel rubbed her hair again. "I'm getting an uneasy feeling about this. I can't mention patients' names or conditions because of privacy laws, but you can tell me. What's the woman's name?"

"Darlene Pratt."

Annabel gasped. "My patient," she stammered.

"Really?! Anything you can think of that would be important to us?"

"Her renal function showed signs of beginning deterioration when she showed up in clinic."

Dustin shook his head. "The Bureau of Criminal Investigation is talking to suspects. High on the list at the moment is the daughter."

"The daughter? She's exceptional. I'd want her or someone like her caring for me if the need arose."

"Sometimes it's the ones you don't suspect."

"I wonder," she thought aloud. "Her mother was living a pitiful existence ..."

Dustin squinted his eyes. "Hmm. I see your point."

Annabel took another sip and then moved the wine to the side. "So much for dinner," she said. "I better go home. I have a houseguest."

"Edgar's waiting too. I'll leave you to tend to your bill. Call us if you think of anything else."

"I will. I still have both your numbers in my cell phone."

CHAPTER 30

Light spilled from the upstairs window of her apartment as Annabel loped up the hill from her car. She felt like she dragged a dead weight from the evening's turn of events. Darlene Pratt was dead … murdered! Gloria Pratt was under scrutiny. The Secret Service Agent, Ben Rogers, nothing more than a pooper-scooper picker-upper who had been hauled away. That would go down as a date story difficult to beat.

As if these developments weren't enough, the two officers from her past came screeching back into her life like runaway Spanish bulls. Dustin Lowe was an excellent officer and a praiseworthy man who was privy to her stupidest indiscretions. How embarrassing, and there was nothing she could do to change it.

Annabel tapped on her apartment door, turned her key, and went in.

Nancy sat on one of the stools, her hands wrapped around a mug. A warm, full length nightgown graced her body and her clip no longer clasped her hair. "How was your date? I didn't expect you back so soon."

Annabel dropped her bag and jacket by the windowsill. She pulled the second stool to the other side of the counter. After frowning, she stifled a sigh. "The guy I met? Our date ended prematurely. No loss for me.

"However, I ran into someone at the restaurant who told me something about one of my recent patients. The best part of my evening was our get-together up the block. Did you have fun?"

Nancy gave her a sheepish grin. "Considering that I may have a future date with a med student, the night was super."

Annabel squared her shoulders. Bob didn't date Karla anymore, but now a relationship could kindle in the future with her own sister. She found it difficult to appear cheery and her heart left out a beat.

"I'm sorry you had a crappy time later," Nancy said, "but aren't you going to say something? Jordan is really cool and I want to come back in the next month or two to go out with him."

Annabel's apprehension lessened. "Jordan Maldonado? He asked you out?"

"Yes. The date stands for when I come back to Cincinnati."

"I'm happy for you. My place is yours for whenever you want, as long as I can have needed quiet for studying. After all, Dad is paying my rent."

Annabel joined her sister in a weak cup of coffee. Later, her eyes closed for the night when an internal medicine book dropped from her hands onto the floor. Nancy looked over from her sleeping bag, put her Kindle down, and went to sleep content about meeting Jordan Maldonado.

Annabel scurried around seeing her patients and gathering lab work for rounds. She grabbed a cup of coffee from the ICU and stepped into the office. The team gathered one-by-one with Bob and Jordan being the last ones to filter in.

"I hate Sundays," Donn said, standing up and putting on his lab coat. "Old news." He motioned to his *USA Today* on the desk. "It's the weekend edition which comes out on Friday. No use by the time Sunday rolls around."

"Sorry to hear it," Bob said, unzipping his backpack. "Knowing that, I bought you a present on the way in." He pulled out a thick *New York Times*.

"Donn's face lightened up in a full smile and he swiped the newspaper from Bob. "These aren't easy to find in Cincinnati except for a few truck-stop gas stations. You aren't trying to influence your clinical evaluation, are you?"

Bob shook his head. "Not at all. I thought to buy it for you because you gave us off yesterday morning."

"Good man. Thank you." He stuck it behind him on the desk. "Bob knows this already from checking on his patients, but Mr. Hogan died on Friday night. I suppose in the end, his heart failure didn't cooperate with him."

"No…" Annabel blurted out. "Really?"

Bob nodded at her. "Yeah. This morning, I missed him sitting by the window telling me his woes or expressing his optimism about springing out of here."

A silence fell in the room as if they each muttered a prayer for Mr. Hogan's demise.

A frown etched across Annabel's forehead and she glanced at Dr. Watts. "I learned more bad news last night. Darlene Pratt died."

"However sad that may be," Chineka said after thinking about it, "her death may be a blessing in disguise."

"Did you read about Mrs. Pratt in the obituary column?" Donn asked.

"No. I bumped into two police officers last night that I know. She was poisoned with anti-freeze and one person of interest is the daughter. The one who sat or slept in her hospital room all the time."

Chineka's mouth fell open and someone else gasped.

"Were Darlene's BUN and creatinine elevated in clinic?" Donn asked.

"Yes," Chineka said.

"That could be from the anti-freeze," Donn said. "Annabel, if the cops need any medical records via legal means, we're here to cooperate."

"I pretty much told them that."

Dr. Schott herded them out the door for rounds. Jordan strutted close to Annabel. "I took your sister's phone number," he said.

"So I heard."

"How did the rest of your night go?" Bob asked. "Were the police officers you mentioned the ones that dated you and our psychiatry attending?" He dared not mention that Nancy told them about her date last night. Perplexed, he wondered how the policemen fit in.

"Yes, it was Dustin Lowe and Edgar Banks. I happened to bump into them in the restaurant. We discussed my rotation and the conversation veered off to Darlene Pratt."

If she did have a date, Bob thought, she wasn't divulging more information; he was dying to know but decided to stop pressing.

Sunday morning rounds remained uneventful with only rehashed patient updates like the news printed in the Friday weekend paper ... except that two of their patients had died and, for the team, that made front page news fit for the cover of the *The New York Times*.

Annabel still needed to circle back and see May Oliver before leaving. Another decision had been made at the conclusion of rounds about May's care. Dr. Schott scheduled her for radiation treatments in addition to the chemotherapy she had completed so far. She found out they could fit her in the next morning.

May leaned over the sink brushing her teeth when Annabel entered.

"Mind if we talk again?" Annabel asked.

"No, I'm always up for talking with you. Are you feeling any better about your dog?" She stuck her toothbrush in a cup and went to her chair ... as if standing was too tiresome.

"My sister brought me some of his ashes this weekend. Remains of our pets are comforting, aren't they?"

"I agree. Although I think my ashes will soon be next ... for my parents to put beside my beloved Misty." She rolled the tray table to the side and sat. Her buzzed-off hair still startled Annabel every time she saw it and her face seemed to be growing gaunter by the day. A sinewy hand went up past her cheek and she rubbed her eye.

"May, you're scheduled for a radiation treatment tomorrow morning."

May stifled a sigh and frowned. Her bulging eyes stared at Annabel and clouded over. "No. I don't think so."

Annabel saddened. Besides learning, it was part of her duty to provide care and treatments, but May Oliver might have been at the end of her tolerance for further medical care.

A juggling noise came from outside the doorway and the drug cart began rolling in. Annabel took a double take at the medical assistant behind it. Gloria Pratt. What was she doing here?

"Dr. Tilson, it's me, Gloria. I was wondering if I'd be seeing you on the ward. I told you I had interviews scheduled for medical assistant jobs and I landed one at my favorite hospital."

"I remember. Congratulations. What a surprise. How is your mother?"

"The bad news is that she passed away. I miss her so much, but she's in God's hands now and not suffering."

Annabel nodded at the information she already knew. She guessed the police were doing their job and had, or would, talk to her again.

Gloria clunked by Annabel and addressed May. "While Dr. Tilson and I talk, I'm here with your meds."

"Pills for what purpose?" May commented. "You and I have had some serious little discussions about my feelings towards where I'm heading. In a day or two I may start refusing those medicines."

"It's your prerogative," Gloria said, "but I wouldn't want to watch you wither away much more or take on more pain. Some natural ways to die are brutal."

"A man a few doors up from me," May said, "told me he had congestive heart failure. Next thing, he was dead."

"That was Mr. Hogan. Good thing he passed before a harsher end."

A nerve twitched on Annabel's temple, especially listening to Gloria's remark about Mr. Hogan. The woman gave her the creeps. How long had she been working on the ward and privy to his medical condition?

Meanwhile, the two women talked like she was invisible. Gloria pressed on a plastic bottle on her cart and spit out sanitizer and rubbed her hands. She plucked pills out of the drawers and prepared May's midday medications. As Annabel watched, dread mounted in her stomach like she had swallowed a whole twisted-up pretzel. An alarm went off in her brain. Gloria Pratt's appearance was too much of a coincidence.

"I need to go," Annabel said. "Nice to see you, Gloria. Sorry about your mom. And May, I'll catch you in the morning before rounds."

Annabel drove home clutching the wheel with a solid grip. Should she call Dustin to tell him her suspicions? She parked and flew up the apartment steps.

Nancy was about to roll up her sleeping bag. "You're later than I thought. Let's grab a bite and I need to hit the road."

Annabel was out of breath and put her hand forward like a stop sign. She slumped down on her sister's makeshift bed and scrolled through her cell phone contacts and dialed.

"Annabel Tilson," Dustin said after one ring.

"You said to call, it may be nothing, but my instinct tells me otherwise." Annabel gulped for air and Nancy lowered down next to her.

Dustin pressed the phone against his ear. "Tell me."

"Gloria Pratt started working at the hospital."

"The government hospital?"

"Yes, as a medical assistant. She dispenses medications along the medical ward. I find that too weird. We had a patient with congestive heart failure die while ready for discharge. Something about her doesn't feel right ... over and above her matronly shoes and hand-sanitizer fetish." She finally slowed her pressured speech and chuckled at the end of her comment.

"What did you say?"

"She gives out medicines ..."

"No, something about hand-sanitizer."

"I talked with her often while she visited or stayed over with her mother in the hospital. She routinely massages ethyl alcohol into her hands."

Dustin's thoughts raced. Didn't the lab report indicate anti-freeze residue in the paper cups at the Pratt's residence as well as a germ-killing lotion on the outside? He thought back to when he and Edgar poked around at her house when they took the 911 call. He noticed Gloria pump Purell on her hands in the kitchen. The caretaker, Marabeth, had nothing to do with Darlene Pratt's death!

"Dustin, are you there?"

"Yes."

"This may be making sense," Annabel said. "Gloria may believe in euthanasia, mercy killing or whatever you want to call it. Maybe she had something to do with her mother's death with what she considered a compassionate motive. But our patient, a Mr. Hogan, was desperate to die, other than wanting to go home one more time to clean up his affairs. He died Friday night and I'm worried because Gloria dispenses drugs."

"I can't ignore even your slightest hunch. I'm more convinced now that she was responsible for Darlene Pratt's death."

"She's working today at my hospital."

"Listen, I'll get back to you. The BCI is overseeing the majority of this case but, under the circumstances, I don't have time to contact them and explain our suspicions. Edgar and I better go take another look at the Pratt residence. I need to get off and procure a search warrant."

"Thanks. You see, she has access to other patients and that's what has me worried."

"I understand. Gotta go."

Annabel put her phone down and stared at her sister. "After you leave, I don't understand how I'll concentrate on my studies."

"Tell me what you can. I'll treat you to lunch and then I have to leave."

Dustin told his chief a sketchy newsflash of Gloria Pratt and had his search warrant in hand sooner than he anticipated.

"What do you think we're going to find?" Edgar asked as they swung on their seat belts.

Dustin turned on the ignition. "Damn if I know, but the woman wearing a halo around her head may be Machiavellian in her treatment of people desperate to die."

"I agree with you, but, for people like Gloria, that may depend on how you look at it."

When they arrived, Edgar rapped on the front door.

"She's not home," Dustin said. "She's at her job at Annabel's hospital."

"Her again."

"I don't know what Annabel Tilson is better at. Getting herself into social trouble with men or being fantastic as a medical sleuth. She's cut out for medicine, that's for sure."

The two men were soon inside. The hospice-like environment they witnessed last time no longer existed. The hospital bed was gone and a simple cloth couch fit against the wall. The wood floor shined and the end table now had a match on the other side.

Dustin strolled to the kitchen counter where pill bottles immediately drew his attention. One of them with a multicolored label were multivitamins and the other a store-brand of nonsteroidal anti-inflammatories. Simple enough. But nothing is as simple as it seems with Gloria Pratt, so he opened the vitamins and turned the bottle upside down. An assortment of pills shapes and sizes splattered out. He exchanged glances with Edgar, put them back in, and spilled the second bottle.

"These are all something else," Dustin said. "We don't have time for the lab to analyze these. Let's go."

Edgar followed Dustin's coat tails and before he knew it, they rushed into a major drug store.

Dustin went back to the pharmacy area. The pharmacist spotted them and stepped to the window before his employee. "Can I help you, officers?"

"I'm short on time," Dustin said. "Give me your opinion about what any or all of the pills are in these containers."

The big bald man opened the gate and let them in. They went to a counter where the pharmacist dropped the contents of the nonsteroidal pain pills into a tray. He moved them apart and furrowed his brow. He picked up an oval off-white pill, walked to a shelf, and compared it with another pill. He stood again between Dustin and Edgar.

"This one here," he pointed, "that's propranolol, a heart and blood pressure pill. These two are diuretics. You know, to make someone pee. I'm not sure about this yellow coated pill, but this tiny blue one is for stabilizing a heart rhythm like atrial fibrillation." He scooped them back into the bottle and dumped out the one remaining.

"Would you say," Dustin asked, "that some of these pills could be a heart patient's medicines? What did she call it … congestive heart failure?"

"I would say 'yes.' People do this kind of thing when they're going on a trip for a day or two. They throw their meds into other containers."

"Something more sinister is going on here. Let's pack these back up." He took the full bottles and slipped them in his jacket.

"On her job, Gloria Pratt kept a patient's heart pills," Dustin said to Edgar as they zipped back to the police station. "And instead of giving the old man anti-freeze like her mother, I think she gave him other patients' pills which may have killed him."

CHAPTER 31

After Annabel left and Gloria finished talking with May Oliver, Gloria dwelled on May's condition. The woman, only thirty-two years old, coughs up blood. Her lungs could bleed her to death, she thought. Every day, her brain grew more alien cells; her bones hosted living, growing cells from her respiratory alveoli cancer; and she could throw another seizure at any time. Her situation was hopeless; she resembled a turtle waiting to withdraw her head into a shell and hibernate into death's wondrous embrace.

Gloria had discovered her purpose; May Oliver must fall under her sublime care. The doctors were wrong in trying to make her go for radiation cancer treatments. Why couldn't the poor woman spend her last days on a sunny beach wiggling her toes in the sand or on a hilltop gazing at a wildflower meadow where she could spot her last deer or rabbit?

It was too late for May, Gloria thought. She would put her out of her misery. Her method was so easy and, after all, she had succeeded with Mr. Hogan. She bought another bottle of cheap vitamins downstairs and by her late day rounds, by collecting pain meds, sedatives, and sleeping pills from other patients, and substituting them with the vitamins, she would deliver May to her maker.

Dustin and Edgar spilled into the chief's office with Dustin waving the pill bottles found at Gloria Pratt's house.

"We need to have the lab identify each pill in these," Dustin said, "and we need to get the list of medications that Mr. Hogan took at the military hospital. I'm betting these pills and his prescriptions will be a match. My premise, or Annabel Tilson's premise, is that he received a deadly overdose from other patient's narcotics and sedatives."

Erickson sat dumbfounded. "Who's Mr. Hogan? Who's Annabel Tilson?"

"No time to explain. Gloria Pratt is working in the hospital and we need to bring her in stat. She could be killing another patient as we speak."

Erickson popped up from his chair. "Another patient? Not on my watch. Go. Get out of here. Bring her in."

Edgar found himself again keeping up with his partner. Outside, Dustin turned on the siren and flashing lights. "Plug my cell phone in so we can talk and listen on the speaker. Call Annabel back. She's the last call."

They zipped onto I-75 as Annabel answered.

"Tell me where to go from the hospital front entrance," Dustin said. "We're picking up Gloria Pratt."

"Go straight. Elevator's on the right; stairs to the left. Take one or the other to the third floor. May Oliver, the woman I'm worried most about, is on the east wing. Room 318."

"Thanks. Looks like Pratt substituted your heart patient's meds. He didn't get what he was supposed to."

"Hurry, then. Gloria should be doing the last round of medications."

The officers stopped the car near the hospital entrance and jumped out. Dustin burst through the front door and ran up the stairs with Edgar at his heels.

A nurse came out of a room by the window. Dustin tapped her shoulder. "Room 318?"

The woman gasped and pointed. The two men rushed down the hallway and turned into May Oliver's room.

The medicine cart stood in the middle of the room and May Oliver was lying down sideways on the bed. Gloria Pratt stood next to the mattress obscuring May's face.

"No," Dustin said loudly. He thought of the literal translation of a "deathbed." Were they too late?

May's leg moved under the covers. Gloria turned and her empty hand flew to her face with surprise. "What's happening?" she asked.

"You tell us," Dustin said. "Have you given her any pills yet?"

May leaned up with one elbow. "I was napping. You all are giving me a heart attack. What's going on?"

"Ma'am, have you swallowed any pills before we arrived?"

"No, not since earlier this afternoon."

Gloria held a pill cup in one hand.

"Give me that."

She handed it over and Dustin put it in an empty uniform pocket.

Edgar put his hand around Gloria's upper arm. "You're coming with us."

By now, a group of curious employees, patients, and visitors were scattered in the hallway as Edgar escorted Gloria downstairs to the car.

"Mrs. Oliver, sorry for the disruption," Dustin said. "We must talk to that hospital employee. I'm sure the medical school student, Annabel Tilson, will fill you in tomorrow morning. Have a good evening. Sorry we disturbed you."

By now, May sat on the edge of the bed. "No trouble. Two police officers in my room is the highlight of my hospitalization."

"You get better, ma'am, or at least try." He crouched down, took her hand, and smiled warmly into her eyes.

On his way out, Dustin found the head nurse and explained that Gloria Pratt would not be at her job until further notice and that May Oliver would need the real pills that the doctors had prescribed for her. He had confiscated the pills that Gloria was about to give her.

As much as Annabel tried, it was difficult to study once Nancy left. Taking the medicine test hovered over her in two more days. The clinical experience and studying up to this point, she thought, better suffice to carry her through for a passing first grade. Best to spend any remaining time reviewing what she already knew and not fight the fact that major events were taking place with Dustin and Edgar, May Oliver, and Gloria Pratt.

She paced the room every ten minutes and finally left the apartment for a run. Maybe that would dispense her nervous energy about whether the officers had reached May in time and if their hypothesis about Gloria Pratt was correct. After a twenty-minute run, she stopped and stood facing south. The sun was disappearing over the horizon and low-lying clouds hung over the Ohio as if they trailed a bulky barge coasting along between the two shores. Her cell phone rang and she wiggled it out of her back pocket.

"Dustin, I've been worried sick not knowing what's going on."

"I'm putting in overtime on this one and the Bureau of Criminal Investigations doesn't know whether they love me or hate me. Edgar and I are wrapping up this case like cement on a casket.

"You want to hear this first, I'm sure. Gloria Pratt was in your patient's room. She held a cup with a cluster of pills, but May had not taken any.

We know what we're going to find when they're examined. Mr. Hogan's drug screen should confirmed what we already suspected."

Annabel sighed with relief and blinked away her happiness that May wasn't harmed. "Sounds like you're sure evidence will come back against Gloria."

"Lab work, pills, anti-freeze and ethyl alcohol on cups, dead bodies will all corroborate Gloria Pratt's confession."

"Confession?"

"Yes. Everything."

"Wow, Dustin Lowe. You did it."

"We caught her red-handed with the pills she was about to feed Ms. Oliver, so her details and her motives came spilling out of her like a hose we couldn't shut off."

"What did she tell you about her motives?"

"Once she started, she told us a lot. She said patients deserve the euthanasia we often afford to our dogs and that some people end up hopelessly sick and disabled to the point that there is no meaning or purpose in their lives. All that is left is great unhappiness and suffering as well as other individuals telling them what they should and shouldn't do, such as the health care system."

Dustin's tone saddened. "She gave her mother and Mr. Hogan their wish: to die when they were ready and to die without pain. She wished she had succeeded with May Oliver."

"I'm glad you stopped her. Medical ethics is a real moral dilemma. Darlene Pratt's condition was atrocious and Mr. Hogan, well, I don't know about him. May Oliver is a young woman for whom medical science has not adequately come up with a cure. We also had an elderly man, a Mr. Harty, who took his own life. I'm sure Gloria would have obliged him if she had met him first." She sighed as the last ray of light disappeared beyond the bridge and water.

"I'm glad she didn't. I'm going to remember Gloria Pratt every time I spot a bottle of hand-sanitizer."

Annabel laughed. "Me too."

"You said a few minutes ago that I 'did it.' No, Annabel, it was you who 'did it.' Thanks to your situational awareness, you helped bring this case to a head."

Annabel blushed like a gorgeous man had flirted with her. "Thanks,

Dustin. I'll take that as a complement. By the way, what happened with Ben Rogers?"

"Probation and a fine. Our chief pretty much predicted his punishment. Hey, perhaps you can put your goofy social life to the side, and try another diner dinner with me one of these days. I think I owe you."

"That would be nice."

"Talk to you later, then."

"Bye, Officer Lowe."

Her own nerves didn't go to sleep with the rest of her body last night, Annabel thought as she took the steps up to the medical ward on Monday morning. There was so much to think about, her nervous system worked overtime. What would it take to clear her brain and only focus on her test? She opened the stairway door and wondered. Some day she should take a meditation retreat to the red rocks of Sedona and learn how to zone out unwanted mental clutter.

As she draped her jacket on a chair in the office, Donn walked in.

"I still have to check on my patients," Annabel said, "but I have more to tell you since yesterday's rounds."

"Tell me. Skip seeing them now and we'll consider it a joint effort on rounds. Plus, we must find out what's going on around here. A nurse just told me the police were on this floor yesterday afternoon."

Bob and the two residents walked in, and Donn let them get situated.

"Yesterday," Annabel said, "I mentioned that Gloria Pratt was maybe involved with her mother's death. Well, she was, and the police were here yesterday to take her away. She could have killed May Oliver the way she killed off Bob and Dr. Watts' patient, Mr. Hogan."

Donn and Bob stared at Annabel like she'd walked off an alien space craft.

"Dr. Tilson," Donn said, "why am I confident that you had something to do with figuring this out?"

Annabel shrugged. "I happened to be at the right places at the right times."

"You spent time going in and out of Darlene Pratt's room. What was the daughter telling you?"

"By her actions, she obviously took illegal liberties, but she did believe that a patient's wish about ending care at the end of life should be respected … that we have an obligation to treat patients with compassion and practice medicine with respect for human dignity, their rights, and their desire to die. She believed in physically helping them along with their death if they are terminally ill or if they are mentally incompetent and in a hopeless situation."

Dr. Schott postponed rounds for an hour. He escorted the team to the cafeteria, bought them all fresh coffee, and listened attentively while Annabel explained the details.

Armed with Annabel's information, the team began rounds and started with May Oliver first. Dr. Schott wanted Annabel to do most of the talking. The cachectic woman walked alongside them into her room after strolling the hallway one time. She perched herself on the windowsill and Annabel opened the curtains for her.

"I heard rumors around here," May said, "about what happened yesterday. But one of those policemen told me that you would explain to me what was really going on."

"Yes, I know Officer Lowe. They have arrested that woman who dispensed medicines. She was not performing her duties in an ethical manner. Please don't worry because she's no longer here."

"That's too bad she wasn't performing her job like she should because she was sympathetic to my medical condition. I liked talking to her."

"May, we'll stand by your decision to go through more treatments or not. Please, however, never give up on hope. You didn't give up hope when you served in Afghanistan, did you?"

"No," she mumbled. "Hope … I can hold on to that with or without medical care."

"Exactly. Are you willing to go for your radiation treatment this morning?"

"Yes, just this one."

"Fair enough. Let's have a heart to heart talk after we judge whether or not the chemo and the radiation is doing you any good or if it's a waste of time when you could be doing something more meaningful."

"Okay, Dr. Tilson." She glanced out the window at the patients down below either coming or going. Either completing their hospitalizations or coming in for admission. She took a big breath, coughed, and leaned towards Annabel's ear so no one else could hear.

"A heart to heart is a fine description. We're two women on different sides of a medical conundrum who share similar personal situations. Misty and Dakota, lung cancer and a history of malignant melanoma, and I'm sure there's something in your dating history similar to my boyfriend taking the easy way out rather than deal with a sick girlfriend."

Annabel giggled. "I have so many stories about men, they could fill up a comedian's stand-up routine or be fodder for that women's dating magazine, whatever it's called."

May squeezed Annabel's hand. Lightly, the only way she could.

As the team went on to their next patient, Donn said, "Dr. Tilson, your rapport with May Oliver is amazing."

"Thank you."

"I second that," Bob said when she fell back and again walked alongside him. "I felt like we were witnessing ideal empathy between a patient and a doctor."

"Bob, you're too kind."

Tuesday morning, the halfway mark of their internal medicine rotation, Annabel, Bob, Jordan, and Stuart took a seat in a classroom along with twelve other students on the mandatory rotation at the same time as them. When the two hands on the circular clock rested on eleven, an attending doctor handed out the paperwork and made himself scarce out the door. A department secretary took the wooden chair at the front desk, opened up a paperback, and gave her audience a cursory glance whenever she remembered.

Annabel penciled in her personal information and read the first question.

"What is PEEP?"

She selected "C." *"The pressure in the lungs above atmospheric pressure that exists at the end of expiration."*

With the second question, she allowed herself to relax. Both the questions she had learned the answers to not so much as from a book, but by learning on the wards.

"What amount of PEEP is most often used in mechanically ventilated

patients to mitigate end-expiratory alveolar collapse?"

The selection of answers were:

'A. 2 cm H20

B. 4 to 5 cm H2O

C. 10 cm H20

D. 25 cm H20

Annabel picked B. She recalled the discussion of the best PEEP to use while she managed her ICU patient with the tricyclic antidepressant overdose. He was the first patient she ever intubated by herself. She smiled to herself and looked up. Bob and Stuart both sat in front of her and Jordan sat across the aisle next to her. She sensed Jordan's arms were not on the desk and she glanced to the side for a moment.

She stifled a gasp. Jordan glanced down in his lap at a pocket-size student handbook. Cheater, she thought, and couldn't believe it. She had no knowledge of any med student who cheated ... until now.

With five minutes left to go, Annabel answered the last question, which asked for the minimum number of measurements to make for a diagnosis of hypertension. Easy enough: two, Annabel answered. She handed her test in at the front of the room and waited for Bob on a bench downstairs.

Her heart warmed when Bob walked jovially across the ground floor lobby of the downtown department's office and signaled for her to keep seated. With the test looming over them the last few days, he'd neglected a haircut and his blonde tapered sides were a bit longer than usual. It didn't matter. He was handsome regardless and, as he smiled at her, she banked on his sense of humor to shine, even after taking a test responsible for a big chunk of their grade.

He turned over her warm hand on her lap and dropped in chocolate blueberries.

"Thanks." She flashed a smile and popped one in her mouth.

"So how did the medical-student cop do on her exam?"

She rolled her eyes. "Not as well as you. But as I told May Oliver, never give up hope. Maybe we scored as well as Stuart. That would be something."

"Yes, it would. There are a few things I hope for, so I'll remember your advice."

Annabel wondered what he meant but dismissed it as they parted. Relaxed, she drove to the hospital ready to tackle the second half of her internal medicine rotation. Their team was on call for the night.

-    End -

FROM THE AUTHOR

Barbara Ebel is a physician and an author. Since she practiced anesthesia, she brings credibility to the medical background of her plots. She lives with her husband and pets in a wildlife corridor in Tennessee but has lived up and down the East Coast.

Twitter: @BarbaraEbel
Facebook Author/Reader Group: Medical Suspense Café:
Visit or contact the author at her website: http://barbaraebelmd.com

The following books are also written by Dr. Barbara and are available as paperbacks and eBooks:

The Dr. Annabel Tilson Series:

Dead Still (Dr. Annabel Tilson Novels Book 1)
Deadly Delusions (Dr. Annabel Tilson Novels Book 2)
Desperate to Die (Dr. Annabel Tilson Novels Book 3)
Death Grip (Dr. Annabel Tilson Novels Book 4)
Downright Dead (Dr. Annabel Tilson Novels Book 5)
Dangerous Doctor (Dr. Annabel Tilson Novels Book 6)

The Dr. Danny Tilson Series:

Operation Neurosurgeon (A Dr. Danny Tilson Novel: Book 1)
Silent Fear: *a Medical Mystery* (A Dr. Danny Tilson Novel: Book 2). Also an Audiobook.
Collateral Circulation: *a Medical Mystery* (A Dr. Danny Tilson Novel: Book 3). Also an Audiobook.
Secondary Impact (A Dr. Danny Tilson Novel: Book 4)

The Outlander Physician Series:

Corruption in the O.R.: A Medical Thriller (The Outlander Physician Series Book 1)

Wretched Results: A Medical Thriller (The Outlander Physician Series Book 2)

Stand-alone Medical Fiction:

Outcome, A Novel

Her Flawless Disguise

Nonfiction health book:

Younger Next Decade: *After Fifty, the Transitional Decade, and What You Need to Know*

Also written and illustrated by Barbara Ebel:
A children's book series about her loveable therapy dog; illustrated with real pictures:
Chester the Chesapeake Book One
Chester the Chesapeake Book Two: Summertime
Chester the Chesapeake Book Three: Wintertime
Chester the Chesapeake Book Four: My Brother Buck
Chester the Chesapeake: The Three Dogs of Christmas
Chester's website: http://dogbooksforchildren.weebly.com